Essential Atrocities

By

George Daniel Lea

www.strangeplaygrounds.com

Essential Atrocities

This collection Copyright© George Daniel Lea 2018

Cover Art by Grace Maria Houseman

All works used by permission.

All rights reserved.

Contents

Dedications

To those of you that still celebrate the strange, most particularly Janice Barry, who I know from experience does.

Foreword

I have admired the style and scope of George Lea's since I encountered his work on various online platforms in my early twenties, long before he was ever published. Over a decade later and I consider him to be one of those rare, deliberate writers, informed as much by poetry as he is by prose, possessing a broad reading across genres and traditions. He pays homage to language, to the complements of structures and sound, to the rhythms of sentences and the patterns of syntax. It has been fascinating to witness his development as an author.

Over the years, I have seen his narrative ideas germinate and take shape as he combined influences from both literary and non-literary sources, ultimately transforming them into something novel and gripping. He pulled together storytelling from various mediums, from William Blake, Stephen King, Clive Barker and Poppy Z. Brite; from television, film and computer games, and formed an aesthetic characterised by a passion for difference and an opposition to the safe, predictable and pedestrian.

Weird fiction, body horror and gothic romance inform this aesthetic, but also a keen vision of something new. In his debut, *Strange Playgrounds*, he showed a fondness for the ecstatic possibilities of transgressive renewal, for the outsider's ability to refashion the world after stagnation. There were stories about reality collapsing, as if Philip K. Dick's science fiction had collided with Lovecraft's cosmic horror. Unlike *Strange Playgrounds*, Lea's ongoing collaborative project with photographer Nick Hardy, *Born in Blood* (up to its third volume at the time of writing), goes in a slightly different direction, one that mirrors the claustrophobia and subjective prison of its subjects, exploring how humanity can be hemmed into its own skull, drawn in a downward spiral of myopia. Here, Lea showed an even greater willingness to push the boundaries of prose and experiment with a style that challenges the conventions of genre storytelling. Again, there is a characteristic fixation on the extreme experiences of his characters, an intimacy that belies the broader, metaphysical implications of the stories.

Essential Atrocities is a unique collection that builds on what came before. An intensely vulnerable book, it represents the most mature articulation of a style and voice, even a mythos, which is as jubilant and celebratory as it is often macabre and bleak. Most of all, it is utterly distinctive. For *if* this can be called a mythos, it is not defined by a stable set of rules to be dully comprehended and categorized, nor even by reliable narrative parameters, but by a universe subsumed in its very indeterminate nature. In stories such as 'Where Our Children Walk' and 'A World Beyond Windows,' we meet with a motif common to a lot of Lea's work—that reality (even at the level of the macrocosm) is wrapped up in subjectivity, and that the mundane is largely the illusory comfort brought on by conservative minds trying to stamp a fake stability on the chaotic world around them. For if subjectivity is the locus of reality, Lea's view of subjectivity is that it is anything but stable—rather, it is contradictory, multifaceted, shaped by traumas, boxed in by repressive conventions, never fully transparent to itself.

In keeping with Lea's distaste for tropes and conceits, in stories like 'Where We Will Never Be' the violent morality of those guardians of normality (the Van Helsings in a world of monsters) is interrogated and aggressively exposed as ultimately an ugly parochialism. Similarly, in 'A Mercy of Minds' the point of view of the possession story is flipped; nowhere does Lea want the reader to settle into the pedestrian playing out of a mere genre piece. And elsewhere in the collection, Lea goes even further, beyond just questioning and subverting specific archetypes, but rather choosing to play with prose and setting out to subvert the readers' expectations about the most basic philosophical assumptions: our grasp of ourselves and the world in which we are situated.

'Where Our Children Walk' is the most ambitious of Lea's pieces to date, both in grandeur and narrative style. It is an apocalyptic tale in line with the truest etymology of that word— not an ending, but an uncovering, a revealing of hidden truths. With prose verging always on the cusp of verse, its deuteragonists Chandra and Crowther are given a real pathos as they wage a

Biblical style war that is not of good and evil, at least not in any generic sense, but of the backward looking and stagnant against a Bacchanalian—if even that word is not too staid—liberation. Fascinatingly, this is explicitly framed as the liberation of a group. I have felt—sometimes, perhaps, to Lea's bemusement— that there is a utopian kernel to some of his pieces, hidden in the horror and ambiguity, repelled by the saccharine and easy sentimentalism of any utopia without a nod to horror. Here this is manifested in a struggle to create a world of the outcasts, a world overcome by a sense of its own becoming and permanent state of reinvention.

If 'Where Our Children Walk' is the most encompassing and emblematic, 'Beautifully Broken' is the most intimate and vulnerable of an intimate and vulnerable collection. Sexuality is explored elsewhere in *Essential Atrocities*, but with Anthony and Robert the tensions between socially inflicted suffering and a yearning to find freedom in another's liberation are most fully realised. It is a piece that marries philosophy with eroticism, to the benefit of both.

This is not a collection that takes itself unrelentingly seriously. There are humorous pieces, too, such as in 'The Breaking Down.' Here a monstrous carnival mocks disaster fiction, as a hellish parade purges the world (in the manner of the Deluge of *Gilgamesh* and the *Old Testament*), but not to inflict some divine sanction on a wayward Creation, but rather to see it cleansed of the very purists that would demand such sanction, the conformists and bigots. The implication being that the horrors are not held back by the repressed, as reactionary horror will insist, but nurtured by them. Likewise, in 'Wasted Day Tarot' a new deck is imagined that provides a transgressive take on prescience; freed from the dull predictions of success in status quo terms, this Tarot becomes a lyrical space in which a fantasy and artistry can explore occult drives and strange imaginings.

Elliptical, dreamlike and impressionistic, *Essential Atrocities* reveals an author in his stride. Whether through a disturbing ocean teeming with an overflowing, rotting, alien (but not quite alien) life in 'A Child at the Loom', or a servant of some pagan god struggling vainly to master his fate in 'Strangest Spite,' Lea seeks to show that speculative fiction need not be bound by merely imitating past glories, that it can be experimental at every level. He is willing to create a transgressive literature that at once puts a mirror up to our own ugliness, but also celebrates in that same reflection our potential for beauty that can only be seen after an eschewal of mawkish illusions.

> – Rowan B. Fortune, of **Rowan-Tree Editing**
> http://rowantree-editing.uk

Where We Will Never Be

Nothing there. *Nothing.*

"Have you been looking up pictures on the Internet?" She asks me, her fingers still in my mouth, tasting of rubber and chemicals.

"No, nothing like that." I lie. "It's just... I can *feel* something back there."

Sighing, pursing her lips, glancing at her computer screen.

"Hmm. Well, there's certainly nothing that gives me concern. You don't smoke, do you?"

I shake my head.

"No. Well... I can proscribe you some antibiotics, but I doubt they'll do much. There is some faint irritation, but that's all."

"Could it be, like, an allergy or something?"

Sighing again, her indifference fast swelling to impatience.

"I suppose it could be. Do you have pets?"

"A cat."

"Hmm. We'll try you on some antihistamines, yes? That might help."

"Okay. Thank you, Doctor."

She doesn't even glance from her computer screen as I quietly leave, trying not to slam the door.

*

Herpes. Throat cancer. Thrush. Oral Gonorrhoea. Pictures sailing across the screen, grotesque, none quite *right,* none looking like what I see when I gape in front of the bathroom mirror.

"There's no damage to the soft tissue, no swellings or rashes. Try gargling with salt water once a day; that should ease any discomfort. Beyond that..."

I check my dentist, not having been for twenty-odd years, finding myself amazed at the advancement in technology: x-rays that appear ten seconds after being taken on the monitor behind me, showing my impacted wisdom teeth, which she says will have to be removed, as and when.

No mention of my throat, though I try to tell her:

"It's pretty much every day, now. I wake up and I can feel it; a *scratching,* as though there's a hair lodged somewhere."

"I'm sorry. I can't see anything unusual. In fact, you've got quite a healthy mouth, all told."

Forty pounds and don't come back for another six months. Thank you.

Nothing. Nothing that even resembles what I see. What they don't.

Home. The cat mewls to be fed (again), mewling to be petted (again), mewling to be let out (again). I oblige all three, a good and obedient slave, the creature bounding up onto the outer wall, hissing at passing dogs and their walkers, chittering at birds on the roof. Later, there'll be gifts: headless sparrows on the stairs, eviscerated mice on the carpet.

I do as they've told me, swilling my mouth with warm salt water, trying not to gag, to swallow the brine. A hideous, stinging sensation at the back of my throat, something tangibly moving.

Spitting, I swill out the sink, head upstairs, to the bathroom with its porthole windows, its glaring, surgery light.

The small shaving mirror is the only one I have, the only one I need. Gaping wide, noting with distress the spreading rawness at the back of my throat. How could they not *see*? The cause of it spread out from where my tongue dips away; the legs of a black widow, some spidery growth, reaching up from my gullet, digging into the flesh of my throat, whatever they anchor hidden in the dark, something I can't see, no matter how I manoeuver the mirror, the light. Twitching as I watch, digging deeper.

I hack, cough, trying to dislodge it. No hope, the thing only battening more earnestly, its legs pricking me deeper.

How can none of them *see*?

I've asked others to look; friends and relatives, some of the guys I meet off Grindr. None of them say a thing, none of them brave enough. As though afraid of offending me, weirded out by the question. The Grindr guys in particular don't care, unconcerned enough by it to allow their tenderest anatomies where the thing sits.

Still there, still the same, after they've finished and gone.
Maybe they *do* see, maybe they're just afraid to say. Too polite,
too British about it. Just one of those things that crops up from
time to time. Best to just ignore it, get on, let it run its course.
Maybe tomorrow it'll be gone, maybe tomorrow it'll seem
different, not so raw, not so *infected*.

I could almost cry.

*

A day off, needed, begged for. I lose patience with it all; the
noise, the shrieks, the stink. The penetrating glares of the Autistic
children from their corners, their isolated spaces on the play mats,
in the classroom's alcoves. Endless questions. Endless
competition for attention and approbation: good boys, good girls;
well dones, gold stars. Straining to explain the simplest concepts
in ways they might understand, called to the Headmistress's
office when I find a way, told it's not proscribed in the current
curricula, the fact that it works besides the point.

A day to sleep. To sit and do nothing. Except worry. To
examine myself in the mirror again and again, checking if the
thing has dislodged itself or gone away.

Swilling with hot honey and lemon, with salt water, the latter
concentrated enough to raise salt burns on my tongue.

But it's still *there*, clinging on.

I feel it, every time I swallow or mutter to myself, every time words rise in my throat: the thing tremors, repositioning.

Trying to dislodge it with a cotton bud, I almost choke myself, spluttering for almost twenty minutes after. The thing still in place, no matter how violently I hack or wretch.

Time becoming molten, inconsistent, a red and swirling haze, not knowing who calls, who knocks on my door or why. Only tears and frustration, rusted saws and ragged razor wire sifting through my mind, my diseased, decomposing body. *Feeling* it, a rot that scrapes me apart, atom-by-atom, that sickens me to the marrow, the soul, that no doctor can detect or medicine treat.

Nothing, they say.

*

The saws and razors don't still, even in sleep: I dream of things crawling from the darkness, invading every orifice, setting up parasite nurseries in my throat, my ears, cockroach things hollowing out my heart and brain, seeping white worms swelling and mating in the loops of my entrails, the frothing bath of my stomach.

Just enough of me left to appreciate the horror of it, to watch through eyes that are no longer mine as they puppeteer my body, carry me from bed, out into the night, to kiss, to bite, to *rape*, their eggs in my spit and semen, *infecting,* to make more walking-hive kind.

The sensation of them crawling, worming and burrowing through my skin, my bone, so vivid, so *real*. Waking to nausea, to scratches earnest enough to draw blood, I vomit black into the toilet bowl.

Even that isn't enough, the thing still there, *still there,* no matter how powerfully I wretch, how forceful the torrent I vomit up. Stinking and pathetic, I collapse against the tiles, my head on the toilet bowl. Sobs no one will hear or pity me for.

*

Smiles and sunshine, azure ties and salmon-pink shirts. Little blonde boys and girls, little dark haired and dark skinned and shuffling and uncertain, scratching their heads as though to burrow through, distracted by cats or butterflies at the windows, by the barks of dogs from the nearby footpath.

"Okay, guys. That's enough for today; make sure you've put the date in your workbooks and… Jamiel, would you collect them, please?"

The boy frowns, sat slightly apart from the rest. Fat and doughy, perpetually afraid. Spoken about, in the relative solitude of the staff room: something not right, we all agree. Something to keep an eye on. Something that makes me roll my eyes and grind my teeth and wish I could drink bleach.

The fright in his eyes at the sound of his name, the look of stunned betrayal on his face: as though I've commanded him to eat the class hamster whole, to cut out his Mother's eyes and bring them for show and tell tomorrow.

The rest of the class bustle about their business, happily chattering, one or two bouts of laughter, quiet titters.

Jamiel slinks from his chair, every motion awkward and uncertain, as though he doesn't fit into his own stretched taught skin, as though every step is an exercise.

Dyspraxia? Some sort of Autism Spectrum Disorder? I don't know. I watch as he breathlessly collects the exercise books, refuses to meet the eyes of the others, glancing from them to the windows, the pictures on the walls, as he ignores their hellos and jokes and gestures.

"Okay, guys, when you're done, come and sit on the mat, and we'll carry on with *The Silver Chair,* yeah?"

Quiet settles, Jamiel seating himself at the back of the group, noticeably apart. Not looking, not focusing, glancing away, to the toy cupboard, the walls, ceiling, as though distracted by butterflies or spiders only he can see.

I begin to read. Where did we leave off? Oh, yeah, on our way to the City of the Giants, through snow and cold and hunger…

On autopilot, for the most part, until the argument, Jill and Eustace haranguing Puddleglum for his misery and mistrust, the class squirming where they sit, looks of consternation…

I cough, a tickle at the back of my throat, Jamiel's eyes on me as I lower the book.

"...sorry, guys; just got a bit of a..."

The boy melts into tears, great, fat droplets rolling down his face, the folds of his cheeks and neck wobbling. I sip from my mug of Fennel tea, which helps to calm the irritation.

The others turn to him, some asking what's wrong, others smiling evilly.

"It's... it's all right, guys. Settle down. Jamiel?"

The boy doesn't hear, continuing to cry, closing his eyes, lightly shaking his head.

"Jamiel, mate, I can't help if you don't..."

The boy *shrieks* so loudly, those seated nearby leap away from him across the carpet, some slapping their hands to their ears, looking to me with expressions of earnest terror.

So strange, so rare. I've never seen this before, not from him.

Rising from my seat, the class parts as I make my way to him. "Jamiel..."

The boy is on his feet, moving faster than I've ever seen, shrieking as he backs away.

"What's wrong with him, Mr. Yentson?"

"I don't know, Connie. It's okay, guys. Just... go back to your seats for now, please."

The class complies, most of them without complaint or hesitation, though they continue to stare, to swap conspiratorial glances, furtive whispers.

"Is everything all right, Mr. Yentson?" asks Alison Fisher, from the classroom next door. Several kids make to answer before I silence them.

"I think Mrs. Fisher was asking me, guys. Everything's fine, Mrs. Fisher. Jamiel over there is just having a bit of a turn."

"Would you like me to take him to the nurse's office?"

"I... yes, if you would. I think that would be best."

The skinny, scarecrow woman sifts into the room, rearing up almost as tall as the ceiling, pale skin stretched across the bone beneath, lending her a certain hollow, skeletal look.

Jamiel shivers, but noticeably calms as she speaks to him, focusing on her.

"There now, there now, Jamiel. Why don't you come with me, and we'll see if we can't make it better, yeah?"

The boy nods, fervently, accepting her hand, casting suspicious, frightened glances my way as he allows her to lead him from the room.

I curse myself after he's gone, in the fractious silence of restored sanity, a question buzzing around my skull like a captive fly:

What did you see, Jamiel? What did you see?

*

An impromptu meeting, after the last of them disappear, with Mrs. Fisher, Claire Houghton, the headmistress, Jamiel's parents. The boy noticeably absent.

Strange glares from the parents as I enter the office, as though I have a Swastika drawn on my face.

"Hello, Kevin. Take a seat, would you?"

I nod a greeting to Mrs. Fisher and Houghton, to Jamiel's parents, who continue to glare.

"We… understand there was an incident in the classroom, earlier today. Mr. Yentson, would you like to give us your account of what happened?"

Your account.

Taking a moment to clear my throat, that hideous, tingling itch, that rasping soreness, intense as always, after a day at school.

"Of course, of course…"

I recount what I saw; Jamiel's strange and preoccupied behaviour, his outbursts that disrupted the class. I select my language carefully, the boy's parents glaring at me like wolves waiting their moment to pounce. His Mother in particular has the eyes of a hawk or buzzard, observing for any wound or opening through which to press her hooked beak.

"He was very, very upset when we came to fetch him, Mr. Yentson. *Very* upset. You said you were reading a book with the students?"

"That's right, yes; we're working our way through *The*

Chronicles of Narnia."

The Mother shifts in her seat, sighing as though the problem is self-evident. "He's... a very sensitive boy; he gets upset easily. Is there maybe something in the book that might have set him off?"

"I doubt it, Mrs. Kahbul. We've already done the first five books and he's not had a problem with them."

"He was saying some very strange things when he got home. *Very* strange things."

Refusing to rise to her implication, reverting instead to placation and protocol.

"I'm very sorry he was upset, but the other children will be able to corroborate: he just exploded out of nowhere. One moment, he's fine, the next, he starts crying and screaming..."

Mrs. Fisher jumps in: "That's what alerted me; I was in the classroom next door."

"There must have been *something*. He wouldn't be this upset over nothing."

All of us exchange glances, the same confession hanging in the air.

"I will say, we have noticed some... *unusual* behaviour regarding Jamiel, of late."

The Mother perks up at this, bristling in her seat, becoming more *angular.*

"Unusual? What does that mean?"

"He... tends to be rather unfocused, very easily distracted."

"I'm sure most boys are at that age…"

"He often seems anxious; he doesn't tend to communicate with the other children…"

The Father folds his arms, huffing something non-committal, though I think it has something to do with the apparent nature of the other children in the class. "No wonder." I catch.

"We do think that it might be wise to seek… specialist help when it comes to Jamiel, with your permission, of course."

The woman dabs her eyes with a handkerchief, shaking her head. "I'm sorry… this is not what I expected today *at all*. First, your teacher terrifies my son…"

"Excuse me, Mrs. Kahbul, but I…"

"… then, you dare to tell me that there's something *defective* about him? You do understand that we're quite close friends with the Lotkins, who are on the board of directors for this school?"

Mrs. Houghton seeths, the room darkening with her temper.

"We're well aware, but what that has to do with your son's wellbeing, I don't know."

"Oh, you will, believe me. I'm not tolerating this, quite frankly."

Clare rises from behind her desk, leaning over it, her eyes serpentine.

"Tolerating *what* Mrs. Kahbul? The advice of people who are genuinely concerned about your son? *Quite frankly,* given his conduct and outbursts, you're lucky we haven't called in a specialist ourselves, which we're well within our rights to do. Mr. Yentson and Mrs. Fisher have both told you what happened. If I need to get the testimonies of the children, I will. But what I won't have is you threatening me or my staff; I happen to know Linda and Carlton, too, very well, as it happens, and I'll be sure to bring this matter up with them myself."

Not here, I am removed from it all, idly scratching at my throat, Mr. Kahbul following every motion, his eyes not quite as frightened as his son's, but…

"I don't think this is helping. Mrs. Kahbul, I've been watching your son for quite some time, now, and he exhibits behaviours that…"

"Excuse *me,* Mr. Yentson, but I've been watching my son since he was born. I think I'd be aware if there was anything *defective* about him."

"Please don't use that word."

Mrs. Fisher, raising her head, fixes Mrs. Kahbul with her eyes. "Excuse me?"

"That word. It's not one we use concerning children who have learning difficulties or special needs."

The woman gapes, gasping as though slapped, glancing between us before rising from her seat, storming through the office door.

Her husband lingers, slowly sighing, shaking his head. "I… apologise for her. My wife… she finds bad news very hard to take. You tell me, yes? What you think is wrong with Jamiel?"

A glance to Clare, for approbation, wanting nothing more than to go home, to sit in silence, to sleep.

Clare nods, sighing as she slumps back in her chair, absently cleaning her glasses.

"Mr. Kahubl, I'm going to assume you're passingly aware of Autism Spectrum Disorders?"

"Jamiel's *autistic*?"

"Oh, we can't say that, yet; it's far too early. But he does present certain signifiers."

The man glances between me and Alison, furrowing his brow, his interlaced fingers fretting and fidgeting in concern.

"My wife... she is going to find this very hard. *Very* hard."

The others likely don't notice, but I do; the way he occasionally glances at my mouth, his eyes lingering momentarily on my throat, before darting away again.

Clare interjects. "I've no doubt. But, for Jamiel's sake, it would be best if he could be diagnosed as soon as possible, then both you and we can start putting special measures in place for him."

The man nods, deflating in his chair. "Thank you. Thank you, all. My wife may not understand or want to see, but I know; I've noticed things."

"We can give you advice on what to do next, if you like."

Already rising from his seat, taking both Clare and Alison's hands, shaking vigorously. "That would be very much appreciated. And I'll talk to my wife; she'll come around, whether she wants to or not."

He returns me after taking numbers and leaflets, a small folder of papers on the subject of children with autism.

"I would very much like to speak with Mr. Yentson alone, if I may."

Clare and Allison share glances. I interject before they can protest:

"That's fine by me; I might be able to give Mr. Kahbul a little more information."

"All right, you can use the office, if you like. We'll go get a coffee."

Allison rises, following Clare as they leave, the looks they throw me pitying, almost accusing. Weary, the day already thrown off-kilter, things waiting back home: washing to get out of the machine, tea to be made, the cat to be fed. Aching to be elsewhere, anywhere other than here.

Mr. Kahbul continues to stare at me, his eyes—that seem somewhat overlarge for his rounded face—unblinking, reptilian in their intense green.

"How long has it been, Mr. Yentson?"

The man taps his throat with the fingers of one hand. Cold, a wash of something toxic down my spine. I half believed them, until this moment; the ones who say there's nothing there.

Automatic denials, feeling so hideously exposed, so *naked*.

"I don't…"

The man sighs, shifting in his seat. "All right, if you don't want to talk about it…"

A strange, wrenching sensation, a shimmering thread, slowly drawn out of my reach. "No! No, I… I don't know. Maybe a year, now."

"A year? Goodness."

The man is genuinely startled, blinking, looking away from me.

"I take it my son saw, yes?"

"I'm not sure, but I think so, yes."

Kahbul grunts, his head lolling back on his neck, raking a hand over his face.

"Damn it. *Damn it.* I was hoping it might skip him, you know?"

"I'm… I'm sorry, Mr. Kahbul…"

"Wilfred, please."

"Wilfred?" I'm unable to keep myself from smiling at the incongruity.

"My Mother was English, she named me after my Grandfather. And I'm sure you *don't* understand, Mr. Yentson. I'm sure you don't. Neither do I, to tell you the truth. But I *see*. Like my Mother could and her Grandmother. Like Jamiel, apparently."

Shaking my head, rubbing my temples, I lose patience with the entire encounter. "Look, Mr… Wilfred, I'm *very* tired and *very* confused; all I want to do is go home and collapse in front of the computer. Will you please just tell me what this bloody thing is?"

The man interlaces his fingers again, looking at me with open and obvious pity.

"I don't know. They don't have names; most people can't *see* them, don't even know when they have them. Some sort of parasite, I would guess. I don't know, Mr. Yentson; I just see things. I've learned to ignore them, for the most part, over the years. I'm going to have to try and teach Jamiel the same."

"So, you don't know what it is. How do I. . ?"

"…get rid of it? I wish I knew, Mr. Yentson. I wish I knew. You'd be surprised how many people have them without knowing it. I've seen this type before, but it's not the most common, not by far."

"There must be people who know how."

"If there are, I've never met them. Like I say: most people don't even realise. For some reason, you do."

Rising from his chair, he pulls on his coat.

"I'll speak with Jamiel. Maybe I can teach him not to be afraid."

The man doesn't offer his hand, understandably, leaving me with a pitying smile.

*

There must be people. Someone who knows. If not what to do, then at least *what the fuck it is.*

Home, weary beyond belief, I leave the washing to moulder in the machine, the cat to meow at her food bowl.

I need to know, to find *something.*

An hour, sifting through web pages, journals and blogs... nothing. Barely even a reference or mention, the ones that chime with my experience idiot, paranormal or conspiracy theory pages that consist of more paranoid fantasy than anything actual.

Though I begin to wonder, the deeper I delve, the longer I pour over them: What if some *are* onto something? What if, beneath the distortions and hyperbole, there's some truth?

That way lies insanity, a gaping rabbit hole ready to swallow me. Ha! Already scrabbling at the edges, soil and grass giving way beneath my fingers...

Nothing. Nothing, nothing, *nothing.*

Maybe... maybe some conspiracy? Someone in power knowing about this shit, afraid it'll cause mass panic, deleting anything of credence relating to it, some program or government agency, editing the web from afar...

Ha! Barely an evening immersed in their madness and I'm already thinking like them, sounding like them in my head; the cranks and crazies, the conspiracy nuts. Why the Hell didn't I ask Wilfred when I had the chance: *what's going to happen to me?*

Maybe nothing. Perpetual discomfort the extent of it, occasional spikes of pain, but nothing I can't endure. Maybe I can learn to live with it.

But at least I know, now, don't I? *At least I know.*

*

I wake in the dark, not the usual tingling itch in my throat, but *motion,* the parasite tangibly swollen and stirring, pricking my flesh with its needle feet, scrabbling up to haul itself free.

It feels larger, much larger than before, as though swollen from recent feeding, or maybe with…

The thought makes me nauseous, gaping wide until my jaw aches, reaching inside with desperate fingers...

I jerk them back with a yelp as something bites, *stings,* almost weep as cold fire spreads through my hand and up my wrist.

A wet, pulsating mass fills my mouth, tasting like rotten fruit and meat left to sweat in the sun. Something forces its way up and out; barbed limbs that creep across my lips, my cheeks, forcing my mouth wide to allow the mass to protrude.

I can't see, too dark, too dark; can only *feel;* the mass slick and foul, hideous, hideous pulsations rippling through it.

Get up. Get up, you idiot! Rip it out, flush it away.

I want to. *I want to,* but I can't; something holds me fast, making me grip the bedclothes as though in the midst of a fit.

I weep as the thing sways and pulses, as some foul matter dribbles down it, across my cheeks, gumming up my eyes.

I feel them: worming, scurrying things, spilling across my neck, my shoulders, so many I can barely discern one from the other.

Several spasms, the protrusion diminishing with each one, until it's barely a scrap of quivering matter, lolling from my stretched open mouth. Withdrawing, it trails effluent across my tongue, the limbs that clamp me open receding into whatever hollow they emerged from.

I want to vomit, to claw myself open and rip the fucking things out of me. Can't, a prisoner in my skull, so distant from the body that has betrayed me in so many ways. Hurling myself against its bone walls, not to escape, but in suicide, seeking to dash myself open, to burst sanity and have it seep out with the rest of the effluent.

Sedative sleep follows, though I fight it, though I...

*

Sunshine streams gold and amber through the partially open curtains. Ayla clambers over me, mewing and purring in my face.

Something surges inside, sunlight-laced blood illuminating every recess.

Laughing, breathing deep, my throat unconstricted, somehow

whole again for the first time in months.

I scratch behind the cat's ears, the animal flopping down on my chest, stretching, pawing at the quilt.

"All right, all right, shit-bag. I'll get you some food. Just let me get up first, okay?"

The cat's eyes blaze in answer, catching the light of the morning. "What time is it? I don't remember the alarm going off..."

I smile at a distant foam of concern in my belly, the kind that would have frothed to blind panic yesterday. Those shores are so far away, now; regarding them as though seated amongst the clouds and storms above, I don't care how earnestly they eat away at the world, how close the cliff-crowning towers come to collapse...

8:15AM. Plenty of time. More than two hours later than my usual workday schedule. I smile, the expression become so unfamiliar in recent months, it hurts my face.

Habitually checking my throat before I brush my teeth, I furrow my brow at what the shaving mirror tells me: nothing, the twitching, partially buried legs gone, the soreness they elicited likewise. Checking from as many angles as possible, I stretch my mouth as wide as anatomy allows. There's no sign of them, not even a stripe of soreness or infection.

Smiling all the more lavishly, I brush and floss and swill, sing in the shower, something by *Pink Floyd,* half the lyrics murmured or slurred for never being known.

I enjoy a glutton's breakfast: three cups of coffee, left over frittata, toast from homemade bread, a banana. Time flows like sludge, every second an eternity in which to enjoy relief, calm, this moment of sunshine.

Far from late when I saunter into work; just less early than usual. Clare calls me to her office before the day begins.

"So, yesterday?"

"Yeah. Listen, Clare, I'm really sorry. I don't..."

"It's fine. It's fine. Jamiel won't be in for the rest of the week. Apparently, his Mom and Dad are having difficulty getting him to come back to class."

"Shit."

"Yeah. Still no idea of what set him off?"

You should speak to his Dad about that. "Sorry, no. It just came out of nowhere."

"Nothing much we can do about it, at this point. If he does come back, I want to start some special measures with him, if his bloody Mother will let us."

"I think that'd be a great idea."

"Glad you're on board with it. Listen, I know it's just one of those things, but try to go easy on any material that might spook or upset any of the kids, okay?"

Sniffing, almost laughing. "It was *The Chronicles of Narnia,*

Clare; most kids have read the books by Jamiel's age."

"Yeah, I know, I know, but I've got to say it; you know how it is. I'll make a record that we had this conversation, blah, blah, blah."

"Ah. Covering our own arses, yes?"

"Exactly that."

Her eyes linger on me, a faint wrinkling of her brow.

"What?"

"Nothing, nothing. You just look good today. Like you got a good sleep last night."

"Thanks. I really did."

"I'll keep you updated on the Jamiel situation."

Her eyes are still on me as I exit the office and head to class.

*

It's a good day. A *great* day; lots of laughs, silliness, but not too much. Lessons made into games that require rearranging the classroom, herding desks and chairs against the walls, which the kids love.

Not a moment, not an incident. Some of the more empathetic—or gossip-mongering—ask me about Jamiel, wanting to know what was wrong, if he'll be back.

Placating, I assure them that he's fine, that he will, sending them back to their classmates smiling, with other concerns (what sweets they'll be picking from the shop on the way home, what games they're going to play after homework).

Storytime, as the day winds down.

The Silver Chair, picking up where we left off; Harfang, the city of giants, our unknowing heroes waiting to be devoured.

Every pair of eyes rapt, none afraid, as we build to the revelation. There are faint gasps and mutters, some shifting where they sit, none screaming or whimpering. How it should be; kids like Jamiel... no hope for them, if they can't cope with something so innocuous. The world itself will be a horror story for them, stepping outside the door or walking down the street an invitation to insanity.

Poor, poor boy.

Some scattered, nervous laughter as we come to Jill Pole's discovery of the giant's cookbook, open at a page that depicts a staple of the giant's Autumn Feast:

"Man Pie."

Looking up from the page, grinning at them, I love the shock on their faces, the smiling, mock-dread in their eyes.

A tickle shatters that smile, something catching in my throat. Setting the book open in my lap, I reach for my fennel tea.

Distant murmurs, uncertain glances, as it comes, rising in my throat: a vomit of scrabbling pins and living needles. The book flies from my lap as it bursts from me, the children shrieking, scrabbling back, protective hands raised to their faces.

No more pain. If anything, a bizarre *pleasure,* almost sexual in its intensity, quivering from my lower belly to my throat, exploding behind my eyes with every convulsion.

Black fluid, glutinous, congealed matter, crawling with parasites, the children scrabbling away, crawling for the doors and windows as it finds them, spattering against their appalled faces, their raised hands.

Barely able to see through tears as I stagger, clutching at my stomach. The children flee, some of them already at the doors and windows, though none without infested foulness clinging in their hair, bubbling on their faces.

I glimpse them through tears as they claw and rake at themselves, trying to peel away parasites that crawl into screaming mouths and gaping eyes, as they collapse and vomit on the carpet where they played and laughed only minutes ago…

"What in the name of Christ?"

Allison, pausing at the door, clutches at it, a hand rising to her mouth. Turning to her, unable to help myself; an arc of black sputum spatters her, a scream rising as a centipede-like thing uncoils from within, seeking out her lips, her eyes.

Those that can flee screaming into the playground, the field behind the classroom. I stagger after them, to the open doorway, out into blinding sunlight.

Others emerge, now; children and teachers from neighbouring classrooms, disturbed by the noise, the sight of children wretching on their hands and knees in the yard.

I ignore them, staggering for the front gate, still quivering in my strange ecstasies, the convulsions diminishing by the time I make it onto the street.

Distantly, people call my name, their voices strained and distorted, the world likewise; wavering and rippling around me, strings of matter, clots of living things still slopping from my mouth.

Home. Impossible; where they'll come for me, sedating me, strapping me down, cutting me open... maybe burning me alive, blaming it on a faulty gas pipe or anonymous arson.

I can't make it, anyway; my legs quiver, seconds away from pitching me to the broken concrete where I'll burst, the things inside scurrying and swarming away, eager to find new hosts in which to make their nurseries.

The car that pulls up is small, bile-yellow, barking and shuddering like it's seen better days.

Wilfred gestures to me from the driver's seat, ushering me into the back. He tears away from the school before I've managed to shut the door behind me, sirens already wailing in the distance.

*

Sleeping, for a time, swaddled in a dreaming cocoon, feeling my wings swell, simultaneously aching for and dreading the moment when I evolve beyond its bounds, take flight…

I wake far less celebratory, the intense evening sunlight burning my eyes, hard, uneven earth biting into my buttocks, the bark of a gnarled, dead tree rasping my back.

Woodlands. Deep, by the look of it, florid with signs of late spring.

Empty, I'm so empty; not the butterfly, but a hideously sentient chrysalis, spent and impotent, now that those pupating within have unfurled and fled.

Hungry. So hungry, it feels like a knife is in my guts, scraping what's left from inside.

Unblinking owl eyes flicker in the murk, a whisper of crushed leaves, stepped-on twigs, a shimmer of heart-racing silver.

"J… Jamiel?"

My voice is strange, deep and croaking, the fluctuations in my throat even moreso.

I try to stand, yelping as I snare against the chains wrapped and clasped around me.

"Jamiel? What the…"

"You wanted to help my boy, Mr. Yentson? You did say that, yes?"

Wilfred ambles into view, the man overdressed, given the warmness of the early evening, rubbing his hands as though perpetually cold. Standing next to his son, he pats him on the shoulder, smiling lavishly.

"What? Of course I do, I…"

I'm his teacher.

I feel it rise; what little is left within, the familiar convulsions, so sore inside, now, my entire body tender, as though from a night's nausea.

An impotent dribble seeps down my chin in black strands, what swims and scrabbles in it barely worthy of note.

Wilfred's smile dies as he urges his son back a few steps.

"Yes, I see that. Well, I want to help him, too, like my Mother helped me. You know what she used to say? No point in telling kids monsters aren't real, when they know they *are*. You teach them how to deal with the monsters themselves, then they're never afraid again."

The boy's eyes are distant and unfocused, the knife trembling in his hands.

"I… I'm not a monster, Wilfred. I… I'm sick."

"Oh, I know, Mr. Yentson, I know; like I said: I've seen this before. Not as many times as my Mother did, but enough. The monster is the sickness, I'm afraid. It's too late, now."

Gently nodding, be puts a hand to Jamiel's back.

"Go on, son. Just like I showed you."

Jamiel frowns, the expression aging his face by at least thirty years. I strain against the chains, the ragged bark grazing my back.

"Jamiel… *Jamiel…* "

The boy walks slowly, stumbling in the leaves and grass, the knife wavering and clumsy in his hands.

"Come on now, Jamiel. Your Mother's going to be wondering where we are."

Consternation flashes in his eyes as he looks down at the knife in his hands, letting it fall, turning to his Father. "I don't want to, Dad."

Wilfred sighs, turning his eyes to the boughs overhead. "I know, son. I know. I didn't, either. But it's for the best. For him, as well! He's not going to get better, you know that? And after what he did to your classmates? He made all of *them* sick, too. We're going to have to help them, just the same."

The boy shudders, shaking his head, starting to weep. His father goes down on one knee before him, taking him by the shoulder. "There's no one else who can do this, son. *No one else.* You understand? If you let him go now, then whatever he does after, whoever he hurts… that will be our fault. It will be *your* fault."

Plucking up the knife from where it lies, he hands it to his boy. Jamiel rubs his nose with the back of his arm.

"Can we get pizza after?"

Wilfred smiles squeezing his son's shoulder. "Pizza and ice cream. You'll have earned it. Just don't tell your Mother."

The boy turns to me with a lunatic smile, the light in his eyes making me shudder, recoil.

Crying out, my ragged throat making noises I didn't know it was capable of.

"Quickly, son, *quickly*."

The boy ambles towards me, the knife so awkward in his pudgy fist.

"Jamiel, *Jamiel*... this is... you can't do this, Jamiel! People will find out! They'll know, and then..."

The boy isn't listening, still grinning at the promise of pizza and ice cream. Nothing else his Father has said taking hold, gaining traction: only that promise.

Coughing, spluttering, something crawling up from my raw and ragged depths, that flaps as it emerges in my mouth, forcing my lips wide.

Wilfred's face visibly palls, growing slack on the bone. He starts forward, but too late, too late.

"Jamiel!"

The newborn flies, a black and ragged moth, trailing beads of matter through the air. Jamiel barely has time to stumble, to drop the knife, before it's on him, fluttering against his face, the boy squealing like a pig.

Straining against my chains, I cry out, the metal biting into the spongy flesh of my wrists.

Wilfred seizes the boy, spinning him around, wrenching his jaw so forcibly the boy cries out, squealing as he reaches into his mouth...

The boy bites down instinctively, clamping his jaws shut. The man pulls away, parting company with his fingers, strings and strands of bloody fibre stretching between them as he collapses back in the grass, clutching at himself.

Jamiel staggers and stumbles, hands at his belly, moaning in the back of his throat.

My wrist slips free, my chest and belly deflating, as though boneless, the organs they contain ferreted to other brackets around my body. The most bizarre sensation, feeling every rearrangement and reconfiguration; organs as they uproot themselves and uncoil, bones as they stretch and swell and make way for them.

Obscene, strange to the point of unpleasant, yet entirely not, making me giggle like a school boy hearing a filthy joke for the first time.

Slipping free from the chains like a snake, I rise to my feet, swelling again. Smiling.

Wilfred turns to me with lunatic pain, mindless fear in his eyes, glancing momentarily at the knife his son has dropped.

"J… *Jamiel…"*

The boy hears, lurching upright, spitting out the mangled stumps of his Father's fingers, glancing between us.

I *see,* long before he does: the boy's dark skin grows transparent, as though illuminated from within by a pulsing, purple light: shapes flitter around his interior like moths caught beneath a lampshade. The boy sees too, smiling, laughing legitimately for perhaps the first time in his life.

His Father wails, sweeping up the knife before I can stop him, hurtling at the boy.

A hideous sound, wet tearing, the boy grunting as though punched in the belly. The light in him flickers, fades, as the Father collapses back, the knife falling from his hand.

I'm on him before he can speak, before he can scrabble away, hurling him against a nearby tree, the bastard no heavier than a bag of feathers, despite his bulk.

His eyes widen as the back of his head cracks from the bark, leaving a dark, wet smear. Blinking, he staggers forward, about to fall to his hands and knees before I catch him, hoisting him up.

The man shudders, raking at my hands, gobbets of meat falling away with every stroke. There is no pain, that matter redundant, now, just like this mask, this life.

"What have you done? *What have you done?*"

Snarling, seeping through clenched teeth, that same orgasmic ecstasy as my stomach convulses, as something squirms its way up my throat.

No. He doesn't deserve this.

Unable to help it, some instinct beyond reason, beyond conscious thought, urges me to throw back my head, to open my mouth wide…

"Mr. Yentson?"

Turning, I see the boy bleeding, but *smiling*. Wet, black

butterflies emerge from the wound in his chest, spreading their newly formed wings, mingling, intermating to form a living bandage.

Wilfred thrashes, wailing in my hands, hot tears pouring down over my new skin.

The boy frowns again, that perpetual mist in his eyes clearing. Blinking, he gasps, looking around as though for the first time, before his eyes settle on his Father.

"Don't hurt him. He doesn't mean it."

Obeying, I lower the man to the grass, where he collapses on all fours, clutching at his throat, wretching.

Stepping away, I watch as the boy approaches, smiling down at him. "Dad."

His voice so *adult,* that of a middle aged man catching his ageing parent in some moment of dementia, some frustrated confusion.

Wilfred glances up, his face quivering, almost melting beneath his tears.

Distantly, a child weeps, not in the woods; deep, deep in the back of my mind.

Jamiel reaches out with a hand that swarms and crawls, his Father recoiling from it in disgust.

"Don't... *don't touch me.*"

Scrabbling back, he stirs up the leaves and soil, so much more child-like than his son, now.

The man they used to call Kevin Yentson peels away, more and more of him steaming on the ground at my feet. It isn't painful; ecstatic, if anything, as though I've been wrapped in smothering, too-tight clothes all my life, their seams finally giving, allowing me to breathe and feel the air for the first time.

I meet Wilfred's appalled eyes as they flicker between his son and me.

"Look! Look, Jamiel! That's what it means! That's their *sickness.*"

The boy turns to me, his skin pulsing translucent once more, the purple light shining through his eyes, seeping through his pores to coalesce as beads of liquid luminescence on his skin.

Beautiful. But far from *finished,* any more than I am: barely a chrysalis stage, neither one of us daring to dream what might follow.

He smiles, sweetly sincere, as others move in the surrounding woods, now, singing strangely familiar hymns.

Taking advantage of our momentary distraction, Wilfred scrabbles away, whimpering like an absconding, autistic child as others emerge from the shadows, taking hold of him, dragging him back.

Jamiel leaps up and down for joy at the sight of them; things that only yesterday would have raised shrieks from both of us now giving birth to smiles.

The two that take hold of Wilfred are as distinct from one

another as I am from Jamiel: a gelatinous, shifting blob of compost-like matter, fragments of semi-human anatomy emerging before being subsumed once more, the other a hunched creature, its lower half that of a woman, naked, beautiful, its upper half swelling into a wasp's nest mass, swarms of albino hornets emerging from its dripping apertures, describing shimmering circuits in the air.

The pair drag the trembling Wilfred back to us, setting him gently down on his knees. Quivering at their touch, at the sight of them, of *us*, he rips a handkerchief from his pocket, pressing it to his mouth.

Others emerge, sifting and slithering between the trees, descending from the boughs, coalescing from mist and smoke, from beams of light. No two alike; all species of one, leaving me to wonder what I might see were I to observe myself through their eyes.

Jamiel turns to me, smiling as though catching the echo of my thoughts, closing his eyes.

A vertical split appears in his forehead, a furrowed expression of discomfort as one of the black butterflies emerges, flapping its wet wings as though newly hatched. Wilfred audibly weeps as it takes flight, landing on my outstretched palm, lingering for a moment before my own coldly lambent skin parts to accept it: a mirror of the same wound, the insect easing its way inside.

A sensation that is simultaneously ecstatic and repellent,

echoing the first time I consented to join another man in bed, the same trembling uncertainty, the same blind want.

Shuddering as the wound seals, Jamiel opening his eyes.

Gasping, I laugh, unable to help myself, my sight *split*, originating from two separate sources: my eyes and his, the pair of us seeing as ourselves and one another, the sensation so strange, it steals my breath.

But nowhere near as strange as what the sight he lends reveals: a creature that's at least three feet taller than Kevin Yentson, tatters of him still clinging to it around the face, the hands: a flickering, luminous thing of pale blue skin, veins and circuitry of sunlight visibly worming beneath, elaborating in response to unknown designs and imperatives, leaving it with the distressing impression of never being quite still, areas where the light bleeds out through orifices in its throat, its flanks, its back. Reaching up with many-fingered hands, it paws and peels away what remains of the screaming, lonely man, the condition beneath pulsing and pregnant, already swollen with life, suggestions of it protruding from the orifice of its mouth and throat; black, scrabbling legs, centipede-like antennae. From its shoulders erupts matter that flows and twists in the air like the skirts of deep-sea fish, arcing with rainbow colour, lashing its back and limbs… *my* back and limbs, cleansing them of the filth that remains.

The man that was, *Kevin Yentson,* still screams, though there's so little of him left now.

"Please, *please,* Jamiel…"

Wilfred sobs, pleading with his eyes, though for what, I can't imagine.

The boy laughs, the others echoing him in their strange and myriad ways.

"You made me so afraid, Dad."

"I didn't mean to. *I didn't mean to…*"

The boy approaches him, hunkering down in the leaves and grass. Portions of him slough away as his back and head swell, pulsing like blisters about to burst.

"Yes, you did. But it's all right; I'm not afraid any more. Not of you or *anything.*"

The man attempts to struggle back as his son reaches to embrace him, arousing growls and moans of displeasure from his audience, including me.

Even now, *even now,* he can't bring himself to do it, seeing how beautiful his boy has become.

Something stirs inside of me, those same spasms of pain and pleasure: labour-pangs unlike any that the Mothers of humanity have experienced, that Fathers ever will: agony and ecstasy intermingled, being torn apart from the inside out, deliriously fucked in the same instance, soaring high on the sweetest of narcotics.

Not denying it any longer, I allow my children to come: slopping from me, wet and newly formed, scrabbling and many-legged, an entirely different species from those Jamiel hosts.

I watch as they unfurl in the leaves and long grass, swarming towards the only host present. Wilfred howls, the terror in his eyes barely dimming as his son takes hold of him, wrapping his arms around him as the swarms emerge, bursting through apertures in his back and head, flanks and limbs.

The pair are momentarily enveloped, the swarms obscuring them as the boy embraces his Father, as the Father tries to prize himself away, denying all Jamiel has to give.

Wilfred somehow struggling free, Jamiel staggers back, calling after the man as he crawls from within the swarm, raking at himself, reaching into his own mouth to make himself vomit. My children find him, rearing up from the grass, mewling ecstasy as they fasten to his face, crawl up his back, beneath his clothes.

Going to Jamiel, I wrap my arms around him, holding him tight as his Father screams and screams, thrashing on the ground. The others step back, allowing revelation to take its course.

Amber and scarlet light shear through the boughs, between the trees, by the time Wilfred grows silent. Time in which Jamiel and I come to know one another better than we ever could have separate in our own skulls and skins. In which we come to know those around us likewise, sharing the children that have transformed us, which we now cultivate inside. Some have existed in this state for years, decades, beyond the eyes and judgement of those that would burn us alive. Drawn here by us, the promise of new children, by what happened back in the classroom…

The children.

Laughter, as those that have been saved emerge through the trees. A handful only, the rest…

Taken, sealed away, hurt and undone in the name of some idiot notion of *purity*. Seeing it, experiencing it in flashes of vicarious memory from those who followed when they were taken, those responsible for stealing them from harm.

Rachael. Timothy. Paula. Raoul.

Four left, from a class of twenty-five. They flock about us, now, each and every one of them beautiful, their own strange works of art.

We laugh with them, weep with them for those they felt die. Jamiel joins them, barely glancing back as his Father stills, panting and quivering in the steaming afterbirth of the man he was.

I go to him, extending my hand. The thing that was Wilfred Kahbul unfurls a head that resembles the centipede-like children that helped him shape it. The tremors of that old fear, of that hereditary loathing: the stink of diseased flatulence in the air, the tang of urine, fading.

A hand like a scrabbling wolf spider's legs envelopes mine, the now nameless thing—as nameless as I am and we all are—allows

me to haul it to its feet, shreds and tatters of Wilfred Kahbul
falling away, leaving it naked, stretching and flexing in its new
condition, staring after the child it once sired as new and more
needing ones take shape in its body.

Yesterday, we were so separate, so far apart; lunatics in our
own asylum-cell skulls, our straightjacket skins. Today? More
intimate than any twins or lovers, more utterly ourselves than the
idiot, biological impositions of our parents and ancestors could
allow.

Following in the children's wake, laughing as they laugh, we
are children ourselves once again, naked and newborn in this
world we hardly know, where we will never be old and evil again.

Lost Moments

Little shit. *Stupid, pointless little shit!*

Hate that burns, a fever in his cheeks, his belly, making him want to scream and puke fire, to hit it and hit it until there's nothing left of its stupid, grinning face.

Its room is only across the landing, barely a few strides. All he needs to do is take a sharpened pencil, his pillow; stab out those blue, blue eyes, press the pillow down until it grows quiet and still for the first time in its life.

He's thought about it before, imagined it obsessively, again and again, when the little shit has stolen or broken his toys, scribbled in his books, torn his comics.

When they've sided with it against him, calling him cruel and selfish and stupid for just defending what's his.

They'll never hear, not find it until tomorrow, when it's too late. His Grandparents… deeply asleep, snores echoing through the thin walls, ragged and rasping.

But they'll *know,* the minute they go to wake the little shit, call it down for breakfast… what he's done, and why.

They'll blame him, like always: the first they turn to, whenever the little shit grazes its knee or bruises its head; always the first they shriek and hiss at when plates are smashed or ornaments broken. As though he has any control over what it does.

Today, a familiar ritual, whenever they visit Nanna and Granddad: a new toy to keep them occupied. He picked one of his favourites, that he's wanted since first glimpsing it in one of Mom's catalogues: *Arachnos,* from *The Drivers of Delirium,* a comic he's collected every issue of, stacks and stacks of them filling his bedroom shelves to near collapse at home.

A fusion of man and spider, black-skinned, many-armed, a bulbous abdomen filled with tiny rubber spiderlings that can be "birthed" by squeezing the toy's midriff.

The little shit has its own toy to play with and ruin: Sagacia, one of the *Restorers,* enemies of the *Drivers.* Broken almost the instant he gets it out of the package, like always. Approaching him, as he knew it would, trying to seem so innocent, though he knows what it wants.

"Can I have a go?"

"No! You've got your own!"

"But it's *broke.*"

"That's your fault, not mine."

Knowing, *knowing* that, if he touches it, *Arachnos* will instantly fall apart.

Mom watches, frowning. "Oh, stop being so selfish! Just let him have five minutes with it!"

"That's not the point, Mom! He breaks *everything.* I can't have anything without him ruining it."

The woman sighs, wrenching the figure from his hands,

placing it in the little shit's pudgy, awkward fingers.

"Now, you be careful, okay? That doesn't belong to you."

The shit doesn't pay the slightest attention, any more than it ever has. A dreadful certainty curdling in his belly the instant it gets up and waddles away, the evil look it throws him, the way it smiles.

Arachnos's abdomen rips open barely five minutes later, the spiderlings scattered across the carpet.

"You *little shit!*" He screams it, bringing Mom and Nanna running.

"*What* did I hear you just say?"

"Look what he's done!"

The little shit hovers behind them, protected by them. How it will always be, he realises, forever and ever.

"I don't care about that. What did I hear you just say?"

"Look!"

Waggling the toy in front of her, trying to make her see.

"Don't throw that thing in my face! If I hear you swear at him like that again…"

He doesn't even cry as he turns and runs from the room, secluding himself upstairs, away from their hateful eyes, its evil grin.

Sobbing prayers into his pillow, snarling them, not caring whether its angels or demons that answer.

*

He can't do it. They'll know. But maybe... someone else? Some*thing* else?

Rejecting the thought out of hand, knowing how *stupid* it is. How can he even ask? How can he make them *listen*?

He's unable to sleep for it, the idea a thorn, burrowing deeper and deeper into his thoughts, growing sceptic, fevered.

They won't come, not here, no matter how fervently he calls: the room proof against them, insulated against their intrusion by years of prayer and accrued ritual.

No, if he wants their help, he'll have to go to *them*.

An idiot notion, a baby's dream: of course he can't go to them! They won't listen, even if he finds them! Most likely, *he'll* be the one devoured, just like always, no matter what monsters he faces.

The night won't leave him be, won't let him dream and wake to a new round of injustices. Lingering, hours dragging to an eternity, the moon rising outside his window, the barks of youths and drunks returning home from the pub up the road filtering through.

He doesn't dare open his eyes for fear that his unspoken invitation has been answered, afraid of finding *them*, splayed across the walls, whispering beneath the bed, silhouetted against the curtains.

Nothing, the room empty, cold and quiet.

Sitting up in bed, he *dares* them to descend on him, swinging his legs over the edge, its old-fashioned springs squealing, metal frame shifting as though about to fall apart.

No hands reach from beneath, curling cold fingers around his ankles, no whispers from the shadows.

Shuffling into his slippers and dressing gown, he creeps to the door.

Something inside screams as he twists the knob, easing it open, peering out onto the landing.

A small space, light filtering through the net-curtained window, hazy and chemical orange, his Grandparents snoring in the room next door. A smell of dust and old pot-pourri.

No sign of the ones he half hopes, half fears to find—no red, smear-headed phantasm flickering before the window, no centipede-thing unfurling from the airing cupboard, no twitching spider's legs creeping from around the corner, pawing at the wall, seeking him out.

Creeping out, shivering, though not with cold, he remembers: *Arachnos,* torn open, his Mother's dull and hateful eyes, the little shit's smile.

Maybe he'll have them do similar to the little shit as it has done to his toys: twist its head off, bite off its fingers, gnaw its face into a shapeless, mangled mass.

The airing cupboard. Strange gurgles and clatters from inside. Just the boiler, they always insist, ever since the nightmares that gave birth to what nests inside.

Maybe true, but not *always*; what they can't see or understand: *of course* it's nothing but old pipes and boilers, *in the daytime,* but after dark..?

He jerks away as he hears it move inside, the thing knowing, sensing him, happy he's come to feed himself to it.

Holding fast, he ignores the urgency in his bladder, the pain that has him dancing from foot to foot in the scratchy, feet-itching carpet.

"H... h... hey. Hey? Are you in there?"

No answer, save more gurgles and hisses, bangs and clatters. Then:

Scratching against the peeling wooden door, nearly imperceptible, but not to him.

He almost bolts, hurtling back through his bedroom door, scurrying under the covers, safe in the darkness behind his eyes, where they can never follow.

Only the promise of days to come holding him fast; days without broken toys, without disruption, without being blamed for everything the little shit does. Days when they'll forget it ever existed, when everything will go back to how it was, before it infested his life.

"I... I have something for you."

The scritch-scritch-scratching louder, accompanied by a low hiss that almost makes him pee his pyjamas.

He sees it behind his eyes, coiled, wet and segmented, pale young clutched in a living ball between its many legs, its antennae waving in the steam-dank air.

Another sound which makes him screw his eyes shut, something on the ceiling above, its tread feather light, but not quite enough to disguise its presence.

He feels it reach down, its legs disturbing the air around his ears, a light, feathery brush at the back of his neck.

It somehow smiles, though it doesn't have a mouth or lips, delighted that the fly it has hunted for nights interminable has decided to surrender itself.

"N... not me, *not me!* Take him! I... I'll give him to you!"

Soft footsteps in the carpet at his back, a chill breath making him shudder. Sighs, a voice filtering into his thoughts: "Suppose we'd rather have *you?*"

A whisper, only; the voice of a dying woman, little breath left to waste.

" N... *no...* "

The scratches and chitters from within the airing cupboard grow more agitated, seeming almost like *laughter.*

Closer, closer: the soft footsteps, the rustling skirts, the pawing legs from above.

"Look! I'll... I'll open the way!"

He opens his eyes, but keeps them firmly on the wall as he edges around, turning the corner to the little shit's room.

"You'll... you'll like him better, anyway. He's younger. And he *cries* all the time."

Feet follow, steps on the ceiling, the airing cupboard door clicking open...

Reaching as gently as he can, he twists the old, rattling doorknob, letting the door ease open. The little shit mutters and murmurs inside, lost in dreams of tomorrow's vandalism.

Sighs of anticipation, the footsteps ceasing, the cold against his back enough to raise goose pimples.

The brush of a frost-bitten, bloodless hand against his cheek, a gentle caress at his shoulder.

Flying, he clamps silencing hands to his mouth, wrenching his eyes from the open airing cupboard door, refusing to see, catching only a glimpse of something shimmering inside, something *moving...*

He stumbles, sprawling on his knees in the threadbare carpet of his little backroom with its cold steel bed, its horrible, horrible paintings of wilting flowers, a little boy crying.

Rising, he wheels around, slamming the door shut before they can reach through, drag him out into the sweating darkness.

Tears come, then, as he slumps against it, as whatever follows scratches and hisses and sighs outside.

Pressing his palms flat to the wood, his forehead likewise, he sobs his most earnest, desperate prayer:

"Take him, *take him!*"

Laughter, a cruel girl, a cackling witch. Shadows skitter in the dim orange light filtering beneath the door.

They can't. *They can't get him.* Not here.

"I... I don't have anything else. *Please.*"

"Oh, such sweet lies! You have *everything,* child. You have *yourself.*"

Weeping openly, now, cursing himself for his stupidity.

"Just take him and go away."

Muffled voices from the room next door, Granddad stirring in his sleep, cursing ripely as he shuffles out of bed.

"Bloody fucking thunder."

The scratches and whispers outside cease, as though their makers evaporate at the sound of his voice.

The click of a light switch.

"What is it now?"

"Need to bloody piss again. Only the third time tonight."

"It's them bleedin' pills what the Doctor gave yer. I told yer..."

"Give over, will yer? Go back to sleep."

His Grandfather's heavy, slumping footsteps drive him away from the door. Diving beneath the covers, drawing them tight, he screws his eyes shut, momentarily so lost in the illusion of dreaming, he *believes* it.

"What the bloody 'ell is this? Aye, Edith, what's all this on the landing?"

A mumbled, slumbering response.

"Bugger ye, then."

The man mutters and murmurs, creaking and cracking all the way to the bathroom, pissing loudly with the door open.

Not seeing, never seeing, the night-things invisible to them.

The toilet flushes, pipes gurgling.

"'Ere, Edith! Our Joseph's door's wide open!"

"Well, just shut it then, will yer?"

"All right, all right! Don't snap me 'ead off! Bloody Hell."

A door clicks shut, more slumping steps, the crick and crack of old joints, muttered protests. A weary body dragging itself beneath covers, settling down to sleep.

He smiles in the dark, *truly smiles* for the first time since the little shit was born, terror slowly seeping from him as he drifts into dreams that already echo with the screams of tomorrow.

A Mercy of Minds

The same games. *Of course.* Too young to know, to remember the world as it was before my fire, before I taught it shame.

None of them recall the Hell of it, the unthinking cruelty of their parents, the bleak cynicism of their teachers. Better that way. No contrivance of mine; no gift to them, though it's within my power to grant such things: a mercy of their own minds, as they retreat and return, as they trick themselves into believing that the evenings grows late, that the days darken and die. They don't and never will. Not in this place: a splinter in time and space, a fragment preserved from the fire.

A gift for them, so that they can play and wonder, so that I can watch and delight in their games.

Cruel, sometimes, like their parents, like the world that birthed them. They are punished for that, though they don't recall, are allowed to see a little of what was, when they stray beyond the fences, when they see the world as it's become: ash and darkness; hollow, seared-black buildings, charred bones littering streets and alleys. The empty wastes beyond.

A glimpse only, a moment in which to hear the whispers of those less fortunate; confessions of pain and cruelty, of pettiness and presumption. Oh, bemoaned and regretted now, when it's too late, after they drew me here, through the filth, through the sewage between states, where realities bubble and burst together, where muck gives birth to muck, a place of fungus and worms and infection... where I walk, sometimes. When I can bear it.

A glimpse is all I allow them, all they can withstand. Promises following the cries and howls, their breathless pleas as they run, *run* from the vermin that have gnawed and wormed their ways through, that have evolved from the dead, formed of their parent's ashes and regrets...

Promises that they never keep, but I can't resist believing: that they will be better, when they return, that they will play beautifully again and be happy to forget the world.

This one, just returning; so spiteful, so jealous of her friend's attention for one another. Taught that much by creators who poisoned her with their affections, proclaiming her the centre of creation from the first smiling moment, the first wordless, idiot gurgle, the original ember of thought.

So deeply ingrained, she reverts to the myth of her memories again and again, no matter how powerfully or painfully recreated, no matter how far I remove her from the child that was.

She stumbles through the gates of the playground tattered, bloodied, ash-strewn, like so many of them, back rent by the beasts that crawl and hunt through the wastes, barely able to stand.

I watch, as the other children go to her, as she collapses in their arms. A beautiful doll, hollow head filled to bursting with new stories, new myths, so that she might be more, when she wakes.

But none that *hold,* none that burrow deeply or intimately enough, that spread with the rapacity of that original cancer: the evil that led her here, beneath my eye.

Tomorrow or the day after or the day after… it doesn't matter; soon enough, it will make itself known, rearing up through the sweeter lies I tell her like a worm from beneath honey. And she will be that same child again: selfish, cruel, narcissistic.

They will turn on her, as they always do, and she will flee from the playground, from beneath my eye and protection, out of spite that they will not bow to and obey her whims, that they won't make her the centre of their adoration, a child idol in an infantile cult.

One of the most lost, who will one day not be able to find her way back, who will forget and become like the other beasts and phantoms… a scavenging thing, half forgotten to itself, but not enough, not nearly enough to maintain sanity.

Its parent's true child.

My burning obsession shifting away from her, to another: the boy who is taller, stronger than the rest, who has known it since he first walked through the gates: a leader, one around which tribes form, legends accrue. A king or prophet born, knowing how to speak, how to manipulate, when to use sweetness, when to use violence. The latter… all he has ever known, all his parents taught him: fear, pain, anger. The shards and stuff of his life.

Something he has fought and fought, that he resists every day: the black bile, the poison behind his eyes, in his belly, threatening to bubble over, boil away composure, make him just another monster...

Sometimes, there's nothing he or I can do to stop it. Sometimes, he is his Father's child, a snarling, spitting beast whose only coherent words are sewage, foulness, who doesn't stop hitting until his fists are bloody, his victim still.

Those ones... the weak and unknowing, the squint-eyed and snot-nosed and asthmatic... I repair, purge of all memory, not allowing them to recall and be poisoned by the violence done to them.

Their abuser I cast out, again and again: allowing him to see me, as he has before, peering down at him through the clouds and smoke, through the swirling ash, as he goes to his knees, as the others laugh at him, mock him for soiling himself, as he weeps, grovels, *remembering*.

Out there, now, exiled longer than previously, for a sin beyond simple violence: for losing himself, for attempting to create something like his parent's ashen kingdom here, in my playground. A sin I will never abide.

I hear him, I *see*, through my eyes in the ash, from the storm above: no longer known to himself, a lost, hunched and roaming thing, twisted and transformed by the broken world where he wanders, by the fractured nightmare his parents have left to him, to them all.

He's a beast, now, perhaps happier in that state: greater than he was before, no longer a child: wiry, muscled, black pelt shimmering in the inconstant sun and moon. Eyes blazing with hurt, insatiable appetite for pain, inflicting it on all he encounters: the lost and exiled ones, his twisted siblings. Displays of such violence, such hideous torment. Like a cat, he doesn't merely kill and devour them, but keeps them alive for as long as he can, hunting and stalking them, reaching out from shadows to rake them across the back or ankles, to rip open their cheeks, allowing them to flee into the labyrinth of inconstant ways, pursing them as long as play sustains. The end never clean, never quick.

Closer, closer with every day. Maybe remembering, in some vague sense: what he was, here, what he might be again. I'm not sure I can save him, now. Not sure that I want to.

Others follow, in time, as they grow bored of the endless games, as they remember a little of who they are, where they're supposed to be. Peeling away to find long lost parents, brothers and sisters, friends and not-quite-lovers.

I let them go, always; not their parent, never making the same mistakes. Fascinated, endlessly fascinated by their contradictions, their absurdity. What they do, when they think no one is looking, when they believe themselves alone. The games they play, the elaborate stories they weave, which transform the small island broken concrete into strange and alien kingdoms, war-torn battlefields, desolations carved by dragons and demons, woodland realms and forgotten gardens of fey and faerie things.

I see as they do, through their credulous eyes: the dreams they weave, the transformations they wreak on the world, still not understanding that they're so much more than ephemeral fantasy, that they are little mad gods in their own rights, spawning realms and realities with every stray thought and inspiration... that I can walk in them as easily as I do here, and will, when this experiment finally fails to obsess, when I grow weary of sustaining it.

Maybe, by that time, they will have dreamed themselves other enough to *see me,* to speak and dream with me without losing their fragile, precious little minds.

Perhaps some amongst them will even become kin, like others I have observed or will observe or never will: when they are weary, so weary of being children, of their endless games and wish a new playground for themselves, beyond anything I can create or suspend.

Or maybe not. Maybe they'll be like so many others; passing fancies that will expend interest long before they evolve to that condition, blinking out, crumbling as I forget and slink my way back into the filth between worlds.

I don't know... only that nothing in all of time and reality obsesses me as much as *this,* here and now, nothing excites my passions or rouses me to such ecstasies as observing their games.

The ache to join them almost irresistable, to reduce myself, find some burned and blasted carcass in the wastes, purge it of carrion poetry, of myths or memories that might still infest it, weave a suit for myself from it; a child-mask that I might go amongst them in, join their games. In which I might even forget myself, for a time, allow myself the delusion of innocence... yes.

So lost in those fantasies, the other states and playgrounds they spark, I barely notice, until she beckons: the one separate from the rest, who takes no part in their games, but wanders, fascinated by the ephemeral worlds behind her eyes.

She smiles up at me, beckoning for me to come down and join them.

Impossible. *Impossible.* The sight of me surely enough to boil her eyes in their sockets, to blast whatever sanity she boasts to shards and atoms?

Yet, there she stands, her eyes whole and flaring amber in the perpetual dusk, clearly not mad or devolving into abomination.

Her invitation more than mere words and gestures: a *desire* so unambiguous, it lodges in me like hooks, drawers on me like chains.

It's so easy to deny, turning my sight from her. But something, *something* will not permit it. I *ache* to be with her, to be like her.

Laughter in my mind, a mind that contains depthless, fathomless realities, in which this playground would be lost— nothing but a scrap of dying creation preserved after apocalypse.

My mind, where a million others like me reside, my undying children, where they fashion realms, dream their own conditions, occasionally bleeding or burrowing out, worms erupting from my skull. My mind, which is so far beyond what they might call the same, as an ocean is to a teardrop, a storm to a breath.

She is so small, so simple. *Nothing.* Yet, I can no more deny her than Canute could the tides.

Already dissolving, I accept her invitation, reach out into the surrounding wastes, casting my eye through the broken, shadowed, shifting streets for something, *anything*... there. There!

Elation mingled with mourning—one of mine, one of the self-exiled; bored of the games, aching for more, not realising or remembering that there is nothing left for them in this world, save what I choose to suspend.

A boy, his body rent, charred and blackened, picked clean in places by the scavengers of those wastes, infested with parasites: echoes that seek to be more, ghosts that partially recall what it is to be flesh, envying it, even in this rotted, stinking condition.

I pluck him up, cradling him like the most delicate of butterflies. So little is left, of flesh or soul. It's simple enough to purge him, even in my dissolving condition—for my dust and powdered bone, my fire and smoke, to flow into him, cleansing him of worms and fungus, fleas and carrion. They scream as they emerge, pulsing formless and empty into the air, carrying nothing with them as they rain back into the darkness below.

The girl watches, fascinated. Others beg to know what she sees, blind to it, mocking her for it.

She *shows them.* Taking the hands of the nearest, she shares her sight. None burning, none clawing out their own eyes or collapsing in convulsions. None fleeing: watching as I come apart, as the stars erupt from my skull, as my heart becomes a sun in which every inch of me incinerates.

So long… so long since I knew this, since I mourned my own passing. Luxuriating in every instant, as my mind and the realities it contains collapse on themselves, as apocalypses beyond count or measure occur in the same span of heartbeats.

A moment… sublime panic, as I realise I may not be able to ascend again, this time; that I may live and die here, as one of the lost children.

I surrender, not allowing that anxiety to undo all I've begun; the girl smiles, her friends likewise: so much wiser, so much more *known to themselves* than I ever saw.

Ha. The same sin, the same *blindness*, as their parents, their makers and masters. Always and forever.

The carcass in my hands shudders as I fill it, as it swells with my light and dust: a vessel for cosmic fire, for memories that no mind of meat can contain. I feel him stir around me, still skinless, but swelling with fresh flesh; a thing of agony as new nerves flare, as they bask in fire and smoke.

The pain of it intense, worse by far than any death I've suffered or shared, but nothing compared to the sense of being smothered, of being constricted and contained within a sack of swelling, living meat.

Passing, I flow, becoming little more than the stuff of thought, an element in his blood that no doctor or chemist might detect.

No longer held, no longer a doll or puppet: *me.* The very essence of myself. No distinction existing between us, now.

Falling, falling, as the last of me disperses, entering his first inhalation, as he plummets like a celestial child ejected from Heaven.

As he sleeps upon the charred, shattered stone, and I dream with him, *as* him, of the games we'll play, the states we'll inspire.

Epilogue

Watching that strange, lonely boy, older than all of them, maybe the eldest. Fascinated by him. Alone now, as ever; while the others play in the red sun, while they dance and whisper secrets, making promises of an adulthood that will never be.

She doesn't know him, yet *does.* As though from a dream, when she was a babe, when she still remembered Mother's arms, the taste of milk.

Before she learned the distinction between awake and make believe. Before she stopped believing in me; the voice in her thoughts, the burning worm in her head. Nothing but a fantasy, a lonely child's imaginary friend. Silent, now, unheard, but far from forgotten.

Alone, in his ragged shorts and t-shirt, alone as the breeze comes, whipping up his over-long hair. Alone, and staring up, at the empty, golden sky, as though there's something there only he can see, or something was, once.

I feel her shudder, slithering through her, eager to erupt; the laughter of a far wiser girl, and far crueller.

Catching her breath, she remembers *seeing:* the monster in the sky, that held the Playground with its eyes, in its burning talons, that led them back to it, again and again, after they were lost or fled from it, after they forgot themselves.

And those memories that are worse, far worse: nightmares of fever and confusion, of running, *running,* of eating filth that made her vomit, made her stomach writhe and her throat erupt with blisters. Sick meat, old bones, poisonous muck and fungus.

So many… lost there so many times, so many girls with her face, returning, after a time, forgetting, by the grace of the beast above, and by mine: the nameless angel of her infancy.

Gone, now, as the boy knows. Yet still, they come: more and more every day, every hour, stumbling through the torn and twisted iron gates, slumping to their knees against broken concrete, blinking in the sun. Guided by their own beasts and angels, their own worms and demons. By selves they have dreamed and lost.

None know. How can they? She tried to show them, once, and they forgot, just as she has. Just as she begged me to make her.

Too soon. Too *young*. Too many games to play, worlds to wander and make for themselves.

But now... time, at last. This little girl's skin and little girl's skull too cramped, too suffocating for what blooms inside.

Rising from where she sits, cross-legged on the scorched and shattered concrete, she goes to him. I unfurl, no longer merely a worm that whispers stories, that sings her nursery rhymes, but a dream that she's never dared realise before, other eyes on us as we swell and crack and bleed, not just red, but luminous white and silver, the pain excruciating, ecstatic: all we're meant to be about to birth itself, but not yet: not without reminding him.

He laughs, this strange, lost boy: laughs as we touch his shoulder, as our light and matter flows over him, as he takes our hand.

My hand.

Wings unfurl inside, beyond the bounds of her skull, her stretched and splitting skin. The girl weeping for her own loss, laughing through tears, as she recalls herself, all we and I ever were, memory that stretches forward, from this point, as well as back, to what we might be, what I might make, after she and I dissolve, becoming one.

He is fire and bone, or was, once: a Father of apocalypse, a child of the same. Oh, the worlds he has burned, the dreams he's licked hollow only to shat or vomit up, to choke on and abandon, to lap up and be poisoned by, over and over again!

As I have. As we all have and will once more.

Some run, the gates of the playground clattering, their screams fading. No returning, after today, no remembering. Going the way of their parents, after all.

But others watch and remember: all they have been, have dreamed and wanted for themselves: the strange states in which they fly while sleeping, the beasts and disgraces they became outside, in the ashes of their makers. They rise and swell with us, even those that do so reluctantly, that cling to this existence, this delusion of childhood, as though it was ever anything more.

No two are alike, any more than we are: my brother and I, my lover, husband, child and destroyer to be.

He laughs as he comes apart, as he rises from himself, to where the boy he wore still looks, a shadow of bones and burning matter staring in horror, in joy, as the thing that haunts every idle fantasy, every waking nightmare, swells before him, kindling the clouds, blazing the sky to fire.

She screams as she comes apart, as I flow from her, others echoing her: a labour-pang choir, as they give birth to themselves, the children they are and never were splitting at the seams, bursting apart, melting from their own bones in ecstatic conflagrations.

The playground cracks and dissolves, no longer necessary, now that we have dreams of our own. Others already coalesce to supplant it: states elaborating under their own enthusiasm and inspiration, whose dreamers already walk there in a million skins and masks, authoring their own apocalypses in time and transcending once more, to this state of perfect potential.

I am with him, braving his fire, as he braves mine, for the first time in waking millennia; moonlight sister, sun-blazing brother; an incest that ripples and rages through time, myth and the troubled sleep of children who ache at their conditions, praying to be more than birth or life or death can allow.

The girl and boy we were realising, in this final rapture, that *they* are the projections and contrivances, the dreams that parents might ridicule us for holding, not mourning that revelation, as others do, not railing against it, attempting to hold onto lives that can never be and never were, but surrendering, in their sorrow and weariness, allowing themselves to be consumed, lost to the flames.

Maybe we forget again, in time, when our passions cool, when we finally part: when he slinks back into that sludge between conditions, the sewer outside of being, to curse the moment either of us were born, that he was ever so foolish as to love me again, to believe anything between us could be different from the million schisms before.

Or maybe not. Maybe, this time, we will be wiser, thanks to

the children we were and whose games we shared, returning to that original state; a single condition, that was once more than either of us, before we tore ourselves apart and became alien, alone and perpetually wounded.

All is possible, dreamed and lived in an instant, in a projection of millennia that spans a mortal blink.

None of it matters in this conflagration, this love-making that sets reality aflame, that undoes all we might have made and leaves us trembling and naked in our earnest unknowing, enraptured by our mutual ignorance of tomorrow.

A World Beyond Windows

A little time. All I want, all it takes.

Stillness, the taste of bitter coffee fading, the creaks of the house, gurgles of the boiler, growing distant. Aches in my joints, the strange tremor of my heart (a new development, not even consciously feeling the organ until recently, when it sprouted wings to flutter against its imprisonment), all fading, fading...

This fog, these scarlet, seething clouds. I tumble through them, still simultaneously *here,* seated on my sofa, eyes open, watching the world through the windows; scuds of purple and yellow across blue, blue sky, passing parents and children on their ways home from school.

Alien desire. Children, family... never wanting them, unable to comprehend the appeal. More bloody grist to the mill of history, more bags of potential misery. Not long enough beyond the womb to understand how pointlessly cruel, how lacking in poetry, this ridiculous excuse for a world can be. Why would I want that? Why would anyone?

Tumbling, soaring, I'm caught naked and bleeding on barbed winds, tempests furious enough to tear cities apart, to sweep up tsunamis that might wash civilisations away.

The winds carry stories of the ruin they've already written, to the dreaming not-quite-gods, the gestating divinities that swell at the storm's heart.

Fables of distant apocalypse, of cities and civilisations having reached states of such saturation, they implode or collapse, erupt or fracture. Of nations and species undone by the most unlikely phenomena, cosmic storms and tectonic shifts, meteor strikes and galactic collisions. The divine unborn revelling in these fables, suckling and swelling on them, incorporating them into their own nascent mythologies.

So many... all their own creations, like me—dreaming or aching or tearing through the grey veils of their original realities. Unlike me, never returning to the withered dreams that bore them, that they ripped open like babes too eager to be born. Some aren't able, having reduced theirs to ashes, for want of self-authored wombs. Others having long forgotten, the memories unwanted, unnecessary, agonising to retain.

I don't hate my cradle, like them, though frustration with it drives me here, beyond its bounds, again and again. Maybe, one day, I'll take my place amongst them. Maybe, one day.

But not today.

*

I hardly notice her shuffling up the path to the front door, not recognising her through the storm. A lost and wandering phantom. I experience a moment of vertigo, of dreaming distance, incomprehension, a look of confusion across her face, of possible offence. Who is she, this strange and shrivelled woman, this shuffling sack of grey and forgotten promises?

I can't help but smile, rising from the sofa even as I tumble, in that other place, plummeting from the storm, carried over the infinite black oceans it stirs, over vast and violent maelstroms that churn continents to powder, in which fleets of ships eternally toss, from which rise the children of drowned and dreaming things. Great molluscs and nests of seething tendrils, leviathans that coil and mate and devour one another endlessly, that combust into blue and green flame before my eyes, consumed to the skeleton before descending into depths where lesser creatures swarm on them, devouring what remains of their flesh or weaving new conditions around their bones from their own matter unwanted matter.

Endless shores, islands, atolls, the horizon boundless, without direction or dimension: the sea that binds us as one, which we all swim, at some point in our lives.

So few remember, for want of retaining sanity. As though sanity ever did us any good.

Depths that reflect the sky in places, becalmed beneath the storm, become the perfect mirror of it: pulsing with drowned stars, the things nestled at their hearts swelling towards apotheosis, twins of sky and sea.

I watch as they're born: tumbling like me from the sky, rising from the depths, some meeting one another in those journeys, impacting, combusting: apocalyptic unions that either murder them at birth or result in something new, which neither could have dreamed alone.

Shuffling from the living room out into the hallway, I fumble to unlock the door.

A stuttered, uncertain, smile, an unsure embrace.

The woman mumbles as she comes in from the cold. "Oooh, you wouldn't think it'd be so cold, would you? Being so bright!"

She peels off her gloves and coat as I set about making coffee, put on my mask and make theatre for her: smiles and hellos, banal wit and dry observations.

Fighting all the while to retain focus, to not slip back, diverted by the shorelines and islands passing beneath: lands to shame any continent on earth; vast plains of broken, black rock, shifting white desert, abandoned, alien civilisations.

Ruinous towers, black and horn-like, fashioned from fossilised bones that erupt from the mountains whose heights they crown, a web of shattered bridges binding them, whatever winged or weightless species built them long, long passed, maybe fled in some exodus, maybe murdered by their own hands. The winds threaten stories of the calamity, which I deny, ignore—terrified of being anchored here, shackled by my fascination with the species' unfolding history (there's no time for it, not any more).

I allow the wind to take me, carry me mote-like out across the desolation beyond the mountains…

She sighs as she sits, glancing about the place, fighting to keep fret from her eyes. "It's been a while since we've seen you. Everything okay, is it?"

Everything okay?

Plains formed from burned meat and molten plastic stream below, which quiver and ripple as though alive, as though whatever doomsday engine authored this apocalypse still churns in the darkness beneath. Shattered remnants of the civilisations that once stood here litter the shifting wastes; areas where ruinous structures still stand, torn open to the elements, invaded and undone, where parasite grasses and fungi sprout, things moving amongst them like maggots, scraping whatever living they can from the diseased earth.

I soar with winged scavengers, things of tar-black, almost molten flesh, their ragged frames barely held together as they swoop and flock, scrabble over the tatters of screaming meat they pluck from the plains below.

They call to me with their strangled, scabrous cries, inviting me to join them in their necrophage feasts, offering me meat that will become mine, that will anchor and congeal around me, making me another of their carrion kin.

I deny their sacrament, the flocks they invite me to be part of, the wastes they'd have me scavenge over forever more.

Rejected, formless, I'm swept up on the diseased winds, carried deeper and further from myself than ever before.

*

"Andy?"

Swilling coffee around the percolator, I absently spoon sugar into one mug.

"Yeah?"

"You've hardly said a word since I got here. Is everything okay?"

A smiling mask, quiet eyes. "Everything's fine. It's been a bit busy, lately; haven't had much time for anything, you know?"

True, true. But also not.

I hand her the mug, her eyes still fretful, though thankful for the lies.

"I know… I know you're working hard right now."

But.

"But it'd be nice to see you, every now and then. We're only down the road."

"I know. Like I said; I haven't had much time, lately, and what time I've had, I've been basically sleeping through."

"I don't know how you do it. How many is it, now?"

"Seven, I think, at the last count."

"Seven. Bloody Hell."

Bloody Hell.

*

Here. Beyond the wastes, beyond sight of the sea, is a city, or was: crooked towers, broken spires, partially sunken, sprouting at strange angles from the twisted, uncertain streets. I descend through architecture that resembles immense creatures, unclear hybrids between humanity and reptiles, fossilised at the point of their cannibal mating, in the midst of giving birth to one another, titanic bones and bizarre fungi, a mote on the howling gale that stirs and snatches up the alien ghosts of this place, whose entire being now consists of lamenting the dereliction they've allowed.

Fleeting glimpses of those that still live, that boast some substance, too ephemeral to make any sense of, my most abiding impressions of tumescent forms, accrued or cobbled together from bubbling black filth, fleeing my attention the instant it turns on them, as though ashamed of their conditions.

My destination becomes clear as I hurtle towards the heart of the city: a structure that might have been shat or vomited into being, an asymmetrical mass of solidified matter, black and shimmering as though lacquered, its wings and cloisters swelling from it like tumors, twisted spires of similarly organic matter sprouting in no particular pattern or clear design from its expanse, twining or spiralling skyward, their structures fluted and hollow, some meeting, fusing as single phenomena at points before diversifying once more.

A familiar song calls through the storm, piercing its howls, the protests and seductions of alien ghosts, singing me stories of who I might be here, what we might make of one another...

Flesh, matter, coalescing in synchronicity with comprehension, both equally unwanted, my mote self railing against the definition they threaten to impose, their hideous, straight-jacket restrictions.

Unable to deny them, the song intent on me, infesting me, every note and lyric a new nerve, a fresh splinter of bone.

Inevitable, but no less hated for that; the reunion to come requiring eyes, requiring hands and tongue and blood, no matter how hateful the whole they contrive.

A scream of defiance, of near birth, as I choke my first breath, as I hurtle towards one of the structure's towers, the gale intent on dashing me against it, rather than allowing me to be...

A window shatters as I hurtle through, skidding across the warped and splintered floorboards, setting small fires as I pass. *Pain,* my new, unasked for carcass already bloodied, crumpling against a great bookshelf, its contents spilling over me. A stink of blood and burning, of rotting meat and sewer foulness. The stench of my own rebirth, a life that already knows more of pain than anything has a right to.

He's here, waiting, as always, somehow *knowing,* attuned to the storm, knowing where and when it will shat me. Staring down at me, her permits himself a feline smile.

"You look like shit."

No worse than I feel; not possible. Broken bones resetting, burns healing, organs swelling and sealing.

Righting myself, a spider unfurling, I stretch my limbs, orienting to this new state.

"Oh, *fuck.*"

My friend sniffs laughter, a cat's kiss, eyes half closing.

"I'll never understand why you make it so difficult for yourself."

Gasping, I hack up a wad of semi-congealed blood and bone splinters. The air in this place... saturated with filth, disease; the myriad ills that reduced it to desolation.

"It's how it's always been."

"But not how it *has* to be. Why can you not understand that?"

Struggling to stand, I use the shelf at my back as leverage. More of its scrolls and volumes tumble around me, scattering on the floor.

"Some of those are priceless, you know; one of a kind."

Everything here is one of a kind, no matter how hideous. Us included.

He can't quite conceal his impatience, for all his apparent composure. Clearly anticipating me for some time, he's had opportunity to scavenge some clothes for himself: a purple and gold robe that clings to his scrawny frame, swirling about him as he moves, black trousers beneath, buckled leather boots.

"Well, where are we this time?"

"I don't know its name. Only that it has secrets."

"Don't they all?"

A sickle-moon smile.

"Of course they do."

Of course.

*

"You look worn out, love. Aren't you due any holiday, soon?"

Sinking into the sofa, I draw hands across my face, pulling my features taught. Beard unkempt, hair too long, Overdue a makeover. "Probably. It's tricky taking it right now, the way things are."

"Oh! I know; it's all over the news. Bastards, aren't they? Taking money from the schools and the care homes and what not."

Bastards. Yes. But clearly not enough for people to tell them so, to hold them to account.

"We're short staffed right now; people are moving on."

She tries to conceal the fright in her eyes, failing.

"And what will that mean for your lot?"

I shrug, sipping coffee, hardly tasting, hardly seeing.

"I suppose we'll have to move on, too."

Rain hammering down, now, forestalling her departure. Both

of us frustrated by that, weary of one another, pricked and invisibly bleeding, as though we both erupt with shards and venomous spines.

I don't want her here, with her watery eyes, her false concern. She doesn't want to be near me, with my unspoken resentment, my disinterest in any of the empty cattle noises that come from her mouth.

Cruel, no doubt, but true, almost beyond my ability to conceal it, to pretend otherwise.

"You'll be all right, love. You'll see."

A placation more for her comfort than mine. In no way will I or any of us be "all right." She knows that as well as I do, but will never say, afraid of what that confession will mean, the dissolution that will follow.

"We'll see."

*

He tuts and sighs as he helps me to scavenge clothes, though it wouldn't be the first time I've had to wander a new playground in nothing but my skin.

Remnants and remains litter the upstairs storeys, negotiating them a suicidal exercise; the floors and stairwells warped, broken, collapsed on themselves, the rest not far from capitulating. The structure is bizarrely tilted, sunken on its foundations, making every step confusing, almost nauseating in its disorientation.

We trespass in rooms infested with vermin; skittering, spider and cockroach creatures, rattish carrion, their bulbous eyes about to burst from their skulls, their scabrous backs sprouting with amber-dewed spines.

Bones. Piles of rot decorating every bed, every floor, as though those that rest here gathered to die in relative peace, rotting serenely, uncaring of the scavengers that make their nests amongst them.

We find a set of robes similar to his still covering the bones of their former wearer, colours vibrant and shimmering, whatever they're woven from clearly suffused with some art that's sustained them against the decay of this place, the vandalism of moths and rats.

I struggle into them, marvelling at their sky blue and dusky amber, not as well fitting as his, but then, they never are.

He already seems so at home here, so effortless, almost floating up the stairwells, over rents in the floor, pausing at windows, at openings in the walls, staring out over the surrounding ruins.

I join him, once sufficiently dressed, the robes quivering against me as though sentient, aware of the fact that I'm not their original wearer, though not resenting me for that.

He gazes out through a rupture that splits the structure's exterior, widening towards its foundations, exposing floors and chambers, corridors and hallways to the elements. From its ragged lips, extrusions that partially resemble wire, partially nerves or veins, systems that might have once had some organic origin. Dead as the building itself, now; dry and motionless, whatever they once transmitted long since bled or evaporated from them.

Below, a ditch of filth, viscous, scarlet matter flowing in a polluted stream, shapeless, boneless things rearing from the effluent, flatworm bodies coiling with tendrils, lesser versions of themselves sprouting from their amorphous anatomies, swelling until they're of similar size to their hosts before violently tearing free.

Though revolted, unable to entirely conceal it, I find myself mesmerised by their vile dance, their grotesque feedings, listening to their hideous songs as they blossom open, hooting and hissing to one another.

"Please don't tell me..."

He grins at me, smoothing lank, blonde hair from his face.

"All right, I won't. It's not like I have to, anyway."

Of course not. *Of course not.* Always knowing, with that strange telepathy of dreams; knowledge sifted from the air, revelation washing my mind with a certainty that my waking self can't conceive or imagine sufficiently to envy.

Our way... following the stream, as it twines into the distance, overshadowed by looming, partially collapsed structures, choked

in places with filth and debris, where the shapeless things gather,
scrabbling over clots of matter that they devour, bloating until
they become almost translucent, spraying excess and effluent
from the orifices decorating their backs.

In the distance is an opening, a cavern, into which the stream
flows. God only knows what's waiting for us down there...

Smiling, he leaps, floating down in defiance of gravity, landing
with a cat's poise, a dancer's grace.

Smiling, I follow, unable to help myself, though I know it will
likely be the death of me.

*

Shuddering in the vile afternoon, I resist a hideous waking.
Nothing of blood, nothing of dreams; just dull intimations, sighs
and suggestions: her mask far more practised and perfect than
mine.

I ache for her to go, screaming for it with my eyes.

And she knows. *She knows,* but won't indulge me, any more
than she or my Father ever have. Not like *him,* my nameless,
dreaming friend; my sibling since before we were born, who I've
never met here, in waking life, but find every night, there,
amongst the dreaming desolations of our species, in the heart of
the storm, the ocean's depths.

"Well, I'd better be going; your Dad will be wondering where

I am."

No, he won't. Any more than he spares a thought for me, beyond what he fears might happen to change what we know.

Kind words, as much as I can muster; obsequious goodbyes, empty promises that I'll visit, when I have a moment.

My moments, which I will never let them steal.

Not ever again.

*

We wade through the mire, stinking and spattered, tattered robes glued to our bodies with sweat and blood. The arterial stream froths around our ankles, the things we pass by, that flop and shriek at us, spray their effluent at our backs, hooting, wailing, horrified beyond measure at our trespass, as though the open sewer they inhabit is the most sacred of gardens.

But not following—they're wiser than that.

Pausing at the opening, smiling at one another as we catch our breaths, we peer into darkness. The *stink* of the place… echoes from below—the shift and quiver of something vast, scraping stone, splashing in sewage. Grunts and wickers echo, distorted and indecipherable.

Markings deface every visible inch of the stone; claw marks, places where it has melted and solidified again, as though beneath some acidic secretion, flaming breath.

Braver than I, always, he's already at the entrance, a step away from shadows.

"Are you sure?"

"Of course not. When am I ever?"

A fair retort.

Joining him, I stand aside from the entrance, peering around its ragged lip.

"Christ, *the stink*..."

Closing his feline eyes, he breathes it in, as though fortified by it, luxuriating in it.

"You don't have to come. You know that?"

I know. I've always known. Yet I follow, always have. Always will.

Better than waking, than sleeping only to never find him again—the price I'll pay, should I retreat in reluctance or cowardice, should I let *their* disease smother the child inside.

No knowing what awaits us down there, what manner of worm ate this hollow from the city's bedrock. What it might do to us, should we meet it.

That ignorance... lightning behind my eyes, in the pit of my belly; a fire to shame any dragon's, that will only swell at the sight of it, beyond my will or ability to contain.

I follow, as he steps into the dark, praying that I never know waking or daylight again.

*

She lingers, though afraid of the rain returning, of me, wanting me to say the words that I don't feel, for the loving lie.

I can't, I won't, not today or ever after. My silence the price she and her kind pay, for their indifference, their bertrayals, the arbitrary births they subject us to.

"Well, it was nice seeing you, if only for a little while. Come down and say hello, won't you? Your Dad would love to see you."

Another lie, the last of a lifetime, enough to fill a series of bibles, to make numerous gospels of contradictory falsehoods.

My Father has never loved to see me, any more than I have him. His grunting, hostile presence an affront, fricative, his unspoken dismissals matched by my desire to be out of his presence, away from his empty eyes.

Eyes whose hostility I'll never know again, after today.

The moment anticipated, specifically planned. Imagined, over and over again, considered from every angle.

The extension cord purchased and practised with, the weight it can support determined. The upstairs bannister reinforced, so as not to snap and make a cruel farce out of it all.

Like everything this world has given, all it has ever promised, this ultimate moment...not one of pathos or poetry, no grand revelations, no metaphysical awakenings. Only a dull impatience, a matter-of-fact process, in which I assemble the necessary equipment, ensure the doors are locked, the curtains closed.

Stepping back, once I'm done, exhaling, a wordless prayer of relief, that there'll be no more wakings, no more want; that the smothering weight of this wasted, endless nightmare will be lifted from me, soon.

I ascend the stairs, each one creaking as though in protest at what I'm about to do, the rain consistent, its monotone music filling the house, my head, leaving me thoughtless, without fear or hesitation.

You'll be all right, love. You'll see.

Smiling at that prophecy as I slip the cold knot around my neck, and step out into nothing.

*

I barely feel the storm that stops my heart, that chars my brain to cinders. A strange swelling in the dark, gasping as I stumble, reaching out for him.

The texture of alien fabric beneath my fingers, the heat of his skin. He stops, turning to face me, his eyes cold stars in the abyss.

A smile, as I regain myself, as I breathe, rubbing fingers that suddenly feel so much more *solid,* so much more *there,* before my eyes.

Unable to contain myself, though I know that it will rouse

whatever burrowed this place, whatever coils in the darkness, sweating or bleeding the vile matter through which we trudge.

Breathless, lunatic laughter, beatification exploding through my mind, as the last breaths come, and the first.

He laughs with me, coming to me, embracing me, the trembling heat of his body more immediate, more scintillating, than any sensation or play of intimacy in waking memory.

"I knew. I *knew* this would be the day."

Why he was waiting, why he blazed the path for me through the storm with his elegy. One not only for me, but for himself. Seeing him, now, feeling it; momentary flashes: the water of a scalding hot bathtub, music playing downstairs, already addled with pills and drink, the green-tiled, cracked and stained room distorting around him, shadows deepening, swelling from their niches...

A silver kiss, cold and enlivening, electric in its intensity, searing every nerve, leaving him bathed in frost, in shimmering fire.

Synchronicity, the sublime poetry of the universe, that same sense of relief, of removal, as the storm sweeps him from himself, as the bath water stains red.

Our laughter one, as he pulls away, as our eyes scintillate together, stars sharing their poisoned radiance, transmitting their poetry and adoration through the dark.

So much here, that we might know and make: feeling them

worm and writhe behind my eyes; stories of old and forgotten lives, that have begun and expired more times than I can number or recollect, always ending the same: in blood, in violence, whether my own or another's, with razors at my wrist or a sacrificial blade in my heart...inviting it, eager to know what stories of despair I can make, to relay to him, when we find one another again.

The urge almost beyond denial; to bear him down, to rake him naked, to set fires burning in his stolen raiment, make love to him in the mire.

A smile, a promise.

"Not yet. Soon, but not yet."

Not here. Something stirring, deep, deep in the darkness, that we brought one another here to see:

Its attention on us, drawn as much by our revelation, our heat and hunger for one another, as our trespass.

Seeing it, as he steps aside, still clutching my hand, the fires we kindle crawling over our intertwined fingers, embers rising to partially light the cavern.

Via their flickering radiance, an unfurling immensity; something that resembles a knotted mass of titanic serpents, locked together in incestuous mating, in ouroboros self-consumption, eyes blazing throughout, peeling open like wounds, weeping equally luminous tears: blazing holes in the darkness, in reality, whose light penetrates, piercing us both, reading the stories we have come to feed it.

"What...what is it?"

An impotent question, flickers of comprehension flaring, revelation kindling like the embers at my fingertips.

He laughs, though doesn't answer, knowing as I increasingly do, but unable to articulate, our language not sufficient.

An old thing. A forgotten thing, that we made this cradle for, that we murdered this dream to feed and cage.

That provides the means of our myriad resurrections, the lives we ache and beg for, come to lament, in their saturation. That we return from bloated with experience, with new miseries to suckle it on, stories of fresh despair to confess.

Older than us; a creature that might have been mighty, that was undoubtedly worshiped in its own right, once. A god of a million forms and faces, of numerous aspect, withered to almost nothing, all but lunatic at having been so forgotten, when we discovered it, when we plucked it from the abyss.

Remembering, now, as I remember the numberless lives that thread from that first revelation, that original trespass.

Laughing with him, crying with him, as we approach, as the nameless, formless thing cries in our minds like a hungry child, its various maws gaping, peeling back to reveal lunatic interiors: fathomless pits infested with cosmic vermin, Hells beyond the imagination of the firebrand faithful, where entire nations of souls writhe and clutch at one another, calling to us for a salvation we can't provide or in plea to sustain their suffering, knowing or desiring nothing else.

Happy to feed it, to open myself and spill it what stories I can, confess the lives I've worn and shed since the last time we walked here; a hundred or more, one following from the next, kindling and forgotten with the readiness of dreams.

The one whose hand I hold, who was my friend, my co-conspirator, my lover, before all of this began, whose names seethe like a vomit of bees on my tongue, behind my eyes -*Verity, Lambert, Damascus, Kirchner*- bleeding likewise, the pair of us shuddering together, as we rise from the filth, still hand in hand, as the infernal god of our own creation devours us, licks us hollow.

Reliving them all, every dream, every lost life, every instant of exultation and despair, in that vile intimacy, these moments of ecstatic extraction:

Every sorry, defeated, forgotten man, every child in love with its Mother, every delirious moment of virginal self-murder...mine again, for an instant, then gone: swirling away into those gaping maws, those weeping eyes.

But not only mine: his, likewise, our confessions co-mingling in common streams, becoming interpolluted masses that we never lived, but perhaps imagined, in moments of idle fantasy, in masturbatory conjuration, whilst dreaming of one another, straining to shrug off the grey restrictions of the masks we made, the roles we wrote for ourselves.

Knowing him, through them; the species of men he became, that he woke to, after every murder or suicide, after every car crash or mid-air collision, every abortion or infanticide.

Far, far removed from those I habitually inhabit: the manner of their disgraces not as a result of despair or passivity, but more extreme: alcoholism and addiction, demagoguery and ideological absolutism: men that poison themselves, slowly, by their appetites, that wither their own sanity and sense of reason in fires of certainty intense enough to burn civilisations.

With him, experiencing the same bleeding-edge reality, as he embarks on a two week bender through the clubs and bars of Brighton, eventually winding up sick and deranged beneath the peer, bilious, grinning manic delight at his condition, not even remembering his own name. With him, when the indifference of his Mother leads him to the conclusion that Mothers are the source of our species' neurosis, of its manifold evils, that the only way to extinguish those factors is to spark a crusade against the casual and ill-considered maternal, a crusade that elicits international waves of violence against women, that he himself commits, at his most fervent, quoting his own kant to them, as they burn, as they are slit open and involuntarily deprived of the mechanisms of Motherhood.

As he is with me for every slow decline, every pathetic, self-authored defeat, every mutilation and suicide.

Confessing and confessing, recalling and recalling, until there is no more; until we are shrivelled and empty, suspended here, before our bloated and writhing child, as it demands what we cannot give, its hunger still acute, still agonising.

Insatiable.

A moment of dizzying terror, that none of our individual, extinguished lives could know or comprehend: the fear of immortals, sensing the possibility of their own extinguishing, the impossibility of oblivion, that has become more and more dissolute with every incarnation.

Then, laughter, as the mechanisms we established long, long ago activate, arts that whir and sing through our flesh, severing and searing away the tongues and tendrils by which it feeds from us.

The old god, our nameless child, shrieks and recoils, its clotted, serpentine form convulsing, myriad minor entities, clutches of young born before their terms, slithering and skittering away from it through the filth.

Curses, familiar promises of what it will do, when it finally swells beyond our control, when it finds a means of recreating itself, and shattering this shell of a world we have bound it within.

Suffering so absurd as to be beyond comprehension, torments so elaborate, they transgress even beyond abstraction, making them frictionless, weightless.

We fall, its claim on us undone, still clutching at one another as we collapse in the mire, stumble and drag one another away.

The child recedes, closing its myriad eyes and maws, to digest what we have suckled it on, and to weave for us the new skins and masks in which we will wake from this most beloved, nursery nightmare.

*

A storm in the night, rattling doors and windows, waking me in the early hours of the morning. Flashes of blinding blue, the cat growling in her cardboard nest beneath the bed.

I rise, every inch of me raw, soreness that surges as I stretch, work my joints. Some nightmare, its absurdity already draining from memory, leaving only impressions: the smell of blood and burning skin, wetness, weariness, something so strange, that coils behind my eyes. A sick man's smile, lunatic enough to split the world in two.

Stumbling to the window, wrenching aside the clawed and shredded curtains.

Beyond the filthy, grime-smeared glass, a molten world, silent, dark-windowed houses and parked cars flowing where they stand, the street a black river, filth and discarded trash carried in the foaming flood.

Sleeping, for now, more to me in this state than when it wakes, the stories it dreams of far greater interest and inspiration than those it lives.

That I have never wanted, in the telling or experience of, whose inevitability brings tears to my eyes, and an ache for silence, for nothing, that I don't know how to salve.

Watching, as the rain hammers down, as lightning licks the rooftops, charring distant fields, splitting trees in two.

Silently praying for it to wash either myself or the world away, and let us be divorced from one another, after so long out of love.

The Breaking Down

She leaves me, as I always knew she would: her hand slipping from mine, my name slurred on her lips as she stumbles back through weeds and uncut grass, the remains of old, rusted bikes and broken toys.

Back into the stinking dark where I was born, slamming the door shut behind her.

There was a time when I would have followed, scuttling after her, tripping, snaring myself on weeds and nettles, screaming and clawing at the door—a time when I did, though I forgot, until this moment.

Most of them like her: running, screaming, thinking themselves safe behind their doors and windows. Men and women, boys and girls. Dogs barking, cats yowling.

Others -like me, a rarer breed- remaining, in awe as the creatures emerge through the fog, the red haze of morning: rumbling, cracking roads and pathways, knocking down telephone poles and street lamps. Cars crushed, vans hurled out of their path.

Impossible. A nightmare, a storybook or horror film nonsense that the world can't sustain, sanity won't allow. Unable to see clearly, at first; only the carnage that sweeps in their wake: speeding cars ploughed off the road, crashing into front gardens and the facades of houses, through the fences of the nearby infant school (memories I'll never make: of being trapped behind them, of hating the idiot play of the stinking, squealing others they set me amongst, the weary, hateful eyes of teachers at their desks).

Panicked flight, screamed pleas and prayers in different languages, to different gods and messiahs and saviours. Many stumble, breaking legs and heads on the pavement, trampled by the rest or mown down by cars. Bodies fly up into the air like ragdolls, breaking as they hit the ground, bags of red pulp and splinters.

She still screams my name through the living room window, the pale-faced woman I've loved and hated, adored and feared most of my life—who I've never truly known.

I turn from her, from the weeping, red-faced sister she holds in her arms. Smiling, as I realise that it's *over*: nursery and friends, teachers and doctor's visits; dentists and shopping trips and her boyfriends (so many, strange faces in the dark, some smiling, some friendly, many not, looking at me as though I'm a rat scurried up from the sewers). That life, with it's uncertainties and unwanted wakings, with its commands and parameters, its denials and disappointments: over, now.

I stumble from the grass, through the broken fence, hearing her hammering on the window hard enough to shudder the glass in its setting. How she screams, how she weeps! But doesn't come for me, not in love enough with her child to risk stepping outside, dragging ot back into the dark.

What a relief it will be for her, not having to play Mommy any more! Knowing, seeing it in her eyes on those days when our crying and laughter, our questions and confusions, are too much: a confession more eloquent than any words, that sears me inside with its abyssal cold:

I wish you'd never been born.

I don't hate her for that, as others might, though I did, once upon a time, when I had nothing else, when she was the reluctant, bitter core of my world, when her poison was my only experience of Mother's milk. No point in hatred, now, no point in remembering scars that will never have chance to become old and obsessive.

On the street, beyond her eyes, tingling with the forbidden pleasure of trespass, as the first emerge from the fog: immense, misshapen things, bulging bags of muscle and limbs, distorted and slumping, poorly put together, as though they might burst or unravel with every shambling motion. None are the same; a nursery art project, salt-clay and plasticine monsters, each sculpted by different hands:

One boasting a head that rises to a flopping point, eyes bulging and blinking all over, red and yellow and streaming, tongues lolling from the mouths that pant and part in its sides, revealing a black and infested interior. Another slithers forward like a slug, leaving a glistening trail in which the others slip and stumble, its head a garden of arms like a great flower, every limb scrabbling and pawing at the air, as though to drag passing angels into their embrace. A thing hidden from view, draped in rags and tatters like old bandages or burial shrouds, wet and stained, glued to its pulsing body by whatever seeps beneath. With every step, clots of steaming stuff fall away, squirming where they land, alive, until one of those that follow crushes them to inert pulp.

Cries, even from those that don't run, hands rising to appalled mouths, eyes watching through interlaced fingers, unable to believe, unable to look away.

Closer, closer, more creatures emerging from the fog, following one another, each carrying great chains that stretch back, clutched in their fists and talons or driven into their flesh, drawing something that rumbles and shakes the ground, something that strains and creaks, as though every scrap of dead wood in the world protests its own murder.

People call my name, neighbours beckon from gardens across the way as I stagger from our house towards the intersection of Lindhurst and Charam, the school where I'm supposed to start this September. Burning, screaming, a van careens off the road through the steel wire fence, into the classrooms beyond.

I hear them, see them through the smoke and flames: figures running, scurrying, crawling through the rubble, black and orange, blue and yellow. They collapse as they reach out, legs disintegrating beneath them. Some are fused and shapeless;

teachers carrying children already still, silent, some wandering as though blind, the eyes melted from their heads. A girl with fiery wings flaring from her back screams as she stumbles across the playground, not yet ready to take flight. A boy who reaches the steel wire fence, clutching at it with blackened fingers, tears streaming down the half of his face that remains.

I know what I'm supposed to feel, that I'm supposed to scream, vomit, run crying for Mommy.

But I don't, won't pretend any more.

A parade, the creatures blocking out the school in their number, become a mass of impossible anatomy, the like of which I've never seen in any dream or video game, cartoon or comic book.

I'm supposed to be afraid of them, disgusted by them; the ones that seep and bleed, the skinless, torn open, with pulsing insides on the outside or that are more bone than flesh. Those with scales, those with mismatched and infested feathers, those made from swarms of spiders or screaming cockroaches. Those that drool liquid fire and weep lightning. But I'm not, no matter how much Mommy's little boy screams inside, demanding my tears, my terror.

More and more appear, so many, they burst through the houses on Lindhurst, smashing walls and windows, trampling conservatories, swarming over ceilings that sag and collapse beneath their mass. I don't run, fascinated, *fixated* as obscuring walls rupture and slide away, exposing sacred interiors: living rooms and bedrooms, landings and hallways. Places I know, in some instances; places I've walked, on the rare occasions my Mom dragged me to neighbour's houses in the times before they inevitably turned against her, when she started sneering and swearing at the mere mention of their names. That familiarity doesn't dilute my discomfort, the strange sense of peering on someone as they undress; these places where people sit and sigh at their TV screens, stand singing in the shower, reading books in bed, arguing over bills and wallpaper and what they might have for dinner... distressingly naked, though not enough to make me look away.

I stop, spluttering as the dust of those demolitions reaches me, tingling in my throat, scratching my eyes, tears blurring my sight as the creatures slump and slither and stalk by. Some of those like me, similarly mesmerised, not yet fled for cover or curled up quivering on the ground, break, fleeing in broken-legged awkwardness, sprawling on their faces in the dust as they fling themselves towards the beasts, crying to be taken by them, carried away or consumed, to be made like them.

Most are batted away, bones broken, organs ruptured, others unthinkingly crushed beneath elephantine feet, trampled by bovine hooves or raked to shreds by avian claws... lost in the dust and filth the parade leaves in its wake.

Still not running, still not screaming. The little boy crying for

Mommy distant, fallen into the abyss, worms rising from it to entwine and drag him deeper. I laugh at his desperate, accusing eyes, at his strangled screams, knowing that I'll never have to listen to him again, after today.

None of those that call my...*his* name come to drag me from harm's way, none loving or desperate enough, become pale, smeared faces behind filthy windows, ghosts whose names I'll soon forget.

Ignoring them, I draw closer, through the dust and grit, the scattered rubble, those sprawled broken and twitching throughout. I've seen before... not only in films that Mom doesn't like me watching; on the internet, in my own nightmares and imaginings: the red inside, spilling out through ruptured bellies and smashed skulls. The way they twist and shudder, as no body can or should.

Laughing through the dust in my mouth, the blood in the air, laughing as those still able blink through red and black masks, reaching for me.

Skipping over them, weightless, my bones become those of a bird, a sparrow, their clutching hands falling from me, slick with blood, too mutilated to hold on. I stagger to a halt at the edge of the parade, so close I can smell the stink of beasts; blood and metal and sweat, the filth that slicks their path.

Wailing sirens disrupt their songs, flashes of blue appearing at the bottom of the hill. Ambulances. Police cars. Laughing so much it *hurts*. What are they going to do? What do they think they can. . ?

Cries. Screams. Gunfire. The beasts force their barricades, brightly coloured cars and vans flying, uniformed and armoured officers likewise. Nothing but toys in a moment of over-enthusiastic play, the kind that makes Mommy shout and swear at me about how expensive they were.

These ones aren't expensive; two more arrive for every one that breaks. Not that it does any good.

Mechanical mosquito hums draw my eyes up to the red sky, helicopters hovering there, bigger, closer to the ground than any I've seen, olive green, their sides opened, weapons slung from inside.

I laugh so hard it *hurts* as missiles scream, as guns revolve and blaze. Sparks churn from the surrounding concrete, the shattered street, the ruins of houses. The creatures caught up in the fusillade burst like rotten fruit, spatter out from themselves, spilling the parasites inside. Few even slow or stop; those that do slumping forward or collapsing into the dust, trampled to smears of filth by the rest.

Mr. Astwith from number 26 at the end of the row—who sometimes talks with us when we play in the street outside, telling us stories of his time as a soldier, a teacher, who sometimes lets us dig for beetles and buried treasure in his front garden—is hurled from his feet as the blazing streaks of white and yellow find him, his cardigan becoming a shredded, black and red mass, still smouldering as he falls and becomes still.

Mrs. Astwith and Lucy, their daughter, shriek from the open front door, reaching out as though to drag him inside, Lucy beckoning for me to join her.

I smile, shake my head, too much in love with it all: watching as one of the beasts—a thing composed almost entirely of flesh like compost and burned black bone—erupts, a missile finding it, burning meat and shards of flaming matter raining all around, some lodging in its sibling's hides, though none of the wounds cause them to slow or comment on its passing.

From out of the red mist come ear-splitting cries: those of great birds with throats of torn and twisted metal. Gasps go up from those that still look on as they emerge: flapping immense, leathery wings, spined tails trailing behind, bodies like masses of skinless meat and muscle, studded with irregular, steel spines, some pristine and silvery, others rusted and tarnished.

I don't see where they come from, only the helicopters manoeuvring to face them, weapons already blazing, sending several down in flames.

For every one are five or six more: no two entirely alike, some with mouths like the pictures of flat worms I've seen in biology books, others snaking, worming masses whose myriad teeth whir and churn like chainsaws.

The helicopters spiral down as the creatures batten onto them, heedless of the rotors that shred their twisted flesh, raking open cockpits to winkle out the pilots, tearing them apart and swallowing them in still-quivering chunks.

I yelp in pain as I'm thrown to the ground, shockwaves rippling the concrete beneath my feet. Plumes of black smoke and orange flame go up in which the creatures writhe and squabble, more concerned with claiming their share of the meat than the fire charring their flesh.

Another falls closer, on the school, glass and dust and metal soaring, a lethal rain that wounds the beasts as they trudge by, sending several onlookers sprawling back with scraps of twisted metal in their eyes and bellies, their heads stoved in and bleeding from chunks of brick or plaster.

Children still scream, impossibly alive, as the beasts that brought the helicopter down thrash and unfurl in the ruins, hurling blazing bodies left and right, plucking up those that screech and writhe, squabbling over and devouring some, though far from all. Some, they pluck up and cradle like dolls, like children of their own, smothering the fires that infest them with laps of multiple tongues, with folds of their own anatomies, drools of viscous matter. They gather the trembling, almost-burned-fleshless things to themselves, pressing them inside through organs and apertures I don't understand, some still visible through translucent blisters in which they float, through swellings and tumors and bloated bellies, a little like Mommy's when Anna was still inside of her, like Aunty Sharon's before cousin Cameron was born.

Bleeding. I feel it run down my leg, my back: hot and sticky, pooling black around my feet.

A time not so long ago when the sight would have had me in tears. Now? Nothing but smiles, forever and ever.

I don't know how or why, but something is *passing* here today; something beyond the parade of beasts, beyond the red fog and what it conceals: a promise of tomorrow, the inevitabilities that I've known and dreamed of from the first instant, but denied, that the cancer called sanity has kept me ignorant of, in order to preserve itself:

The first attempt... a day shy of my thirteenth birthday, a razor from the shattered set I've been using for a year, now. My fingers cut from forcing its plastic casing. A bath almost bubbling with heat; the best way, or so the internet tells me.

Downstairs, the TV, turned up high so as to half obscure the voices hissing and snarling beneath. He'll leave for good, this time. I know he will. The only one... the only one I've ever loved, who has treated me with anything like humanity. She'll chase him away, with her jealousy and her spitting, slurring rages, her petty thefts, her casual cruelty. And that will be the end. I'll never see him again.

I can't bear it; the thought of being stuck here with her, of being forced to work whatever shitty job a thirteen year old can get to pay her fucking bills.

Stolen from, again and again and again: every birthday, every

Christmas: anything that might be mine, in gifts, in cards. Denied when I confront her about it, every accusation eliciting the same shams: mock surprise, feigned insult, a play of incredulity that I could say or think anything so vile of her.

Even when caught red-handed, her grubby fingers in my wallet, rooting around inside my coat pockets, my drawers and cupboards, returning my stolen bank card to its rightful place.

I fucking hate her. I fucking hate this. Lies and thefts and disappointments. A world of dirt, getting filthier by the second.

I don't cut deep enough.

For a delirious, blissful moment, I think I've done it; severed my chains and escaped. The pain sears through, blistering me, momentarily wiping out thought in a white apocalypse.

Then I drift, deliriously down, into the strangest dreams; of what never came, the infernal parade that murdered this day...

Waking, though I fight the dawn like an autistic child flailing against a Doctor's attentions, wrenched up through dreaming depths, though I'm happy to drown. An echo of original indignity, which I can only recall here, in the non-space between living and dying.

Waking not to welcomes or sympathies, but scowls and recrimination: the selfish bitch and the selfish fucks that call her friend, family, all waiting to spew their poison in my face, to tell me what a horror I am to her.

Wishing I'd cut deeper, that I'd torn myself open, so the

bleeding couldn't be stopped.

My first job... a few days a week at the local bakery. I fall into it by accident, a work experience placement, finding a knack for it, liking the place, the people. My boss, Sean, is a decent guy, off his face on MDMA most of the time; some rich kid from London, decided to jack in his life as a banking executive to start over again here.

I like him. He loves me. It's an illicit affair, my first, my only; one that occurs behind the counter, in the kitchen, the alley behind the shop. Everything is new to me, never having known this kind of comfort, this contact. He teaches me... how to be, away from her and home. He even keeps me, for a time: nights spent away, which she hates me for, believing that I have a girlfriend, that I'll leave her and sister Anna to fend for themselves.

Half right, at least.

The little thefts... I get used to them; a hundred pounds here, two hundred there. Whenever I confront her... nothing but frothing, spitting abuse, reminders of being at her tit and heel for the previous ten years or so.

I change my bankcard, my pin number, set up security that she can't breach. She hates me for it, just as she hates me for the crime of being.

Sean... it can't last, not as it is, as I am. Too much of her in me, too much poison in my blood and brain.

Suspicious, paranoid text messages and phone calls, invisible chains I wrap around him, constrict him with, that I'd weave through his flesh and lodge in his bone, if I could, to have him with me always, to know that he'll never leave me.

The first in a long line of broken loves, forced back home, to her; the font of corruption, the living tumor in my soul.

Other jobs, other boyfriends. Some so far, there are oceans between us. Yet, she's always with me: a ghost wreathed in cigarette smoke, sneering unhappy smiles.

I love them, all of them: the rich, the poor, the healthy, the diseased. Black eyes and blisters in my throat, loving the ones that provide them most of all. Until they tire of me, until they hurt me too deeply.

Never still, never stable. One moment, the secret affair of a movie star heartthrob, who keeps me in gin and chocolate, a palatial home, for the gift of my silence, the promise of my mouth around his cock. The next, trading blowjobs in the backstreets of LA for the price of a cup of coffee.

Dying. No message of it, no address to send it to; hearing almost by accident that she's passed.

Suicide. Emulation of my failed efforts; slit wrists and vodka in the bathtub, a brood of bastard siblings screaming for a day or two before neighbours broke down the door.

I laugh. Washed and fed and tested by then: a case of Herpes, of Gonorrhea in the throat. Treated, thanks to the man who has plucked me up, dragged me from the gutter. It doesn't matter; myriad deaths follow, alien to comfort, to stillness; less able to bear it than the violence and uncertainty of the streets.

Letting them take me: starvation, freezing to death, injecting myself with shared needles in some stinking, abandoned place, floating away in heart-stopping bliss before the man who would be my angel finds me...

I double over with laughter, tears, almost going to my knees, no longer a child, save here, in this idiot, unfinished body. So strange, memories and projections of what will never be filling its skull, swelling me beyond my brain's capacity to rewire itself.

I feel it try, as the parade trundles on, as the beasts grow in number, size, variety; as some even turn from their labours to regard me, beckoning me to join them in their blissful slavery.

I smile refusal as blood seeps from my nostrils, my temples throb. I'm not ready, not in this state and skin: too easily broken, my heart too easily stilled or ruptured or ground to pulp.

Pulsing, my head, my back, my belly; the red mist fills me, whispering stories into my mind beyond the ones that echo back, that I remember, though I've never lived them. Contradictory gospels, lives that fly in one another's faces, becoming a common slurry of miseries and disappointments, punctuated by bursts of salvation that feel like love, but dwindle and flicker out far too quickly.

None endure, none make me mourn their loss—not even those

that paint the prettiest pictures, in which the loves of my lives find me in my teenage years and never go away, never reject or abandon me.

As for the worst... the ones where I never leave home, where she battens and swells on me like a leech until the day she or I die... I laugh, knowing they'll never be.

It comes as they ebb, the last, lost life flickering like a candle in a blizzard; the red mists part, my skin with them, tears in my pulsing back and head and sides, the pain nothing, *nothing,* next to my desire to see:

What emerges through the mists, as they boil and part, as they peel open, layers receding like curtains to some unimaginable theatre:

The beast's chains linked to an immense engine, a creaking, pulsing thing of black matter and machinery, of great wheels, grinding the muck and rubble. Atop it, a mass whose immensity, whose lack of form, murders what little is left of the boy I remember, the child who falls screaming into its own abyssal maw.

Impossible, impossible to define, the shapeless, shifting state before my eyes: portions of it blistering, bubbling with new arrangements, organs and configurations before they rot and recede, withering like flowers, like clusters of fruit at the coming of frost.

Eyes. Eyes in lunatic number and variety: eyes of beasts and insects, vermin and parasites, men, women and children; mouths the same. Nests of worm-like tendrils, snaking out to lash the ones that carry it, to pluck up those that watch, dragging them into fang-rimmed maws or snapping beaks, into puckered, dilated orifices. The machinery upon which it sits bound to it, a part of it: conveyance and creature inseparable, parts of the same lunatic anatomy.

Falling to my knees as it grinds closer, as more and more and more of its immensity emerges from the mist. Raking at myself, screaming as what little remains of the boy sloughs away, the whimpering worthless, lost little boy that this lost, whimpering, worthless world would have me be, over and over, forever and forever, until whatever machinery suspends it, in whose effluent my new Fathers were born, breaks down.

Seeing it, as I see every failing, flickering potential, every day that will never be: no more revolutions, no more expansions and contractions, no more births, deaths and rebirths.

I know in that instant why they're here, why they eat their ways through, why they seed and gather us, their cuckoo-spawn, parasites in the womb, both of and not of the flesh we resemble, the species we infest… a certainty that I've never felt outside of dreams, knowledge convulsing me with the violence of lightning's kiss.

New and ancient purpose, brain and body fruiting with new states, even as the old and unwanted burn.

Emerging, a blissful sensation; cool air on new, wet skin, unfamiliar senses flaring, the world a riot of shape and scent, of taste and colour.

Nothing more beautiful to my reconfigured senses than the ones that have come to remake me.

Behind, shattering glass, screams. Lucy descends on silvery threads and filaments that erupt from her translucent skin, shreds and tatters of the girl she was streaming behind her.

She smiles, though she no longer has lips with which to make one. Returning it, as we embrace, as our shifting bodies melt and bleed momentarily, any distinction between us disappearing.

Others, our heretofore unknown siblings, already in flight, slithering or swarming to join the mass, to flock around those that drag it forth.

Those that would have condemned them to the old cycles, that no longer have any claim over us, call and cry out, trying to hold them, beat them back, murder them, rather than let them fly free.

None succeed. Their world is over, the engines they've slaved themselves to on the verge of breaking down entirely.

Lucy and I tear apart, though it wounds us, one of her coiling, luminous tendrils still clutched in my talon, our flesh fused.

Taking flight, our songs rise with the screams of dying Mothers and Fathers, their impotent, defeated cries, familiar condemnations. My Mother's voice amongst them, cursing the day she allowed my absent Father to spit me into her belly, that she didn't drink bleach while I gestated, failed to strangle me at birth.

Abrupt silence, their bleating cattle-hymns, their engine's dismal, dying roars, drowned out by our songs as we spiral and soar, laughing, watching the empty, impotent world they made for us come apart, making way for one we'll dream for ourselves, that may be of nightmares, but that will be *ours* at last.

Strangest Spite

We've come so far together, she and I. Yet, she still doesn't trust, still suspects. I see, though she does everything in her power to hide it; plays of gratitude, of sisterly love for the one who snatched her from the altar, who plucked the sacrificial knife from her Mother's hands.

I slit the woman from breast to cunt before her eyes, yanked out her black, infested heart to display before the appalled eyes of her faithful.

Barely a day passes when she doesn't thank me for it, doesn't try to show her affections in ways I can only deny.

"Don't."

The first time, coming to me at dusk, in plains of strange, swaying plant-life, their bulbous leaves and fronds set with luminous blue blebs and crystalline growths that shimmer and tinkle as they dance in the breeze.

The only means she knows of expressing gratitude or affection, the way her numerous brothers and cousins taught her: with all that she has, all that she is.

Her scarred and wasted body of no interest, save in how far it can carry itself.

"I'm sorry."

Her apology barely masking the resentment that her usual

gambit hasn't worked, my denial more shocking to her than any physical harm I might commit. The beginning of her contempt, of the dreams in which she stabs me through the throat, in the eyes, drags me away from the fire for the wolves and worms to devour.

Dreams only, in that place where no wolves or worms reside, the only animal life we've glimpsed the great, wheeling things in the scarlet skies; webbed wings, long necks and tails, their flights leaving glittering arcs against the night, their calls sweet and soothing, the creatures occasionally diving to pluck prey from the hills and plains.

She covers herself, hurriedly donning the rags and tatters that are her only concession to clothing: the remains of the ceremonial robes in which her Mother would have murdered her.

"You have destroyed me."

"Hmmm?"

"You... you have destroyed me."

The fire flickers, the nameless beasts singing their strange hymns. Something snuffles in the undergrowth nearby, distressingly human voices rising in animal chorus with one another.

"I took the knife from your Mother's hands."

"It was meant for *me*. If you'd only..."

"You wanted to be slit open and bled out, did you? You wanted the woman to reach into your chest and pluck out your heart?"

Cold fire in her eyes, a murderous frost. "It's why I was born, what I've always wanted."

"No; it's what they wanted of you, what they taught you to want. There's no Great Mother, no Goddess who would take your sorry soul to her breast. You would have simply bled, then *died*. And your bitch Mother would have gone on to live another lifetime."

The fire flaring, the frost in her eyes vicious enough to freeze mine in their sockets, the blood in my veins. "You're lying."

"No, I'm not. There *are* Gods, or at least, things you might call that, but your Great Mother? No—she's a child's story."

She turns away, her eyes on the heavens as strange stars wheel, as alien moons rise.

Far, far beyond the valleys and wastes where her people scavenged and scrabbled for their living, where she and her brothers and sisters hunted for meat and metal, for the devices that are all that remains of whatever world went before.

"You miss it, don't you?"

"I've never…" *Never known anything else.*

I shiver, drawing closer to the fire, shuddered by her silent, fervent prayers that I'd never come into her life.

*

The flowers sing, crystalline petals shearing the orange light into spectacular rainbows. Insects of a similar composition dart and swarm in the air, descending to sup silvery nectar from the flower's hearts.

A shift occurs shortly after dawn, after the last of the fire dies and we move on.

Still hideous, that familiar vertigo, the ground receding, tumbling away, distance distorting around us, flickering like an illusion of light and water.

Taking my hand, she clings close to me, though I feel her sickness at the intimacy, a crawling antipathy that leaves her resisting an urge to scratch herself bloody, the sensation like vermin scurrying beneath her skin.

Happy to be the vessel for her hatred, if that's what she requires; for her to pour into me all of the pain that abuse by men and mothers has fostered. No other who can, none she might turn to, make the idol of her resentment.

My born victim, my intended abused. Why I sought her, took such pains to find her, trawling through the sewers between states for some sign, some omen in the filth: a creature that knew nothing but trauma from birth, shat out bloody and unwanted, save in the sacrifice she might provide. Taught to define by her proscribed fate, to celebrate in it, no matter how profound the hurt or deep the disgrace.

So many potentials, so many who it might have been…

But *her*…the rarest creature, singing the loudest, the most desperately: the one who will be most beloved, when we reach journey's end.

Not that it ever ends, for me.

The plains shimmer and dissolve, a moment of transition in which we are lost amongst the shit and filth, in the black, infested mires where abortive god-things swarm amongst the corpses of dead and dying realities, where they bloat on filth and desperation, listening and sniffing for sign of fodder-souls, the open and wounded psyches in which they might find anchor and drag themselves from the pit.

Vermin divinities, cockroach, maggot and spider gods.

I know them, having been like them, once. Before finding myself again, before recalling the desecrations and disgraces that cast me amongst them.

In an instant of hideous realisation, the girl sees me as I see her; transparent to one another here, our dreams and agendas, our possibilities and potentials, obscenely exposed.

Horror dawns on her face, in her eyes, but she doesn't pull away, doesn't attempt to flee into the surrounding abyss.

Knowing better, remembering from our last transitions, how I almost didn't find her again in time, how they followed her, cornering her, their filthy hungers and vile designs scrawled in the shit and diseased filth they seeped, in the tainted stories they sweated from every pore and orifice.

I burst them apart, sending them scattering: a breath of black lightning, tears of blue fire. None of them were whole or strong enough to defend themselves, mercifully: if they'd been more than mere scavengers, one of the bloated Mothers or Fathers of their kind, the outcome might have been different.

I lead her through, as before, though she weeps, though she gnashes her teeth, promising the hurt she'll do me when we wake and walk in sunlight again.

"Don't dare sleep again. Don't dare turn your back on me. I'll cut you open, I'll make you bleed. Lying *shit*. I'll watch them eat you alive; the things in the deserts, I'll feed them your fucking eyes and heart..."

I laugh at her, shaking my head. "No, you won't. You won't even remember."

"I will. *I will.*"

Oaths she's made before, but never fulfilled. My uniquely faithless child.

The vermin gather, scenting us; the raw *reality* still clinging to us. Hideous chittering in the dark, things unfurling from the filth, the pitted and seeping stone like immense centipedes, worms fashioned from corpses, a thing that squats atop a mountain of shit infested with weeping, mouldering forms; those that were once its worshipers, its faithful, that it no doubt promised some measure of salvation, beyond the lives they fed to it.

Laughing, beckoning as we pass, promising such pleasures, such obscenities, she and I stumble beneath their assault on our minds.

Another's song guides me, her silken threads shimmering. A sweet voice in my mind, a lover's voice, sighing a summons to a warm and welcome bed: *so long, so long to go, my sweet boy. And the night is almost over…*

I know, I know.

Almost dragging the girl, the things swarming at our backs calling us away, away from the light, away from hurt and uncertainty.

I feel it before I see: one of the vaster, more legitimately divine specimens rearing up from beneath the muck of aborted creations at our backs: an immense, worm-like mass of cancerous flesh, its torso vaguely human, limbless, every inch of it pock-marked with irregular wounds and growths, lesser parasites battened onto it, tumbling away as it sways and convulses.

A blind, eyeless face, masses of tumors pulsating where its eyes might have been, tears of filth seeping down its cheeks, anointing the up-turned faces below.

Cankered lips peel back from yellowed and broken teeth, the god-thing hissing as it cries in the voices of plague-ridden babes, of diseased children herded en masse into immense pits, pleading for the fire to scour away their trauma.

"Go. *Go.*"

All but hurling her through the rupture in the wall, the girl protesting as it swallows her, as she disappears into waking light.

The thing vomits a spray of infected blood and bilious matter, of worms and filth. Hurried motions in the foetid air, my hands leaving burning and shimmering patterns upon it, their light causing many of the lesser vermin to hiss and recoil. Minor abjurations, not enough to disperse the assault entirely, but at least to partially *deflect* it, streamers and rivulets of the infectious filth turning course on contact, returning to their point of origin.

The god-thing howls as its own matter bursts against its ruinous face, sore and pock-marked features partially melting.

Smiling at the small victory, I hurl myself back, away from its retaliations, the rent dilating to accept me.

I scream silently, coming apart, a thing of motes and ashes, each carrying a measure of sentience, singing to the rest, desperate to fly from them, to become the flickering seed of its own dream, its own universe: a scrap of sceptic filth or fungal spore in reality's matter.

Inevitability defeats those designs: every aspiring scrap of me hurtling back together in hideous cataclysm as I tumble back, through black dust and silver sand.

Spluttering, heaving, I'm disgusted at my wretched weight, the coherence of my own body.

It's never easy to be whole again after divine separation, to be singular after being many.

The girl waits for me, cross-legged amongst the dunes. Red and blue lightning flickers in the bruised sky, licking down to char roses from the ash and sand.

So far, so much further than I dreamed. Here, at last! At the end and the beginning; the world whose name I can't recall, but which I murdered, whose dying screams I stoked to call her down: The Moon Mother, The Leering Hag, The Hanging Sew.

I hear her, so close, now, singing her lullabies to me from across the wastes. Singing of all she'll show and give; the secrets I'll learn in gratitude for my gift to her.

The girl plucks up the sand, letting it sift between her fingers, cocking her head to one side as though seeing something in the silvery streams, listening to some unheard music...

"I've been waiting."

"For how long?"

"I don't know. Everything's different, here; the days... they feel broken."

They are. Everything is; the engines we made, towards the end... they dissolved everything: time, space, dimension. This... the best facsimile we could construct of what went before, that she holds together, from the last temple, at the edge of the wastes. But even she can't hold it indefinitely, no matter how strong her webs, how numerous her children.

She must be fed.

"Are you ready?"

The girl allows the last grain of sand to tumble from her palm before dusting off her hands, rising, surprisingly strong and certain on her feet.

She turns to me, the amber moon reflected in her dark, dark eyes.

"Are you?"

*

The wastes roll on forever, to the distant mountains, black and shattered as the ruins that rise from them, the remains of cities that were.

I don't know them any more; too long travelling, too many years since they were whole. Dreams... dreams of being, only; returning to me, sometimes, in sleeping fevers, in unguarded moments: places I maybe walked as a boy, before she first sang to me from the filth and emptiness. Before she promised me eternity, all worlds for the price of one.

I never regretted, never bemoaned that bargain; not even now, the truth of her long since revealed to me.

Hardly believing, at first; that she might be just another wanderer, another exile, more like me than she remembers, than she'd dare admit. Her myths lost to time, but found, oh, found, after a long time searching, after so many tormented and murdered and driven mad... worlds burning for the price of a rumour, generations sacrificed for the whispers of insane and unseen things that claimed some knowledge of her.

Now I know: her name, the world where she became what she is. I've walked there, amongst the haunted ruins, the perpetual storm of dust that whispers through them. The structures her people erected from that place... unlike anything I've known; more grown and sang into being than constructed, their designs better resembling flowers or coral, bone or seashell, than any tower or temple.

She reduced it to rubble, long, long before I arrived, what little remains haunted not only by the ghosts and echoes of those she murdered in her apotheosis, but by the children she left: those that seek her out, as I once did, that she devours or sucks dry, taking the most promising into her womb, her belly, to remake, to shat back into being as he agents, her loving prophets and prodigal messiahs.

Their purpose the same as mine: to find what that world can no longer provide, the meat she craves, the *minds* she hungers for even more desperately.

The vast majority are lost or forgotten, now—no more children, no more prodigals. I learned that out there, in the worlds beyond her dominion: that they might be *more* than she ever intended, that the shard of divinity she shared with them during their remaking might be hewn and shaped, coaxed to swell within them, under the right artistry, the appropriate inspirations.

Though they all resist, so in love with being their Mother's children, with sharing her shape and aspects. Those I've perverted...that have perverted themselves, in their separation from her, agonised by the process, fleeing me, denying every revelation, until they had no choice but to surrender and abandon all she imposed and inflicted upon them.

Powers in their own rights, now, those that survived with some semblance of sanity; largely forgotten to what they were, with their own churches and temples, their own worlds and peoples.

Owing me for their freedom, their divinity, as well as whatever disgraces they've endured along the paths to both. Debts I intend to collect, when beyond their Mother's eyes, perhaps as a means of releasing me from her attentions altogether...

I spin my own webs, catching myself up in them, during those rare moments when she sleeps and dreams of the worlds she'll never create, when she communes with conditions I can't conceive, beyond stars or the blackness between, beyond power or creation.

And she?; So far from the absolute thing I presumed when she first descended, when she tore her way through from the muck and mire, when this world shook and died around her, cataclysms toppling cities and empires that had endured before any recorded history, her presence alone enough to inspire them, along with a madness that infected every living thing, the species-spanning lunacy that followed still recurring, in nightmares, in moments of unguarded recollection.

Still such a little thing, in the estimation of many: a small and petty goddess, an insect they might take the time to stamp out, were she worthy of the attention.

No doubt she regards me in similar terms; I and all of the other desperate, crawling aspirants; the ones too wasted and worthless to even devour.

This girl... so much more than I was, when I first came to her, the child that found me in the shape of a man I fell in love with almost on sight, at the first words we shared. Who taught me the worthlessness of that condition; who cultivated and delivered me to her as just another sacrifice, a morsel-soul, despite genuinely adoring me, the life we built together, the promises we made. Still professing love and apology when I lay before her in the ashes, my mind half lost, her attention like swarms of her kin scurrying behind my eyes.

I called her through at his behest, via means he provided. So much revealed to me, through his words, through our love-making, our journeys beyond the veil.

A pity that she'd long since grown weary of his ambitions, his constant mockery of her, when he thought her eyes and ears were elsewhere.

That strange contradiction of horror and black joy when she plucked him up, when she raked away the skin of humanity he wore, exposing him to me for the first time... wondrous, a delirium that I ache to have again, at some point in my sad and sorry being.

"Look!"

Taking the girl by the shoulder, feeling her shudder at my touch, I point out across the distant dunes:

A soft lambency pulsing on the horizon, a haze that arcs and coruscates into the night sky like cracks in a mirror through which alien light bleeds. Silhouetted against it, the shards of her last temple, the only place where she's still worshiped, where she can sustain herself.

Laughter bubbling up inside at the sight of it. Years? Maybe decades since I last walked there. A place that resembles great, black shards of jagged glass and crystal rising in strange angles from the wastes, in perpetual motion, grinding against one another, as though to sharpen themselves for some celestial surgery.

I hear her on the wind: a sweet voice, softly sighing, singing to me: *Hurry, hurry, sweet one. Moon time is almost over—we'll be dreaming again, soon.*

I don't understand her words in my head, most of them not words at all, but a jumbled kaleidoscope of alien impressions— concerns and experiences I can't fathom.

Only her *urgency* is clear, whatever license to roam I've been granted coming to its end.

A small thing, a scrap of meat too wretched for her to devour, perhaps, but not entirely powerless. I've learned more than one or two sways at her many knees, at least enough to make me useful to her, many more during my wanderings, my encounters with her prodigal and outcast children, the rivals and lovers and siblings she would murder me for consorting with.

Even feared and venerated in my own right, under certain guises, in certain states, though I have no presumptions or delusions as to my status, at least for the time being.

I bring the girl to a halt, her dark eyes turning to me.

"Stay perfectly still and don't be afraid."

As though she's still capable of fear, of any emotion beyond resentment.

Dragging my leg through the sand, I draw a great circle around us, using a little in the way of art to keep the contradictory desert breezes from obliterating it. Words accompany every inch, some blistering my tongue and throat, others pricking my balls and entrails with their potency.

A tangible shift in the air, by the time the circle is complete; the winds no longer trespass within its boundary, leaving us insulated in an oasis of unnatural calm.

Already, I feel how powerfully this will cost me, hoping that my Mistress has a little to spare, after my delivery is made.

Going to my knees, I thrust my fingers into the sand. Ripples of intent pass out through it, terminating at the circle's edge. Inspiration, energy, flow from me. I focus on them, not allowing them to run riot, but directing and controlling, threads and flickers of will swimming their currents like salmon in a stream, all of one mind, intent on controlling the flood with their sheer volume and fury.

I reshape the substance of the sand, charring it into a single mass, a great, shimmering mirror that bubbles and boils before settling, the girl falling to hands and knees on the crackling glass.

Rising, my fingers streaming with molten stuff, I focus every ounce of will on binding the one that stirs, that uncoils from its warren beyond shape or waking. One of the lost ones, an abandoned would-be divinity, its name rarely used, hardly remembered, now, save in ancient fables and fairy tales that will be forgotten themselves, when their last tellers finally succumb.

"Lotahn!"

The creature answers with hissed laughter in my thoughts, coiling through the air around us, through the storm of sand at the circle's edge.

"What is it?"

I ignore her, the creature likewise, likely not even aware that she exists. Its eyes only for me, its tongue flickers, its gullet gaping, Hells beyond the most vindictive fundamentalist's imagining boil in its belly.

All yours, shit-soul. Cunt heart. Sewer-born, fungus-dreaming, filth-eating... It spews a barrage of epithets, more than mere words; a sensory assault, promises that scour every nerve, that evoke moments in which I writhe through those states and experiences, a worm-soul, flayed, bleeding, shrivelled and devoured, until it shats me back out once more, whole and shuddering, fresh for another round of torments.

"Lotahn."

The thing writhes at the use of its original name, its true name—a thousand wards flaring through its un-fashioned body, blue and green fire kindling in the swirling sand. Anatomy knits before our eyes, the girl gasping as it emerges from the squall, flesh for the first time in aeons, from its perspective.

Blazing blue eyes peer, their predatory hatred so cold: frost in the desert, shimmering scales, nacreous arcs of colour passing through them, its great, serpentine head swaying, a black tongue flickering from its lips.

I beckon it forward with a gesture, the thing compelled to obey.

I could swallow you, now. Snap you up, as though you were nothing; a lizard, a rat in the sand. Oh yes! I would enjoy that... feeling you squirm and scurry, listening to you beg, going mad in my belly...

The slightest twist of my hand and the thing's length convulses, rents and ruptures opening along its flanks, black blood seeping to the dunes, sand sifting from its wounds.

"No time for theatrics today, Lotahn."

The beast slowly stills, though it continues to shudder, unable to contain its indignation at the disgrace I dare heap on it.

In a hiss of compliance, the creature bows its great head,

brilliant blue eyes fluttering.

I open my clenched fist, releasing it, though ready to blast it to the sand it came from, should it decide to turn. There's no telling with these old and forgotten ones; most of them mad from dejection, barely remembered outside of distorted stories and old myths… they lose themselves, as Lotahn did, before I found him, before I cultivated some facsimile of his old faiths again.

I go to the girl as the serpent encircles the great, glass disc, as it battens onto its own tail, forming the ouroboros that was the most prominent symbol of its murdered cults.

I seat myself alongside her as she trembles and casts about in wordless amazement, watching the serpent slither, twisting on itself, the glass trembling beneath us, rising from the sands.

A yelp, a quiver, the girl clinging to me, taking my arm. Her fear is a pleasant contrast to the contempt she usually radiates, however impotent: "It's all right. I won't let anything happen to you."

A familiar promise, I've no doubt; one uttered by brothers and keepers and surrogate Fathers a thousand times over, proved a lie in the next breath or heartbeat.

Lotahn's motions stir the desert, a storm kindling around and beneath, the glass platform rising. The old one whispering in my mind: archaic incantations, verses in a language I don't know, that none remember; maybe from a time when he too aspired, like me, when he walked on two legs and required the aid of others, long forgotten, to fulfil his designs.

The storm churns the dunes to nonsense, their motions a boiling cauldron, ripples and waves passing beneath us, the serpent's voice rising higher and higher as it continues to slither, to spin on its axis.

Then, a moment of impossible impetus, the glass platform becoming static in the air, while the surrounding desert and horizon dissolve, flowing as though scrawled from coloured chalk in a tempest, blasted away in the gales we've called into being.

The girl cries, clinging to me hard enough to bruise, her eyes streaming with tears as she looks out, as she silently pleads with me: *Don't let me fall, don't let the storm take me...*

Laughing as I smooth the hair from her brow, caress her cheek. *Almost over, sweetness. Look! Can you see?*

I point beyond the storm, to the shard city, the pulsating, pink light on the horizon as they draw closer, accruing in size and detail before our eyes.

A fleeting moment of abjection in which I'm certain Lotahn has betrayed me, that the disc will carry us into the structures themselves, shattering, shredding us to a rain of meat and bone.

Then, in a tangible cessation, the storm dies, the surging, swirling nonsense coheres. The disc descends beneath us, already coming apart, streaming sand from its edges as the art that holds it in place slowly, slowly dissipates.

I cling to her as it comes apart, spilling us to the dunes on the city's outskirts. No cries, the girl up on her feet in a heartbeat, kicking sand into my face, screaming at me with what breath she still has: "Fucker! Shit-hearted bastard! What were you doing?"

The sand stings my eyes, grating in my mouth, between my teeth. I tremble, weary to the point of dissolution, after that expenditure. Somewhere distant, Lotahn hisses in the back of my mind, laughing at the ambition he tastes, the desires I sweat.

Soon, I promise him, *soon, you'll never laugh at me again.*

I allow the art that holds him in place to dissipate, the flesh he has dreamed of and begged me to weave for beyond decades dissolving around him.

Smiling at his hisses and howls, his fading threats, as he slips away back into formless oblivion.

Rising, though it pains me, though I split and bleed beneath my ragged clothing, I stop her with a raised hand, invisible fingers lightly constricting around her throat.

"No more. Understand me?"

The girl struggles, raking at her own skin in an effort to dislodge my hold.

"If you speak to me like that again, I'll crush your heart in your chest. I'll burst your eyes in their sockets. I'll boil your blood in your veins. Do you understand?"

The girl snarls, baring inhumanly sharp teeth, nodding.

Lowering my hand, I frown indifference as she drops to the swirling sands, coughing, clutching her throat.

Turning from the desert, I exhale at sight of the city I haven't walked in so long, there were times during my exile I believed I never had, that it was nothing but an idiot's fantasy, an escapist's delusion. That the only way I might return is by cultivating the same strain of lunacy, allowing it to swell and consume whatever delusion of sanity I entertained.

Barely a fragment of its original expanse, according to testimonies I've heard, the stories I've scavenged: a time when it spread from horizon to horizon, when the desert was a garden of shards, when it swarmed with light and life.

Before she came, weaving her nurseries and conspiracies in its quiet and forgotten places. Before her emergence and the apocalypse that reduced its people to ash and echoes.

Remembering, at the sight of her, the carnage that we wrought together, calamity beyond my wildest, most nihilistic fantasies: dancing at the heart of a storm that she sweated and exhaled, wreathed in its lightning, laughing as they fled from me, as my lover, her child, watched and urged me on with wild words. Revelling in their miseries, as they ran, took flight, as they fell screaming into the abysses that opened beneath them, were swept up into the boiling skies. Singing the hymns she taught me as her children came, swarming from their warrens and nurseries, laughing as they consumed all in their paths.

So many apocalypses, since then, inspired in her name, as part of the threads of intrigue she weaves throughout reality, from this place, at the heart of the web.

As to her ultimate intentions...I likely couldn't comprehend them, even were I beloved enough for her to confess them. Most likely, their alien elaboration would melt my mind, reduce me to another of the mad, lost morsels wandering the streets beneath her immensity.

Falling to my knees in her shadow, I'm barely able to look at her, to *comprehend*, to tear my eyes away. A creature that should not, *cannot* be, that all sense and sanity revolts at the sight of:

The source of the pink, pulsating light that threads through the city, that arcs and coruscates into the diseased sky; a point where reality sags and fractures, threatening to burst, as it did when she originally emerged into this state.

So many names, so many titles… almost all forgotten. But not to the same degree as Lotahn and his ilk; still worshiped, still adored, not in many places beyond this, but by those that infest it: her bastards, the children that scurry and scutter across every inch, that spin their webs and nests between the shards. A clotted network of shimmering silver runs throughout, strung with swollen larders, where victims scream and struggle, where sacrifices to her wither, draining of vitality and inspiration, blood and marrow. Pulsating nurseries, tended to by loving handmaidens and midwives, await the moment of emergence, when new generations will hatch to be introduced to their adoring Grandmother.

Many descend at sight of us, as we disturb the air, the threads of their nests and webs: emerging from the shadows of shattered and ruined spars that jut from the surrounding desert, some closer in resemblance to the Grandmother: bloated, arachnid things, ranging from grey white to deep black, their forelimbs in the air, tasting our natures and intentions. Others are more humanoid, extraneous limbs breaking from their backs, their flanks, from around their waists, vast and numerous eyes swelling their skulls beyond proportion. Some, the rare few, are almost devoid of familial resemblance, save for strange patterns on their skins, a darkness in their eyes.

The Grandmother shifts her weight, those scurrying across her belly shaking loose, descending on silken threads or curling into balls of limbs as they fall. The structures between which she rests shudder and grind with her sudden activity, her great limbs extending, talons immense enough to shear mountains to rubble coming to rest in the desert beyond, carving new pits and canyons amongst the dunes.

Too enamoured of the one who plucked me from misery, who taught me all, elevated me from the lost and dreaming boy I was, so certain of his worthlessness, to spare the girl the slightest attention, the merest whisper of interest. Though I'm certain that her mind and body betray her at the sight as mine originally did, that she soils herself, collapses in the ash and ruins, gibbering nonsense denials.

"I... I did as you asked, Grandmother."

Not like the rest; not kin to her, save in what she has given me; the venomous revelations she trickled into my soul, the ichor she allowed me to drink like Mother's milk.

The entire city sings a chorus of hootings and whistlings, hisses and chittering as she answers; a wave of purest adoration, almost enough to smite me to the ground, make me weep and rake at the sand in its intensity.

I know. I see you, child. Always.

I force myself to raise my head, though it swirls and sifts, though it feels made from smoke and light. Force myself to meet her eyes, that blaze down on me like amber moons. What they reflect... other whens and wheres, distorted visions of places far beyond; yesterdays and tomorrows that might have never been, that may never be, that are as certain to come as any whispered or written prophecy.

"Please. Take her. She's..."

A slither of ice inside, invading, stealing my breath. No mere blade, I've long since been elevated beyond the state where something so pedestrian might do me harm. Something *imbued,* sacrificial, splinters of frost breaking away from it, tangibly trailing their cold fever through my flesh, my blood.

Fear. So old and abandoned an emotion, I almost don't recognise it.

The splinter withdraws as I scrabble at my back, its wielder still clutching it in her trembling fingers.

Black blood spills against burning blue and cold silver. I know it: the same blade that would have carved out her heart, had I not plucked it from her Mother's hands.

Laughing, as cold and pulsing numbness fill me. I see, now, though it's far, far too late: the game she has played with me from the beginning, so much more subtle than mine. I almost applaud, almost smile.

Black brine fills my throat, rising foul in my mouth as I reach for her, as I crawl towards her through the ashes.

"G... Grand... motherrrr?"

Hush. Hush, child; it's been so long since you knew peace, hasn't it? I've been unkind, asking you to wander so far, so long. You must be weary...

"No... please, no..."

Distant laughter hisses and wails: not just Lotahn, but the thousand others I have uncovered and bound, straining at bonds that give way, one by one, as my flesh fails, as it seeps and bubbles on my bones, sloughing away.

Watching as my fingers blacken, as my borrowed and stolen and scavenged flesh goes to what it should have been long, long ago: filth and rot, spattering the ashes. The girl steps back, glaring down at me with contempt profound enough to escalate the process.

Grandmother, please...

Don't fret, sweet one. This isn't the end for us. At least, it doesn't have to be.

A single thread, the slightest strand of spider silk, shimmers in my thoughts, that I might grasp and tear myself from the yawning abyss.

So many… so many I've hurt and disgraced, enslaved and humiliated: forgotten gods, bound demons, mad angels. Spirits and spectres and nameless, formless things. All awaiting me, to tear what remains of my soul to tatters, to devour and torment me until the end of time.

One chance. One bargain: the same that so many others have made.

Of course. *Of course.* I always intended this; why else would she have come to me, why else would she save me from myself?

I almost spit the bargain back in her face, hurl myself into the abyss, the waiting arms and coils of those that hate me beyond all reason, that know nothing else other than their dreams of tormenting me.

Shuddering as I grasp the thread, its light filling me as I'm torn from my rotting, failing carcass, that goes to dust and muck before the girl's appalled eyes.

One last glimpse of her, as I'm drawn from it: up, up, into the Grandmother's yawning maw, as I'm swallowed, filtered, sifted through the ineffable systems of her body, not into one of her myriad stomachs, but her *womb,* a black and burning place where

I writhe and am remade, where I'll coalesce and be born again, by and by.

Where I'll dream, for now, and happily forget what it means to be anything other than her child.

Epilogue

The first face I saw, the most beautiful in all creation. Tearing me free from nightmares, from hideous confusion, unwanted memory. Fading, fading, in the first few heartbeats, my earliest, adoring moments of being.

My beautiful midwife, the Mistress I follow, away from my brothers and sisters, out across the great wastes, the burning horizon, beneath the suns and moons of other places, where she makes different faces for us, different names.

I love her. I've loved her from the moment I opened my eyes, since the first thought. There is nothing else; nothing that nourishes in quite the same way as the sight of her, nothing that exhilarates as much as her eyes, her hands on me.

Cruelties. Such cruelties! I miss them… my kin that I barely know, my siblings and Mothers… the Grandmother most of all, who still sings to me, when I dream, who sometimes calls me back, across the sleeping voids, through the filth between states, to sing with her, to tell her stories of where we wander, what secrets we learn. Such wonderful moments; some of the few when

I can be dreamless, when I'm not haunted by that idiot boy, that lost and loveless ancient, with his ridiculous aspirations to her status, with his gods and monsters.

Oh yes, I remember him, and so does she. We speak of him, sometimes, in the blood and ashes, amongst the burning bones, the crumbled spires: speak of what he was, what he wanted for her, what he might have been. So strange... little more than an infantile dream, now; a nightmare man, fast fading from memory.

I am happy. Truly, deliriously happy, to be with her, out amongst the waning worlds, the wastes in waiting, making stories with her, carving myths, opening the ways for my kin to follow.

And, maybe one day, we will return. Maybe one day, when the ways are open, when Grandmother's webs thread from every spire and tower in creation. When all dreams are one dream.

Maybe then, we'll walk the paths home to her, and allow ourselves to be adoringly devoured once more.

Until then, we wander, we roam; we make love and murder and sew our secrets. We dance in fires, sing with ghosts, calling the ones we love, the new and beautiful children, from their aimless play.

Hymns that will never be forgotten linger long after most have gone to echoes and silence, which we sing to one another, in the aftermath of anarchy and apocalypse: lullabies for the unborn that swell in her belly, who will make ruin their playgrounds, in the strange days to come.

Beautifully Broken

Of course now, *here,* at the edge of all creation. Where else?

Where else?

It feels barely days since I used to walk here… so long ago. A student, so young; a *boy*, no matter what age insisted, the plays of sophistication I affected.

So tired, even then—tired of trying, of failing. Of *being*.

Him. I survived because of him. If we'd never met, if I'd refused his invitation to coffee, as every instinct screamed…

Light rain raises sweetness from the grass and soil. Wild flowers jewel the hill's flanks. These stones… immense, arranged by natural phenomena or the hands of many, many men, welded over centuries by mosses, lichens, wild growth, trees grasping at the sky from their heights.

We used to come here, to *climb*; we spent hours, days… picnics and bottles of wine, sometimes from morning until the day died, when the chill came, even in high Summer.

The only one, the only one I really spoke to, who fascinated with his own tales. Who *heard me.*

"Where are you? Where are you now?"

Not here—only the rain, the flowers, the whispers of old ghosts. Our ghosts. Long dead, now: the both of us.

The wind… sharper, more hateful than I remember: joints and muscles groaning, veins pumping molten lead. Everything is so much *harder* than it used to be.

Once, we found a ram's skull, set in the centre of a circle of ashes, the icon of some occult rite or satanic ceremony. I still have it, on my study desk, its eye sockets speared with pens. A manifest memory, evidence that it's more than a myth or story I tell myself.

Where are you?

Idiot fantasies; that you'll come, answering some unspoken call, that I'll find you there, beneath the tree where we used to sit, swap theories and confessions…

Nothing, ghosts in the rain.

The tree, *our* tree, is still here, skeletal now, gnarled and charred, as though set alight in recent memory, licked by lightning or ignited as a beacon by some lost soul.

I breathe it in: damp stone, wet green, rain in the air, charred wood. My own sweat.

Nothing like the old Summers, eh?; The world a different place, now. Not made for us. Never for me.

I seat myself, the stone cold, less comfortable than I recall— grinding bone, bruising skin. So much older, now, but no less lost.

A storm threatening since the morning's early hours, sullen and cancerous in the sky. Growling; lit from within by flickers of blue and yellow, veils of black rain billowing over the distant hills. It will be here, before long. Maybe the lightning will lick the tree at my back, char it to ash and fill my veins with blue fire.

Burn ghosts and memory to nothing.

Please.

*

"… just the *sensation* of it. Can you imagine?"

He sprawls, cat-like, comfortable on any perch, swilling *Cabernet Sauvignon* around his glass.

"No. It's absurd."

"That's the point; that's what I *want*..."

"But it's something you'll never have; you can only *imagine,* and that's it."

It's a consistent argument, my desire to fly pierced by his faith in gravity, my lust to be a living fire doused by rains of reason.

A different day… *so* different; a gold-white sun glistens, insects swarm in the air, refracting gold into rainbows with gossamer wings, sweat sewing the shirts to our backs. A cigarette flares, offered to me, but refused.

"You're setting yourself up for disappointment, if that's what you dream of…"

I laugh, sighing. "I can't help it; it *is* what I dream of, all the time."

Shedding my skin. Becoming fire. Sprouting wings, becoming an angel or dragon. What it might feel like to be mist, rain, smoke: a torrent filled with spawning salmon.

"You'll never know."

The constant retort, "It doesn't matter; like I said: I can't help it, any more than you can pissing or blinking."

A serene smile. "I know. That's the tragedy of it."

Green, green eyes burn colder than winter stars.

It never happened, not this way. But it does, now. Maybe because we both wanted it, once, because my anxiety, my *cowardice,* kept it from being.

Let me go… the ghosts inside shackle me to the present, telling stories of possibilities that never were.

Rain, the storm overhead bruise black, so heavy, *so heavy…* lightning, blazing blue.

"That's the miracle."

A strange man, the pair of us kin, in that; physically as well as in thought: wiry, almost *wasted,* clothes hanging from his angular hips and shoulders as though poorly cut, perpetually about to slip from him or give at the seams. A white Summer shirt, almost translucent in the sun, trousers the same; leather sandals poorly suited to rambling or rock-climbing, though it didn't concern him on the way up. A garish kerchief around his neck, a number of bracelets around his wrists and ankles, lend him a gypsy motif, the look of a transient, new age shaman.

I envy his grace, his comfort in his own skin.

It was a lie, a fantasy of my insecurities, as I learned, far, far later: a revelation that will never come again.

So different from the boys we were: the ghosts of memory, that insist on themselves, even as they fade; we are able to be our own ideals, here.

More wine, our third bottle, the sun suspended, allowing us all of time.

Sitting up, craning his neck, his eyes are half closed as he sighs. "My Mom seems to be under the impression we're sleeping together."

I almost choke on my wine. He smiles, amused at the sight of it drooling down my chin. "What the hell gave her that idea?"

"Well, it's not like you haven't slept over before..."

"In separate *beds!* And only because I was too pissed to get home."

He waves his hand. Incidental details, apparently.

Not like this; a conversation we never had, outside of my head.

"She likes you; thinks you're a good influence on me. She *hopes* you are."

Silence, whatever responses I might give snarl in my throat. All save one, "A shame she's going to be disappointed."

Sinuses prick, joints ache. *Idiot. Idiot! Every chance, every offer, always denied out of wittering anxiety...* thunder rumbles overhead, in the stone below. Blue tongues of lightning lick the storm's belly. Let it come! Let it char me, fuse me to the stone; let others find me, a black, shrivelled testament to my cowardice. Let their trespassing fingers break me, scatter my ashes to rain and wind.

"That's cruel. There's no reason she has to be..."

Close. Closer than he ever was, in waking memory: scents of wine and warm cotton, spice of sweat, exotic aftershave.

"...is there?"

The moment... the ghost shuddering fit to tear itself apart, appalled by its self denial; the damnation it set in motion with just two words, "I'm sorry."

Idiot. Idiot, idiot, *idiot child.* Were it living, were it flesh and blood, I'd tear it from my head like a cancer, dash its soft skull against the rock.

But it isn't, never will be.

He laughs, not making it out to be a joke, but refusing to pursue the thread further. Things go on, pleasant enough days, fewer and fewer, as our time winds down—distance, disappointment. A slow, slow divorce.

Not here, not in this rain, this sunlight.

Here, *I* laugh, not in derision or denial, but invitation, raising a hand to his face, skin burning beneath the unkempt beard. Eyes flutter, heavy lidded, as though I might lull him to sleep with my touch.

"Anthony…"

He eases himself down, laying his head in my lap, curled on himself like a boy weary from play.

"Just for a little while… just… let's sit here."

A hand on his flank, a momentary shudder, then stillness.

Lightning, vicious rain. A trespasser here in my own past, not a ghost, but flesh and blood.

Not true. Not real.

What the fuck do I care? Let disappointment drown, let the rain wash us away.

My hand moves in the sun, more confident than it ever was, could have been, when I was this man, this dead boy. The curvature of his flank through warm cotton, hips bony, angular, ribs the same. Heat radiating, summer-born pneumonia. Smiling, though I can't see.

"Enjoying yourself?"

His shoulder, his neck; the rush and pulse of blood.

"Are you?"

"Yes."

Unambiguous. Another quality the ghost envies, the lie adores.

Not here, not with you.

Where, then? Out there, older, out in the world, more in love with it than I've ever been. Always a ghost, imagining itself a man. A lover.

No matter, not any more.

I crane my face to the rain, the rabid, wounded sky. Its growl in my bones, my entrails, threatens to shudder me apart.

Good. *Good.*

Blinding, sun so white, kisses so eager they bruise. I break away, breathless, wine-tasting spit trailing between us.

Why not? What good is memory, anyway? Just a graveyard; the ashen womb where disappointment is born.

His shirt... struggled out of, torn away, fluttering into the grass. His skin the same shade as the cotton, freckles dusting his collarbone and shoulders. His chest reveals pale-blonde, downy hair, alight in the sunshine, woven from it. His lips are at my throat, his teeth, his tongue... burning, grazing, eager for the breath and blood beneath. Fingers trace the seam of his spine, raking his shoulder blades. He shudder, arcing against me, his bites and kisses enthusiastic enough to mark me.

Never so urgent, never so confident as this, not in any of the sporadic, momentary love affairs that followed my ghost's refusal, the tragedies and disappointments that litter dying memory, already distant and dream-like.

Straddling me, weightless as a bird, hollow-boned, he laughs as the stones shift beneath us. Not caring; the ripples of an earthquake in Okinawa or Tokyo; a hurricane in Kansas. My shirt snares at my ponytail, his guidance easing it loose.

His hands at my chest, trailing through the dark mat of hair there, palms and fingertips burning, tracing invisible tattoos to mark their passage.

An imagined touch more intimate, more exhilarating, than any I've known in flesh, in memory...from every ghost, every single one: the fled and lost lovers, the one-night, anonymous and faceless fucks... nothing; mist and tatters, fading further with every kiss...

His hair, scented of coconut and burning November, Summer lightning earthing in my spine as his lips find my nipple, battening, traces of tongue and teeth.

"Why?" I ask the rain. "Why can't *they* be the lie?" The ghosts, the grey years they haunt. Why can't the sun, *this* sweat, *this* hair, *this* skin, be real?

My bellowed fury is met by denials from the Father that condemns us.

Fuck you. Fuck you.

There as here, my fingers fumble with wet buttons, damp denim and cotton.

The rain doesn't care, any more than the angels and demons I once prayed to, begged to pluck me up, drag me down... anything to be away from this life. Either way, it didn't matter.

Still doesn't.

Lightning, so bright, so beautiful, betrays the child inside: the writhing, whimpering thing that he shrivels with his kisses, terrified and resentful of his affection. Illuminating the surrounding hills, fields, valleys, revealing no one and nothing, no eyes but his and mine: those of the angels in the storm, the demons beneath the stone. None are more intent, more *fevered*, than ours.

Burning, febrile lust, for this spittle, scorching my throat like alcohol, for those eyes, these bony, angular hips... the heat and hardness between us, grinding together as though intent on becoming common dust. Lighting inside me, kindling every nerve.

Time was, I would have glanced away, terrified of his attention, ashamed at my cowardice. Not today.

Today, my eyes drink his light, devour the blue, flickering with their fire, that might any second burst from them, engulfing him in rapturous flame.

"Are you..? Christ!" My teeth are at his throat, gnawing, bruising. "Ha... are you sure... this is what you want?"

I laugh at his courtesy, at the bite of his teeth, gnawing my shoulder ragged. An answer in kisses, dragging him close, not caring that the rock rakes and grazes my back, that insect legs and butterfly wings tickle my skin. Let them come, let them watch and know.

Spiders, beetles, centipedes, stream from their nests and nurseries, disturbed by the apocalypse we promise with every heave and shudder.

I was like them, once; this play the province of others, impossible, no matter how much I dreamed of or ached for it...

belonging to an alien species I could barely converse with.

The sounds I make, *here,* in the rain, there in dreaming sunlight, *soon to be a memory.* Rain in my mouth, tasting of him, as I imagine him, washing away the lingering traces of the false loves between then and now, reducing them to smoke and fantasy, despite their realisation in flesh.

Nothing but boys and betrayers—ill-fitting, soiled bandages for a wound that never, never stopped bleeding.

The storm upon me, all around, the air sparking blue, every inch of me shuddering, inside and out; nerves fray, entrails unravel... thoughts burn in their azure inferno. Swallowing the world, the sky is beaten black from horizon to horizon, its abuse far from over. I want to be there, to make love with lightning, be charred to sludge and washed to the bone by rain. To have hurt and loss and masochistic memory sluiced away.

But he won't let me; the heat and light and *scent* of that place; no despair is sufficient to tear me from it, to puncture or dissolve the dream.

Standing from me, struggling to disentangle himself, the sun streaming around him, rain intruding, refracting it into faint rainbows. My heart is a hammering lunatic, butterflies and lacewings shimmering in the air. Fumbling with his cotton trousers, shrugging them away, his erection straining against the grey boxer shorts beneath.

I imagined this so often, in the wine-fuelled frustrations of all-night benders, after the bars and clubs… staggering home, silently begging him to call, to knock at my door, to share the sweat and fever that followed. The reality, the *realisation,* here at the edge of everything, is so different—so far removed from masturbatory idealisation…

"Fuck."

He smiles, wanton, guileless, casting his eyes about as though he cares if anyone sees. Happy to provide a show for them; something to dilute or distract from the grey of their lives.

Stretching, his joints cracking as he cranes his neck, clenches his fists. Laughing as he turns to me, kneels on the stone, hands on my legs, my thighs.

"Can I?"

Trespassing between. Gasps, noises the ghost, the *child,* can't imagine making.

Reaching down, I run a hand across his cheek, smiling at his sweet perversity. Reaching up, grasping at rain, at knots of cloud, threads of blue lightning, fingers pass through as though *they're nothing…*

Synchronicity, waking now and dreaming then, rhyming as I fumble out of jeans, no helping hands in the former, nothing to cushion the stones against my back and buttocks. Only this: a ghost that made itself, begging the lightning to kiss his face, sear out his eyes, to let him love in imagined memory, forever.

He's more urgent than I imagined, almost violently eager,

hoisting up my legs, tearing jeans open, casting them away. The boy was never seen like this, not back then. He doesn't know, thinks I'm like him: so feline, so versed.

Far from it, the cold of his eyes on me almost enough—enough to make the lightning spill, charring us to ash and smoke.

No more courtesy or questions; his face between my legs, nuzzling like a cat's, deep breaths, inhaling my sweat, my heat, his lips and tongue burning. Sensation intense enough to make my sex molten, becoming its own liquid state: a mercurial sea into which he might tumble and happily drown.

My eyes rise from him, to the white sun, the warm rain.

Nothing is left between us, now; flesh to flesh, his kisses, his tongue, his teeth, causing me to rake at the stone, as though I might tear it with naked fingers, rip it up at the foundations, carrying us to where the rain is born...

Words. I don't hear, thunder and lightning swallow them, the rain between my legs as cold as his lips are burning, and as welcome. The storm's fingers... skilful as a whore's, at work on me... what children might we make together? Hopefully a happier species than either of us.

My hands on his head, in his hair, feel the thoughts swell and burst through skin and bone. *Beautiful.*

"Fuck... fucking *Christ*..."

He slows, pulling away, smiling, lips glossed.

"Having a good time, I take it?"

Laughter is my only answer, the storm behind my eyes, in my throat—the lightning in my belly, not allowing more.

His fingers grasp me, a slow working, his lips tracing the seam of my balls with kisses. The sight of him, pale and naked, in love with his abandon... almost enough to wrench me from storms and wind and shivering cold, to strand me forever in sunlight, that other state just a fading dream, a dead growth on the rocks.

Rising, he trails kisses from crotch to navel, from navel to chest, settling at my lips, rain on his back, rain on our faces.

Tears, burning, freezing.

"Stand up."

A wild smile.

"Is that an order?"

"Yes."

He does as commanded, as I lever myself into a sitting position, the scrape of stone at my back (*jealous ghosts, their impotent, ragged talons*), his musk, mingling with the scents of rain, wet stone, charred wood, wild flowers.

Yes.

Taking him by the hips, turning him, my hands on his buttocks. Not fulsome, but bony, attenuated, yet beautiful, for all that—my attention on them coaxing sighs and shudders.

On my hands and knees against the stone, rain searing my ragged neck, waiting for the lightning to lick me, spit me through, char me where I kneel, making me an icon for other wanderers, other lovers, to come worship at…

Naked, I kick away his underwear, a moment of concern for our discarded clothes, soon dissolving.

Skin on skin, the lightning between us enough to turn the storm overhead, in that other, half forgotten place, to fire.

"Go on, *please.*"

A sweeter, more plaintive plea never heard, none more desperate from the lips of a serial killer's bound and bleeding victim.

The taste of his skin… every lick and kiss is saline, spiced; trembling beneath, crying as I bite, his skin yields, leaving darkening bruises, red wheels on his buttocks. Raking him, my nails making stripes that thread the tapestry together. Strings of silver, sloping from between his legs, teach me what he loves; what he'll never deny or admonish me for.

A ringing slap, hard enough to startle the butterflies, makes him yelp, leaving a red handprint on his skin.

He glances over his shoulder, eyes pooling, reflecting the lightning, the love and wrath of the storm.

Licking the surrounding stone, charring the moss and grasses that pelt it. A sharpness that puts me in mind of burning out electronics; celestial machinery that holds together the failing world. Heart a lunatic swarm, battering itself bloody against the cage that confines it. Not afraid of this, of dying, but of losing it: the memory, the fantasy, dying first…

There. *Here.* This body, this meat; these buttocks, the dank, ridged space, so pungent, so certain to the touch and taste.

Dividing him, probing, the scent and taste and damp, honeyed heat of him. Imagined, but never fulfilled; never knowing that the act would wash over my mind like a tab of *Ecstasy* shorn of chemical qualities, more *sincere.*

Grinding against me, legs shivering, his voice rises to almost female expressions of delight.

Never knowing that I might be capable of this, might author such pleasure...

The strings of silver from between his legs catch sunlight like the rain. Too detailed, too *pristine,* to be anything other than a dream.

"That... that was..."

Beautiful. Incredible. No words; none sufficient. Instead, stroking fingers where my tongue passed, playing in my wetness, pressing, pressing...

Glancing back over his shoulder, his breath catches. "Deeper." *Deeper.*

Stone gives way, a crack widening between my hands, my knees, as rain sheets and streams over my naked body. Filth and sweat and regret wash away as the abyss widens, as I sink into it, riding a freezing stream into darkness.

Pain, a rag-doll, bouncing from stone to stone, broken and torn, moments of blinding agony, explosions of empty white, none

*profound enough to sear away that day, that sun, his heat
enveloping me.*

Unable to stand any longer, laughing, his legs gone to water,
he hunkers down to kneel over me, his head between my legs,
every lap, every stroke of his almost fluid interior, coaxing
moans, pleas through gritted teeth.

More.

More.

There is no slowing or cessation, not even when his
expressions become wordless, yelps and groans that might be of
pain as much as ecstasy. I don't care. The whole world could
collapse, ground giving way beneath, sky splitting, raining down.
Neither of us would care or stir from our communion.

Only this, only this matters, no matter how the storm howls,
how the ghosts scream.

Somewhere deep, deep in him, *deep beneath the stones; a
natural cave, dank and dark, so dark… where I am; where I've
always been, since the lie that calls itself memory, that I'll no
longer allow or tell myself.*

*The lightning inside is enough to illuminate this world, seeping
through my eyes, lips, pores and prick, allowing me view of this
seething kingdom, this realm of snails and spiders.*

Sun. Blinding, burning. His body. His scent. His taste. His
heat. The weight of him atop me, the slick quivering of his skin…

Deep, deep inside.

Transgressions the child inside will always deny, as it always has, wallowing in its shame and self-disgust, perpetually out of love with itself.

Why? Why has it always denied itself, why does it refuse delight?

Unworthy. Always, always unworthy, of even the smallest pleasure.

His tongue is a calamity on my nerve endings, his throat so deliciously enveloping... it's almost enough to make me molten, make me flow...

"R... Robert! Slow... slow it down, just a little..."

From rainforest heat to faint chill and rain, as we gasp for breath between sighs.

"Are you... close?"

Laying my head back, letting the sun and rain wash my eyes.

"Yeah. Not yet, though; I don't want to be done just yet."

His hands are still on me, eyes fluttering in drugged-out bliss as I press deeper into him, moving over his quivering folds and ridges, seeking the spots that make him squirm.

"God... would you have believed... we'd be doing this, if I'd told you this morning?"

I smile. "Why the Hell did we wait so long?"

"I don't know. I don't know..."

I do. Blinking in the dark, storm raging overhead, stone and darkness whispering around me. Rain streams through the rent above, scuds of sky visible, flashing cold and hideous blue.

No one knows, no one will come. No one I want. Only ghosts and spiders; the lies that dream one another, when wanting is done...

Something inside... wet, hot pulsing, shards grating and jangling through my body with every breath, glass and grinding stone.

Finally, beautifully, broken.

Hauled up, I stand now, the rain colder, more earnest, as though to wash away sweat and the filth to follow. The day isn't darker, but brighter, the scent of stone and growing things and our intertwined bodies delirious, narcotic.

Kneeling behind, working him, every kiss sacred, wanting to be inside of him so badly, to melt and flow into him, nestle in those places that children never will; to be born out of him whole and ready to fuck myself back inside again and again... a new Ouroboros.

"You... want me to fuck you?"

Breathless, barely able to answer. There are no eyes to be enticed or appalled by us, save those of rabbits and pheasants, sparrows and foxes. Not caring if otherwise.

"Yes."

No protection... the notion of disease absurd, a fairy-tale horror, in this enchanted place. Hating myself for even thinking it; that there could be anything so pathetically vile under this sun.

Always envious that he finds it so, so easy; the seductions, recycled, meaningless bed-mates, two or three weekly, at times, always grown bored with, abandoned in days.

Seawater in my throat spills over my lips, an endless well, slowly filling the dark. The spiders fearless, their fluttering footsteps mingling with the ghost's wandering fingers, hands that will have me, soon enough.

Here, with him; the lover that never was, that always will be, *yes; smiling, even as I drown...*

Sun and the burning scent of his hair, our sweat comingling, his grooves and ridges, slight resistance as I press against him.

"Take it... take it slow. Let... let me..."

The urge to be brutal, to press him against the stone and fuck him 'til he screams almost undeniable.

Easing back, slowly, slowly, gasps and gritted teeth, until his buttocks meet my thighs, until I'm lost in him.

Christ, *Christ*—the heat and fluidity, the silken strokes, the butterflies swarming around us in their mating frenzy.

Unable to help myself, I grasp his neck, thrusting into him; long, slow strokes, rejoicing in every flute and ridge of him.

Cold hands, cold lips, on me in the dark, feather light, so eager for a little warmth.

Rain and blazing sun, cries echoing around the stones, the surrounding hills and fields. Lost to all things, except one another.

This moment... let us die in this moment, this mindless

Heaven. What else could we or anyone, ask?

Wordless, breathless bleats, grunts and gasps, professions of love more eloquent than poetry can contrive, prayers more passionate than the most faithful can utter. Want keen enough to shatter the world, to slit its seams and make reality spill.

The stink rises from us… I drink it, luxuriate in it—animal and ripe and intoxicating. Splayed out, hands against the stone, my hands on his hips, straying between his legs…

Their lips on mine, so cold, their fingers around my throat, stealing breath. Many cold mouths, many cold cunts and assholes envelop me, demanding my last, dying spurts.

Lightning overhead and lightning inside. No one will know, until this place surrenders to time, humanity surely doing so before, leaving nothing but more ghosts to see, more ghosts to join the cold and desperate orgy.

Smouldering spools slick my fingers, his coming cries the bleats of a lamb scenting its slaughter, my teeth at his neck, his shoulder, breaking skin, his blood in my mouth.

Blinding blue and white, eclipsing us, searing us away, the lightning finds us, taking with it the stones, the hilltop, the sun and storm, leaving us sealed in that blood and honey place where all is intensity and sensation.

Weight and flesh and heaving exhaustion coalesce around us, the rain cool on our backs, the sunshine warm… *the last breath plucked from me, happily given, the ghosts retreating with their prize, the storm peeling back, silent now.*

Awake, truly awake, for the first time. I'm still inside of him, spurts and seepages, catching breath between laughter—the only thing we know.

Breathing so hard... a dark dream drains from me; some dying lie, thrown up by my fevered mind. His cock still in my hand, deflated, slick with cooling sperm.

"We... can't stay like this forever."

Kisses where bites previously passed. "I don't see why not."

Pulling from me, his absence is cold, invigorating, strangely welcome. Somewhere below are old eyes; of a dreaming lie, closing, at last. A childhood horror, easily forgotten.

Collapsing, our naked bodies warm against the stone, laughing even as the rain comes, washing away what remains of the lie below, leaving only this dream, more real, more *wanted*, than any before or after.

Wasted Day Tarot

I.

Desecration's Dawn Bird

Hateful, synthetic shriek, machine-throat song. Wingless, cageless, featherless. No beauty in its cyclopean eye, only demands, insistence: *Rise. Rise. Rise.* An elegy for dreams, no matter how beloved, how desperately clung to. Dissolving like wet sand beneath its hymn. For nightmares, too, equally mourned, against the pale glare of its light, the sun coldly blazing in its skull and stomach, threatening dawn without end, day without respite: a death to dreaming.

II.

The Dreaming Beast

Coiled black, heaving in animal slumber, its cruel dreams: oaths of the atrocities it will commit, when it stirs; of the babes it will devour in their nests, of the appalled Mothers it will devour after. Heads bitten away at the necks, bellies opened, innards strewn across the ground in its play. For the Great Child it will make gifts of its victims; the Child that, for all its immensity, lacks the teeth and talons to claim its own meat. Stirring, its blackness ripples, eyes of green fire flare, talons raking where it lies. No knight can slay it; only the cruel children its Child fears and the growling engines that speed across stone rivers that it must cross to reach its hunting grounds. No maiden can tame it, indifferent to love, innocence its meat. Insouciant affection for its keeper, whose tongue and eyes it will eat, should he never wake again.

III.

The Sorrow Hours

Whispers in the dark, scrabbling inside: spiders made of misery, worms born of doubt. Infested, every evil, parasite thing waking with me, bloated on bad dreams, hungry in the darkness before dawn. Biting and stinging, their venom cold, feverish in its frost, narcotic visions of older times, that might never have been, that I've done all I can to drown and forget: corpses of old shames and betrayals, of idiocies and embarrassments; of rejections and humiliations and every poisonous moment... stirring, now, not caring how deeply buried, how assiduously drowned: corpses beneath the mire, rising with its filth in their rotted eyes, their black and drooling mouths. Not to devour, but to *remind:* to tell me their stories again and again and again, until sanity slays them once more or chokes on their excrement.

IV.

The Empty Man.

Maybe at prayer, maybe its antithesis: deep and desolate thought, undoing the mind and works of God in his earnestness. Naked and moaning, taut and straining, every thought a contraction, giving birth to frog-spawn hosts of children, cockroach-purses of nascent ideas, that swell and scurry and scatter, in the fullness of time. Sweating, stinking in the synthetic light, the buzzing dawn, as the beast stirs, as its eyes find him, as they *demand, demand, demand*. Sighing, moaning, as revelation comes, he curses the filth of his being, the knowledge that the beast and he are of common blood.

V.

The Stranger

A moon-window onto another place, a distorted when and where. Walls and floor set at crazy angles, a strange non-place, where I will never walk, save perhaps in dreams. The only inhabitant... not merely of that distorted room, but of the distorted *world* it occupies, a strange and haunted man, peering out, begging with his eyes: *Help me, help me, please, let me through.* I would, if I knew how—if I could reach through the silver and take his hand, could smash the window and open a way between our worlds. How beautiful would that be? To drag this alien man through or to swap places with him and walk the fun-house mirror world he occupies? A lost dream, a wasted hope, the despair unbearable in the stranger's eyes, and in mine.

VI.

Meat for the Beast

Stinking meat, the stuff of daily ritual, no telling its source, where it was culled from: a rotting, stinking mass, unfit for flies, but which the Beast demands, following like a shadow, always at my heel, until I make my offering, and the hideous feast begins.

VII.

The Dead Day

Grey abortion, weeping at its own waste. Sunless dawn, no burning skies, only ashen desert, inverted above for the angels to walk and wonder at the atrocity we unleash on ourselves.

Wanting to walk there with them, in the whispering ash, the weeping rain, to look up and see sad, hanging heads, the upturned eyes like stars shimmering, smiles and tears of children, of lost and abandoned lovers, of the perpetually unwanted. But no; anchored here, in the same mire, the same filth, where I'm just another unwanted memory, where the clockwork dawnbird breaks my dreams to make my offering to the Beast, where the thinking man murders angels with every inspiration and the stranger in the moon-window laments every waking moment, silently begging to be away from the twisted world he was born to. I can do nothing but envy those who walk the wastelands in the sky, where there's no denying despair and they watch as the stories of unwanted days unfold.

A Child at the Loom

He was a child that couldn't bear to be, for whom every thought was a coil of barbed wire. No wonder he made this, knowing or otherwise. Too long ago for me to recall, now.

His delight, the fluid darkness that washed his entrails when the door first opened... I remember that, so keenly; a sensation like being in love, invited into the bed of one adored or lusted after. An end to all else, or so he assumed.

It seems insanity, now, that he should have emerged; that the world could have summoned him back. That he ever answered.

"What did you want? What did you fucking *expect*?"

Breathless, slurring questions as I climb, hands outthrust against the corrugated walls, rivulets of lukewarm fluid flowing beneath. The stone is warm, faintly pulsing, as though beating hearts are entombed within.

No answer. Of course he doesn't fucking know: a masochistic, self-mutilating urge, slicing open a vein to see what colour it might bleed. But one that he surrendered to, disbelieving, begging himself not to, even as he descended, step by step, back towards the world.

I never thought I'd see it again, not after I abandoned it, letting the door close at my back, sealing me here, in the place that made it necessary. Granted a miracle, a self-made release, I let it go, opting instead for the old wastelands.

Never. Never again. Though the climb is harder than before—the boy who bounded these steps long, long since gone, the steps themselves no longer as certain—I make it, inch by inch, feet slipping beneath me, sending me sprawling, until I crawl, penitent on hands and knees.

The door. Carved wood dark, corroded with damp-rot since he... *I* last stood before it, its surface pulpy and splintered with fungal infestation, fruiting in places with parasitic flowers. The carvings it boasts almost obliterated, the figures they portray—men, women; beasts, monsters, dancing, feasting, fucking—warped and distorted beyond recognition, leaving only fragments and suggestions of their original anatomies.

I lean my forehead against it, its softness giving way, clots crumbling beneath my touch. Sobbing more profoundly than at any point over the last few days, at the litany of tragedies TV and radio and internet provided. Mourning for an abortive world, dead before it took its first breath.

Not mine, anymore.

My hand grips the door handle, its metal painted black, spared the corrosion that has claimed much of the rest.

The mechanism jars, grinding. Lightning in my belly, the urge to piss almost undeniable. Christ, what if it doesn't open? What if it strands me here, in this worm-hole, this maggot burrow between worlds?

Then, a life in semi-darkness, living off the seepage and condensation of the stones, whatever fungus the door might sprout, making meals from crawling, swarming, parasite things, grubs swelling in the walls, worms writhing in the dank.

Panic fades as I realise: even that would be better than returning to the cemetery-state below.

The mechanism grinds, complying beneath my weight, the swollen door sticking momentarily before bursting inward.

I stumble after it, into a room scented of wood and sweet dust—the faint, saline tang of sea filtering through from the open balcony door.

On my knees, the rotting portal seals itself behind me. An unfamiliar click, the mechanism locking. Gratitude, relief as the old beast on my back, embracing me like a great spider, its fangs buried in my neck, disperses. Its venom lingering, still lacing my blood, my thoughts; there'll be tears, sorrow for my lost children in the coming months, but soon, even that will fade, becoming little more than stories to tell, dreams to forget.

The room. Almost as I remember it: six walls, some boasting windows, the states beyond alien to one another: a great, dusk-lit forest of pine and fir, the moon overhead bloated and amber, silhouetting the citadel that rises high above the tree line. A blasted city of white stone, its ruins silent, save for the faint breeze carrying the ashes of its builders, the whispers of its ghosts... An ashen wasteland, swirling with storms that whip up the black and grey dunes, sewing smeared, ephemeral forms from their detritus that all but obscure the fevered horizon.

Doorways punctuate the windows; three in all, sealed against escape or trespass. Ways to the deeper and further places, where the dead boy who made all of this once wandered. I can barely remember those journeys, the places I strayed, the people I met. The old wasteland's sickness has eroded them, made them vague memories of childhood games, contrived fantasies in which plastic action figures were cast.

Allies, enemies, lovers… faded now, all but forgotten.

But I'll find them again, by and by.

The sixth wall different from the rest, glass doors flung wide, curtains parted, billowing in a storm's breath, carrying promises of lightning, traces of the black sea beyond.

At the centre of the room stands a contraption of strings and mechanical limbs: crab and spider-like, flowing contours of carved wood, the extended necks of guitars and violins. Dust dances in the air, layering every surface. So long since it last played. Maybe twice as long before it will again.

The storm's breath rises, carrying a saline spray into the room. The instrument's legs and strings twitch, thunder rumbling in the distance.

I rise, wiping away the sediment of tears, tongues of blue lightning lashing between sea and sky on the horizon, the thunder deeper, closer with every heartbeat, shuddering the room.

How does it *work*? I remember having to *learn*—plucking at the legs and strings like a child at a loom, the technique, the *art*, lost on me.

It was an age before I realised that no amount of plucking, no flesh and blood *fingers*, can stir it. That inspiration is enough, when it senses the right species. That it's capable of producing far more than just music: the states beyond still echoing with its symphonies, the renaissances and apocalypses it once played, strains that even now sift and sigh on their dead breezes.

Smiling at the boy's ghost as I see him moving around it, resisting the urge to reach out, to touch its strings, knowing what will become of the worlds he's created, the music he's conceived, if he does.

Learning, by and by: the chaos beyond the doorways and windows responding to his performances, sculpting itself, coalescing into some semblance of shape and order. Raw and doughy creations, at first: ephemeral things that last no longer than the music that inspires them.

Elegies following, the device responding to sorrow and despair as much as vision and desire. The conditions it shapes from them harrowing, though he'll come to wander them, too, when he learns the love of nightmares.

Tears welling, the boy soon lost, become something other, as transformed by his music, by the worlds that reflect it, as they are by him. So in love with it all, when he first trespassed here, when he first found the engine, realised its function.

So vicious, when the Choirs descended, demanding he abandon it, return it to its Maker, their Master.

Shuddering in recollection of the violence that followed, the fire they visited on his worlds, the children that played upon them: the dissonance and dischord that he used to shred their perfection, to disturb the burning systems and perfect hymns of which they were comprised.

Having forgotten the weeping of angels, until now.

Temptation draining from me, at that; tears flowing freely, as I remember, as I see them dispersing, dying in droves, hurtling from the skies around the tower, the windows, their burning eyes blind and streaming embers, their sunlight-wheels stuttering, breaking apart.

The one that came to him descending upon the balcony, clothed in the skin of something beautiful: a burning youth, little older than the state the boy himself affected, its pristine skin rent and broken, seeping blood and liquid sunlight with every shudder. Wings formed of the same flapping, shedding lambent feathers, as it stared up at him in the most guileless, earnest plea:

No words, only waves of sensation, washing his nerves, his thoughts:

We hurt. We sorrow. Stop this; give us silence, we beg...

Unable to comprehend or endure the creature's pain. Not understanding what he did, when he trespassed in this place, when he toyed and played with a device Heaven itself had forgotten, believing long lost...

Unable to break it, unable to stop it, then; the cacophony having its own impetus, its own intent: the boy-angel coming apart before his eyes, in his arms, as he tried to silence the engine with every fibre, as Heaven fractured and fell from a million skies, as the towers of Paradise crashed down, as the absent Maker's throne cracked, buried beneath the rubble of its own temple.

Why he fled, why he returned...to that world he hated, to the grey Hell he'd done all in his power to escape:

The only place where he could forget himself, whose banality and daily miseries might prove fitting punishment.

Where the few, vengeful survivors of the calamity he wrought might not find him.

Whatever temptation I feel...to take up those old songs, to make amends...dissipating, going with my tears on the sea-scented breeze.

As for the boy...I allow him to go the same way, dispersing him like cigarette smoke, what echoes of his hymns remain finally, finally silenced.

Away, for now, out onto the balcony, into the spray carried by the warring winds, the marrow-biting chill of the storms lashing the distant ocean—a different air, different winds and waters.

A different world. Maybe the leavings of some more ancient,

despairing soul; the state that they hailed from, left to storms and drowning. In the distance, ships ride the swells: alien, skeletal things, fashioned from the carcasses of dead krakens and leviathans; monstrosities dredged from beneath the waves.

Dead a second time, now—the ships empty, broken, half-drowned flotsam. I know each and every one; I've seen them a thousand times, from this spot, from far, far closer. From *within*. Memories of their ghosts: alien sailors, pirates and explorers, entities far removed from humanity, even in life, a welcome company for it in death.

Laughing with the thunder, stretching my arms as the rain comes hard and warm, driving against the cliffside, the structure carved from it (ruinous; derelict long, long before I set eye or foot on it).

Already fading; the dead and abandoned children, the idiot stories of brutality… soon, the boy I was and the man I am will be one again, all distinction between us abandoned.

The strings… their first tremors, plucked not by fingers, but by thought, emotion—pure *inspiration*. A conscious and willing perversity, after my recent resolution never to touch them, never to play again. The storm sets its fires in me with every lick of lightning, every howl of wind and rain. They kindle music in their turn, a dim, ominous tune, building in tempo and complexity.

I feel them move; the limbs and digits stirring, shrugging off coats of dust accrued over many, many decades of neglect. I'm sorry, for all of them; for every miracle I made, murdered or abandoned.

To my forgotten self most of all.

"Never again."

Thunder, closer than it's trespassed before, blue lightning illuminating the cloud overhead, reflected in the black ocean. Defying my oath.

"Never again!"

It calls and I follow, hurling myself out, out, over the balustrade, tumbling towards the black waters, the foam-laced rock... *caught up,* carried by contradictory gales—weightless, a feather, a droplet of spume. Music and lunatic laughter follow in chorus with the storm.

Denied. Always; my suicide, the forgetting that will follow. They won't allow it; the ghosts of angels that still haunt this place, that howl amongst the rocks, that sift and seethe amongst the waves. That scream their accusations into my mind, even as they claw and rip at me, no longer able to kindle, to make good on their threats of immolation.

Still laughing, in the face of their violence, the vile stories they pour into me, that transform me, even as I soar, as I careen and tumble and bleed. Out, out over the immeasurable ocean, its fathomless depths, watched by the gestating ones, the children swelling at the hearts of drowned stars, for whom I am just another story, a dream they will forget, upon waking.

Thankful, even in this tattered condition, this self-shedding disgrace, thankful, as what remains of my mind comes apart:

To be away from doors and temptation, from remembering, and a world that will die unwanted.

Where Our Children Walk

Old ways, wet, dark, winding. Walked since I was a child, for as long as memory itself has existed. Yet never *familiar,* shifting around me with every trespass, no two tunnels or chambers ever the same.

Like the dreams they host, the nightmares that infest them. A state beyond sleep, where I *belong,* the waking world so grey, abortive by comparison, no matter what horrors I encounter in the dark, what absurdities the sick and broken minds I trespass in give birth to.

Stories linger on the dank air, telling tales of other places in strange tongues; of other dreaming worlds beyond the walls, where I might walk, lose myself, never to wake.

Sweet, sweet seduction: to never have to walk *here* again*,* in the shit and foulness of my own sleeping mind... almost enough to have me sprout wings and soar from myself, to plummet through the rents and ruptures that gape in the ground into some other delirium or follow the distant strains of music and laughter, become a happy trespasser in a healthier psyche's bliss.

But no; there's no despair deep enough to seduce me, to have me abandon myself.

These caverns... vaster than most, pillars of twisted stone rising into the dark, their shapes distressingly organic, as though formed from flayed and petrified things, intertwining in hideous, cannibal love-making, fossilised in the midst of congress and slowly eroded over aeons until only the merest suggestions of their anatomies remain. Viscous matter flows down their contours, through flutes and folds, enhancing the impression of things once living—perhaps living still, small pools forming around the pillar's roots or trickling away in streams across the cavern floor.

The *smell*... deeper, more pungent than mere stone and seawater: blood and sweat, primordial swamps, the secret space between my legs. Alchemist's chambers in which abortive things gestate, in defiance of all nature.

Pausing, closing my eyes, *letting it in*, I listen to the whispers in the dark, the distant grinding, as of great, ancient engines in the walls, the scrape and slap of naked bodies against naked stone.

The stories—always, *always* the stories, the air and stone freighted with them, breeze rank with them. Enough to glut me, to invade and eclipse my own, leaving me like others wandering the ways; lost and unknown to themselves, lunatic and muttering fragments of old songs, old prayers; the gospels of others.

Monitoring my intake, the most exacting of addicts, allowing only precise measures of poison into my system: a fleeting echo, a short memory: S*hivering and streetlamp light, cigarettes and wet pavements, dirty pools forming in rents and potholes. Cries in the dark. Screaming women. Barking men. Spit still hot on my neck...*

Shuddering. Enough. *Enough.* Exhaling, allowing the story to leave me on the same breath. Opening my eyes.

Light. Pale and sickly in the whispering darkness, incandescent fungi sprouting from the walls, the broken, undulating floor underfoot: so many species, none quite like the other: fluted and billowing, bulbous and suggestive, flowering and raw and grotesque. Great genital clusters, straining in profusion against the stone they protrude from, their luminescence pale and yellow, sickly and stinking. Others akin to bizarre flowers or the many-lipped maws of strange lizards, peeling back to reveal wet and painted interiors from which feverish light pulses. Some are surrounded by clouds of shimmering spores, some burrowed in and out of the stone, knotted like skinless serpents. Their colour and intensity is as various as their forms, intermingling to contrive a false, feverish dusk in which the shadows dance and distort, the anatomical qualities of the surrounding stone hideously emphasised: the uneven walls, the piles of rubble and matter heaped against them, protruding from them, heaving and writhing, straining and pulsating.

So much more than mere rock; fossilised *bodies* returning to life, the stone becoming soft and wet and rippling, the forms comprising it no longer distinct, but fused and melded, becoming new creatures, new species, whose names and natures even they themselves have yet to learn.

Others stray here, too. Not always, but often; a trio of hunched and shrouded shapes, bent on their knees around a grey, bulbous mass; something anchored to—or protruding from—the wet wall, the majority of its anatomy burrowed into the rock, the rest obscenely naked, heaving with hideous contractions as its attendants coo and whisper, their hands snatching blindly at the air, as though to snare answers to their prayers.

Passing by, I pause, the pregnancy-swollen thing raises its hair-shrouded head, peering blindly at me with a single, luminous eye, the pus of septic stars running like tears down its face.

The mid-wives do not notice or care; too intent on the birth they orchestrate: a labour that makes the Mother-to-be howl, her voice a choir of mutilated cats. Her abdomen tears open under the strain, a wound that stretches from crotch to sternum, stinking, steaming filth pouring from within. The mid-wives scrabble and chitter to themselves, desperately gathering the matter into surrounding bowls and vessels, preserving the most sacred of essences.

The Mother's screams rise to silent extremes, her luminous eye flickering, still on me, silently pleading: *End this, please.*

The mid-wives cackle delight as the child comes, raking its way from the womb with casual violence, laced in skirts of dripping filth, its Mother's matter trailing in rags from its teeth.

It calls to me as I hurry away, echoes in my thoughts; not merely words, but suggestions of its wishes, the secrets it might teach me: S*tay, pretty one; stay and play with me.*

Hideous games: rape, torture, watching me ripen and twist and swell on its seed, as its poor bitch of a Mother did, before she was even that.

The newborn a diseased animal, nothing but the cruellest appetite pulsing through its pale flesh, black veins, its distorted soul.

An urge to peel it open, pluck it apart with a look, a word, painting the air and walls with its confessions. To see its worshipers in disarray, lamenting their faith in what is far from some infant divinity; just another lost and lunatic thing, reliving the same cycles of self-siring rape and rebirth, becoming more monstrous with each idiot incarnation.

I leave them—and it—be, not knowing if I can, not willing to jeopardise my journey by trying.

The walls in the tunnels and chambers beyond… more *organic,* the shapes of barely born babes worked into them, comprising them, as though sealed inside before they could take their first breaths, their expressions varying from despair to tempestuous fury at being denied even that.

Never trespassing so deep before, feeling their faces in the filth beneath my feet, lining the bed of the polluted stream. Whispers, stories; not confessions of past sins and shames, but laments of what will not be, of lives never lived, barely dreamed in the womb, broken for the purpose of building this place.

Desperate, the unborn echoes grow cruel in the dank and dark, the perpetual forgetting: smeared, stretched and wiry forms stalk through the shadows, reaching across the walls, unable to touch me, though they ache to, wishing to grasp and hoist me up, throttle the breath from me, pluck my limbs from their sockets like a spider's.

And far, far worse: Violations they scream and whisper into my mind, promises of perpetual mass rape, in which I will be both victim and Mother of my own abusers, the unborn Fathering their own flesh in my womb, where they'll swell together, before tearing themselves free and beginning the process over and over again.

Others have allowed it, singing with them, now; dragged into the Hell they've sustained down the ages, forced by relentless abuse to forget the lives they'll never wake to again, through torment that will never end: the babes become their murderers, monsters in their turn.

Denying the urge to linger, not even to taste what dreams they still have of tomorrow. Dangerous, if they manage to find traction, if they identify some flaw in my wards.

Unsure if I can defend against them, in such numbers, in such depth of spite.

Deeper, then; deeper than I've ever wandered, to places where sanity itself is a fairy tale.

*

I walk a contradictory path, looping on itself in places, though I
don't divert or change direction; new tunnels and warrens leading
to familiar chambers, passed through only hours or moments ago.
Old ways opening onto new destinations, familiar rents and
wormholes blossoming into great caverns and theatres where
before they remained narrow or diverged into branching paths.

I follow, weary feet knowing the way, even if the rest of me
doesn't—if the rest refuses.

Plenty to distract at every turn, in every corridor and chamber:
stories that are stronger than most lingering in the air, stretched
out in the dark like great, invisible cobwebs, entangling me as I
stumble into them, invisible predators alerted by my unwitting
vandalism, stalking me, waiting for a distraction or weakness
before embracing me with their many legs, gifting me with a
venomous kiss.

A *rocky cliff, a storm-tossed sea, despair so deep as to be
liberating, dissolving want and desire, concern and anchorage.
Sailing, as the lightning strikes, the thunder roars, suspended in
that eternal moment between land and sea, neither flying nor
falling, praying that no angel descends to pluck me up, to save me
from drowning...*

*Waiting. Waiting. So patient, barely able to contain the
Christmas morning bubbles in my belly. The windows showing
nothing, moors made molten by the rain. Knowing that he's*

coming, that he's out there, cursing my name, yet just as eager for our reunion...

Ridiculous. Stupid, worthless bitches! Fantasies of lifting them up bodily, of impaling them on the broken branches of surrounding trees, watching them writhe, listening to them scream...

Sweat and heat and scent. Dark and skin and tongues and teeth. Not knowing, not realising, until the first bite, until I bleed...

All so desperate, so eager to be known. I hate them for that, denying them. Flailing and raking at me in their resentment, attempting to rip open my mind as they have so many others, reduce me to gibbering delirium.

Their parasitism having no more purchase on me than what I allow, the confessions and vicarious experience I take from them little more than sips of stimulant, narcotic measures that ease my transition through this place, this *condition*.

A time, perhaps, when I might have been easier prey, a willing host, even, like many of the others that share it with me: so infested, so lost to themselves, they can no longer recall their own stories, even in waking.

A time when I was a weaker thing, that even the child of before, who ran and danced through the ways without doubt or the slightest concern would lament:

Anxious, fretful, paranoid, the rodent-woman of yesterday.

*

Rising breathlessness, the bus packed and stinking. Body odour, unwashed clothes, chip fat, the grease-sheened sausage roll clutched in the pudgy fingers of an obese toddler.

Chatter, static, cockroach hymns, filling my skull with grey snow and ash. I can't *think,* can't breathe.

A long time since the last attack, since it's been this bad. Some short circuit in my mind, some stripped and fraying wire in my brain...

Idiot. Idiot, idiot, *idiot.* What's wrong with you? Knowing, in any rational sense, that this is absurd, that the frothing, electric wave washing my entrails is illusory; a by-product of some more fundamental fault.

But no amount of reason calms or quells it, no form of self-chiding severe enough to ridicule me out of escalating panic.

The woman beside me shuffles, shifting the burlap shopping bag in her lap, knocking me with her bony, trembling elbows, offering no apology as she endlessly fidgets. The toddler in front stands up in his seat, wailing some cartoon song at the top of his voice as flakes of half-chewed sausage roll slope from his mouth, his Mother apparently unconcerned by the display, too busy with her own ugly, inarticulate phone conversation.

An urge to stand up and scream, beg the bus to stop, hurl

myself with breathless gratitude into the rain.

Denying it, this time, though I've surrendered so often in recent days, unable to face the world in all of its appalling sterility, its crumbling red brick and old stone, its cement and rusted steel and sun-bleached plastic.

A cemetery state, where we're all dead things, whether we know it or not.

Work waiting. An hour early, as always. Afraid that I won't have time, that I won't get things done; that others will whisper behind my back, call me inept and lazy and pointless.

I don't know why I even care. Doltish, dreamless, hateful things, for the most part. Were the building to burn down before I arrive, were I to find a still-smouldering pile of ashes and blackened bone where the library once stood, it likely wouldn't move me much beyond a sense of guilty *relief.*

But I do, anticipating, projecting every judgement, every disapproving eye, every whispered condemnation, as I always have, afraid that some rumour will take root, some rot will spread, until my name is a cancer, until the entire institution is united in its disgust of me.

Even those I don't know, my fellow passengers, who likely don't even notice me, barely glance my way...I'm afraid of them, afraid that I appear strange and awkward and absurd in their eyes, that they see something I cannot, concealed from me since birth: some hideous scar or disfigurement, some drooling, dislocated jaw. A sense of being naked and not knowing it, all others ignoring the transgression out of politeness or fear of my apparent lunacy.

That rising tide...above the level of my entrails, now, washing my heart in sewer water, every breath a struggle, white stars flickering across my field of vision.

I can't afford another day off work, especially on such short notice. Another hateful, fretful, wasted day.

The bell desperately ringing, my fingers acting before the scream can leave my lips.

The old woman beside me sighs, muttering something under her breath, shuffling to get out of her seat.

Eyes on me, now; not merely paranoia, but clear and evident: following me as I stand, as I shuffle past the old woman, the press of bodies in the aisle. Impatient eyes judging, fire-ants scurrying beneath my clothes, biting me feverish.

The bus pulls to a halt as I push past those crowded at the front, the driver glaring at me as I stumble off into the rain.

No courtesies, no thank yous or goodbyes. Only *relief,* the rain cooling the fever inside, causing the polluted tide to recede.

"Thank you, *thank you.*"

Calling not up, into the Heavens, to angels I've never believed in, whose attentions I wouldn't court if I did, but *down,* into those dark and familiar depths, not beneath the earth, the cracked and weed-sprouting concrete at my feet, but deeper and further, into dreaming ways.

He hears me, of that I've no doubt: always there, these days, so rarely absent and awake. Even maintaining a flimsy presence in his waking hours, a trick that I've yet to learn, despite his best efforts to teach me.

"Chandra?"

Distant, an almost inaudible whisper, distorted by the spaces through which it echoes.

"Yes! Yes, it's me! Can you..?"

Aware, acutely aware, of how lunatic I must appear, casting about in the rain, spraying it from my lips with every word I mutter to myself.

"I hear you, but not clearly. Where are you? Can you..?"

Fading in and out of audibility, an intermittent radio broadcast.

"I...I can't do it any more. I can't..."

The rain hammering down in earnest, frothing to muddy torrents in the gutter, welling out of cracks and ruptures in the pavement like filthy, diseased blood. No others to share the street with, none to witness this moment of disgrace. Not caring, even if there are. Already imagining the ways I might do it: waiting for a speeding car or truck to happen by, stepping out into its path, seeking a bridge that runs over a train track, waiting for that tell-tell metallic whine and rumble before leaping into emptiness.

All considered before, some of them even attempted, though I've always managed to snare myself before taking the terminal step, reminding myself of what waits beyond sleep, of what might be tomorrow.

"...don't...I'm....done. Come...me. Let me...you."

Fading, fading, as though tumbling away from me, into depths where I can never follow.

Standing in utter dejection, soaked to the bone and shivering, I stare up at the grey, broken sky, around at the grey, broken buildings, wondering at what grey, broken lives they host.

Not my world; not one I would've chosen to be born to, given the option. One I never imagined to still be languishing in, after so long.

Tonight. If we can't make something new together, if I find myself forced to wake again... I won't waste breath trying to save myself.

At least a mile away from work, easily within reach before my shift starts, at a brisk enough pace. I laugh at the very thought, at the phantom faces that coalesce behind my eyes, glaring at me in such reprimand as I turn away, and begin the long trudge back home.

To bed.

To him.

*

This chamber...I recognise it, but from where? The rock here black, a faint iridescence shimmering throughout, lending it the quality of snake's scales, some deep-sea mollusc's hide. Matter drips from the ceiling, flowing down the lumpen, misshapen walls to pool around my ankles, becoming a foul froth in which scraps of shapeless, boneless life squirm, snaring against spars of stone, tearing, becoming multiple lesser entities that surrender to the current.

Piles of refuse pulse and quiver against the walls, trash-heaps of abandoned humanity, things forgotten, even to themselves, barely able to remember, to *sustain,* what little flesh clings to their exposed bone black and gelatinous, compost-matter, fungus-sprouting, swarming with parasites. Forms indistinguishable from one another melded in rot, wounds bleeding into wounds as they writhe, gasp, their hideous stories similarly cross-contaminated, the confessions of one seeping into or super-imposed over the proclamations of another; this one's suicide note sifting into that one's prayer, this one's remonstrances resonating with another's contradictory love poems.

They rake broken, bloody fingers across the black rock as I pass, across *one another,* recording what they can no longer speak in scrawls and hieroglyphs made of wounds and gouge marks, of blood and bodily fluid. The most desperate attempting to tear themselves from the mass, to regain a semblance of their lost identities, others resigned, allowing any violence or indignity done to them, flopping and flailing, boneless as rag-dolls.

Some coherent enough to note my intrusion, wet, almost fleshless faces turning in my direction, eyes empty or luminous, burnt black or weeping rot.

A rare few succeed in liberating themselves, though the surgery required leaves them universally traumatised, rising to their knees or trembling feebly where they sprawl, none managing more than a few steps or to crawl a matter of inches before slumping forward in the mire.

Pleas rattle from their matter-choked throats, slurred, wordless; gasping and incoherent, of the like I've heard a thousand times before: prayers to be woken, for the nightmare to *end.*

Impotent, empty sorrows, the one who called them here, to this depth of dreaming, not allowing them to rouse, just as he won't allow me, tonight.

No monster or beast; just another wanderer, another dreamer. Like me.

So *young,* maybe a year or two my junior, maybe not. A boy: malnourished, pale as though with some blood sickness. Harsh angles of bone prominent at his shoulders, his hips, overlong limbs lending him a spidery aspect. Features half hidden beneath a veil of dark hair, what little is visible tapering, feminine, an uncertain smile beneath deep-set, hooded eyes.

He stirs from his throne as I stalk into his presence; a living seat of intertwined forms, the same species that litter these caverns, lost to their own dreaming. The structure heaves, those that comprise it impossibly alive, all too conscious of the indignity done to them, though they likely invited it, after he dripped enough serpent-honey in their ears.

The boy more familiar, more *real* than anything in this place: the sight of him almost painful in its intensity, as though every mark and stroke is made in luminous paint, as though he would remain solid if the rest melted or crumbled to dust around him.

"Chandra."

"Crowther."

Not names given or imposed; names we *chose*, more true to us now than those we reluctantly answer to in waking.

Tatters of his throne cling to him as he rises, lapping tongues and clutching hands peeling away, his eyes moving lazily around the chamber.

"Do you like it? It took me longer to make than most…"

I recall his previous displays and exhibitions, the miracles and atrocities he's crafted for me. A love-struck adolescent, writing poetry and sketching romantic nonsense for the object of his misguided affections. Concepts he can never realise in the waking world.

Laughing, kneeling, I reach out to one of the lost, the skinless, gasping thing mirroring my gesture, our fingers meeting. Wet warmth, but cold inside; a billow of venomous desperation, the creature having nothing, knowing nothing, beyond this pain, this disgrace: everything lost to it, save for the most futile splinters of self:

...sunlight, the smell of grass, a warm smile...

...shame. Shame and tears, disgust in previously loving eyes...

...the smell of diseased shit, sickness, blood in the toilet bowl, *congealed filth spurting from its insides...*

Unable to tear away, our fingers fused, one wound healed to another, making us a single knot of pain.

I do so regardless, uncaring if I mutilate myself. I laugh at the pain, the creature's clutching desperation as it tries to hold me fast, to make me a vessel for its every confession.

Others reach, peeling away from their mounds, their abandonment, crawling across the chamber floor, calling to me, begging the same boon: *Please! Please listen to our stories, take* *our confessions, know us as we can only be known...*

Hearing them, tasting them; whispers of fables in my thoughts, across my senses: states I've never lived, alien experience, the strangest fantasies, rendered even more obscure by their fragmentary natures:

Following, so desperate, sprawling on my face in frozen earth *and grass as I reach for it, the colour and scent it trails falling on* *my upturned face, my outstretched fingers: a luminous hybrid of* *bird and woman, her heavy breasts raining almost vaporous* *strands of glowing milk, her eyes reflecting an amber moon...*

Scrabbling. Gnawing hunger, agony, tongue and mouth *ragged, the rest of me futile, nerveless, senseless legs, organs*

spilling from me, unspooling to become meals for other, less
particular souls. I ache, hungering for her meat, as I always have,
before she even led me here, with promises of all we might do and
know beyond Eden's gates...

Lightning over ocean, the ship beneath me tossing and
swaying, soaring and diving, water so cold it feels like knives in
my flesh washing over the sides, shoals of luminous fish in the
depths, matching the lightning with their effulgence, calling me to
the drowning I intend for the brother who steers us through the
squall...

"One of your finest. One of the *very* finest."

Those half-lidded, serpentine eyes fly open, stars wheeling in
their depths.

"Sincerely? That's... that's..."

Snarling, unable to express himself, the boy stares into the red
waters burbling around his ankles, unable to meet my eyes.
Coming to me, he sweeps me up in an embrace so earnest, the
angles of his ribs bite into me.

A kiss, tasting of blood and cumin, of burning bone and the
rarest, sweetest meat.

Letting me go, he staggers back, repentant. Smiling, I take his
hand, its fever pulsing in my fingers.

"Don't be sorry."

Stars blaze, a cosmic apocalypse in his eyes.

"This is *nothing*. Come on! Let me show you!"

So much a child, here, and perhaps beyond too. *Who is he, in waking? How old? How alone?*

He leads me past the writhing, reaching throne, away from the chamber and its nightmares, down a corridor whose walls and ceiling stir, what initially looks like configurations of black, wet stone breaking apart, revealing human forms so densely entangled, so intimately, impossibly embraced as to become a single mass of dreamers, gasping, breathlessly shrieking at being woken, reminded of what they are.

Crowther barely pauses as he drags me along through the burbling stream, the stirring darkness, old doubts gnawing at me; wonderings at what we'll make of one another when we finally meet beyond these ways...

I gasp as cold sunlight spears from the distance, almost blinding after so long in shadow.

"Wait."

He brings us to a halt, resting a hand on my shoulder. Something moves in the light, a vast bulk slouching and slumping, gurgling wet, tainted breaths. A rancid rhythm of cracks and squelches, as though every motion wounds it, requiring it to perpetually stitch itself together or come apart, the sound of tinkling bells, light and silvery, glinting in the light, threaded through its tumescence on fine jewellery chains, through the tatters of priestly robes trailing from it. Pulsing, purple light in its masked and hooded face, occasionally obscured, as though vast parasites crawl and skitter across it, the sight of them making my eyes sting, my temples ache.

"Now!"

A silent cry as I'm grasped by invisible hands, simultaneously dragged and pushed, becoming weightless; reduced to a shimmering shadow, sifting around the shambling figure that casts and swipes blindly about itself, vile matter bursting from its every inch as I hurtle out into the pale day.

Blind, the light burning my eyes, setting white fires in my skull.

The sense of weightlessness, of insubstantiality, dissipates, leaving me flailing in empty air, grasping for hands to arrest my fall.

No angels to oblige, here.

The impact steals my breath, a million tiny cuts and scratches as the bank of matter beneath me shifts. An avalanche; blackened bones, abandoned seashells, the dried skins of things swollen beyond their confines, giving way, trickles becoming streams becoming torrents.

Sliding, I scrabble at the shifting bank, bloodying my fingers as it carries me down...

A feverish hand grasps mine, hauling me up, no more concerned by my weight than it might be a doll's.

Crowther grins as he gathers me into his arms, holding me steady. Below, the bank continues to erode, tumbling and tinkling down into the lower valley, until the shells and bones lie shattered, silvery vapour rising from their destruction.

I blink in the strange light, shivering against him as he shivers against me. His touch… at once welcome and repellent, an animal urge to cling to him, to kiss him until we bleed; to bite and gnaw his flesh, lap at the red springs that burst from each wound. Another, equally urgent to rake his grinning face open, claw his eyes, hurl myself back over the edge, to break amongst the scraps and shards below.

A frustrated roar bellows from behind, that of a failing engine, great furnaces in which living beasts burn as fuel.

We turn as one to face it, glimpsing the guardian in the darkness.

Crowther laughs. "Don't worry. It won't come any closer."

The creature lingers at the very edge of shadow, occasionally straying over into sunlight, flinching back as though burned.

"Can you stand?"

Steppping away from him, my legs trembling, I ignore the urgency in my bladder, one hand still in his.

"Good."

He leads me from the cave, across a lip of vaguely yellow stone, its shape and contours bizarre—not broken and jagged, but flowing, curvaceous, redolent of coral.

Blinking in the light, my eyes painfully adjust:

An immense valley stretches before us, banked on each side by

black hills; piles of semi-molten refuse, still smouldering, as
though freshly vomited or shat from the bowels of demons.
Curving, organic shapes decorate their flanks, resembling
humanoid forms so hideously dissolved, they're barely
recognisable as such. Structures rise from them in fungal
hundreds: shattered temples, great spires, curling, corkscrew
towers. All of different origins, deriving from alien traditions:
some resembling churches and temples I know in waking, gothic
or byzantine, constructed from brick and stone. Others entirely
beyond my frames of reference: things that look to have been
grown rather than built, hewn from the bones of long dead titans
or fossilised dragons, great seashells, hollowed and decorated
with numerous external supports and scaffolds, coral-reef accruals
elaborating like tree branches into the sky, as though reaching to
pluck the sick, pale sun from its scrutiny, drag it down amongst
the filth and ruin it obsesses over.

The hideous, feverish yellow sky is swollen with tumors of
storm cloud that broil but never break, the jaundiced sun's light
seeping through rents and ruptures like pus from infected wounds
in the underbelly of Heaven.

Winding through the valley, a wine-dark river, fed by
numerous streams and tributaries pouring or seeping from
hollows in the surrounding hills. Things rove and swarm
throughout; clouds of buzzing, darting insects, mosquito-like,
with abdomens swollen and translucent, their faces distressingly

human, save for the proboscis forced from their wide open mouths, the immense, compound eyes that burst from their bloodied sockets. Thick, ropey worms twine in the swell, where the blood-river foams and coagulates, mating or tearing at one another, their mouth-parts consisting of hideous, flailing appendages like black spider's legs, their shrieks of pain and pleasure echoing as they engage in their cannibal congress. Hunched, muscular forms rove amongst the flanks of the black hills, their ashen pelts ragged and patchwork, punctuated by areas of scar tissue and disease, swollen tumors and sceptic boils. Lupine heads sway to and fro as they taste the air, growling strange songs at one another, scrabbling down to lap from the blood stream, stalking malformed prey through the desolation.

Lining the shores of the blood stream, perhaps the most hideous of all: piles of the same semi-human refuse as within Crowther's throne room, the caverns that preceded it: flayed, fleshless forms, dumped as though little more than shit in sewer water, more specimens adding to the banks and hillocks by the moment, crawling or spilling from the same distressingly organic apertures that feed the stream. All still living, their motions sluggish and desperate, trembling hands rising to the sky, scrabbling at the stone or one another, as though to claw some salvation from where there's none to be had.

Crowther is breathless as I, his skinny chest heaving, his arousal plain. He smiles in the sun, beatification so broad as to outdo its luminosity, clearly in love with all that he's made.

Laughing, unable to contain his joy or express it any other way. Laughing with him, his rapture infectious. The boy almost jumps as he takes my arms, drawing me to him.

"Please tell me you love it. *Please*."

A sheen of such sweet desperation in his eyes: a boy's need for Mother's approval.

"I do. *I do*."

His smile outstrips the previous, silvery light blazing in the pits of his pupils, the feverish, warm breeze swirling around us, stirring his hair, carrying motes of ash and filth.

A smile that dies at a wet, agonised roar from behind.

I turn from him, finding an atrocity not meant to be seen in even this pellucid light, its malformation made for concealing in shadow. Convulsions wrack it as it drags itself towards us, portions of its hide blistering, bursting, filth pouring down to spatter the stone at its feet, stinking vapour rising from its wounds. The purple star flickers in its head, reduced to little more than a candle flame in night's smothering cold. It stumbles as it approaches us, something in one of its legs giving way, the gatekeeper groaning as it grasps out at the stone cliff for support.

A subtle prickling of my skin, lightning in the air, Crowther summoning some cruel art that he intends to spit or hurl at the thing...

Embracing him from behind, I carry us back, over the edge of the slope. Crowther cries out, screaming laughter as we plummet, impacting the scree below like ragdolls, bouncing, tumbling, still clinging to one another even as we break, as shards and fragments bite into us, slice us open, splinters worming their ways into our flesh.

I hardly feel it, wounds healing the instant they're carved, the jagged, shattered glass-agony of broken bones, the profound, nauseating torment of ruptured organs, a heartbeat's complaint at most.

Crowther laughs in my arms as we slide and gambol, as we almost tear apart, grasping one another all the more fiercely, even through wounds that threaten to break us.

We splash into the red waters, their warmth sickening, currents pulsing and arterial.

Laughing as they fill our mouths, *tasting* them, adding our flow to theirs. I hear him reknit; a hideous crunching, cracking, wet squelches as skin and flesh and muscle become whole again.

Shuddering in the same throes, I twist in my skin, gasping as bones reset, joints pop back into place, spitting blood and gobbets of meat that rise in my throat.

I'm able to stand in a matter of moments, trembling as the thing above roars its frustration, slamming its bulk against the stone, as though to bring the valley down on us.

Crowther still laughs, an interloping child at a farmer's impotent threats, stumbling to me, the river frothing pink around our ankles, motes and strings of silvery life caught up in it, trying to twine around and anchor themselves to us, carried away in its current.

Still laughing, he takes my hand as he swipes blood from the corner of my mouth.

Strange... nothing like before, like anything we've ever shared. So brave tonight, bristling and beaming with it, a black star in his belly, blazing through his every pore.

He leads me from the river, to its shores, scarlet coagulating there to a diseased black around the masses of our fellow dreamers, lost or abandoned here, piled in banks of bleeding and broken refuse.

The most coherent, those that still remember, reach for us, plead wordlessly for aid, even if it means their deaths.

No apology, barely a second glance: we can provide nothing, even if we have a mind to.

Up, up the broken, pockmarked valley-side, leaping weightless from foothold to foothold, almost tumbling back as perches give way beneath us, as stone crumbles to white sand and ash.

Other caverns gape all around, hollows eaten into the living rock. Some still inhabited, their makers emerging at our passage; a white-pelted spider-thing, its back decorated with human faces, all squealing in common frustration, a rose-headed worm, its elaboration quivering with wetness, festooned with mismatched eyes that follow our ascent with lunatic obsession.

Amongst the towers and temples, now, those sitting lower on the slopes in greater states of ruin than those that rise from their heights, shards and fragments protruding from the ash, mere suggestions of the structures that once stood here.

Other things have made their homes here; lost ones, the self-abandoned, though not quite so surrendered as those below: cowed, for the most part, wrapped in rags and tatters, as though ashamed of their conditions, crouching amongst the ruins, staring down into the muck and mire in which they stand or up into the sky, as though the dead sun might provide some answer to their conditions, some salvation from them.

Some raise bandaged faces at our trespass, though none challenge us; the majority too obsessed with their meditations, their *miseries,* to pay us any mind.

Those that do… sick smiles split their ragged masks, filth seeping from the corners of their lips, between their cankered teeth. Attempting to stand, to approach us, they stumble to their knees, sprawl on their faces, spattering the stone with their tainted matter.

Away, before they can address or touch us, their despair a *disease,* as infectious in this place as any virus.

Higher, *higher,* chancing glances at the valley behind, its expanse growing more and more distant as we stray amongst the higher pinnacles, the spires and towers that have retained some of their original conditions; whose makers still dream of them, even if it's only in unguarded moments of fantasy or instances of idiot nostalgia.

Hollow, now, for the most part, whatever engines they might have contained long since run down, whatever congregations they might have hosted become apostate.

No two alike, each alien to its neighbours, as though the original creators had it in mind to emphasise their strangeness through contrast and contradiction: some erected in worlds or states of being where laws of physics diverge from ours: structures in motion, comprised of flapping fabric, like ship's sails, shifting facets and components endlessly rearranging like great puzzles seeking some ultimate solution. Others flowing, semi-liquid, woven from strands of gelatinous matter or *living,* knots of quivering octopi tendrils, billowing with bodies that swell and deflate, changing colour and texture with every heartbeat, structures of bone and ligament, muscle and organ, chambers like great hearts pulsing on their exteriors, their heights boasting lightning-wreathed brains, eyes blistering from them in diseased profundity.

Maddening. Yet fascinating to the point of obsession, of lunatic love. Unable to look away from them, lightning in my brain threatening to sear sanity to ash.

I see it, long before he brings us to a halt at its foundations; taller, more intact than the rest, an edifice of coral, of sea-shell stuff, nacreous and shimmering, elaborating impossibly, twisting and twining around itself, hollow in places, its interior exposed to the elements, betraying alien machinery, wet and shimmering swarms of kaleidoscope-winged vermin. Branches and off-shoots erupt from its height, each laden with lesser structures, fruit and fungal growths, my abiding impression more that of a great tree than a temple, perhaps the *first* tree, of which all others are merely rumours and echoes, around whose roots the serpent twined, from whose fruit every dream of humanity was born.

At its pinnacle, a vast, spherical chamber that looks to be constructed from wax frozen in the midst of melting, only portions of its exterior remaining.

Blue light burns within, liquid trails of it streaming down the tower's exterior, pulsing through circuitry and channels carved into every inch, spilling or gouting from points of damage or erosion, blazing like fire from rents and ruptures. Even here, so close to the tower's foundations, it bursts into the air in fiery gouts or flows in liquid streams through systems in the surrounding stone. Engines rumble below, siphoning it away, their processes stuttering and arrhythmic as hearts beating their fervent last.

Unable to keep myself from reaching for the fire, *touching* it, in defiance of all waking cautions, all parental tenet, as it licks the air. It doesn't burn my skin, despite part of me shuddering in infantile terror of it, but *soothes*, blissfully cool in the desolation's fever. What little pain still pricks me from our fall -and the subsequent climb- fades as the fires lap at me, seeping through my palm and fingers, coiling around my wrist.

I laugh as embers writhe and flicker on my skin, even after I retrieve my hand.

Crowther comes to me, taking it, kissing my palm.

Such a strange, unexpected gesture, his lips lingering, shudders passing through him, as though words that he cannot speak seethe in his throat, stinging him senseless from the inside out.

A sigh, my fingers cupping his chin, urging him to rise.

Who are you? Will I still love you, when we wake?

Maybe. Or maybe we won't have to. Isn't that what it's always been building to? *Transition*, abandonment of the waking world, in all its grey absurdity.

An embrace as fierce, as urgent as when we fell, his erection burning against my belly. Holding his gaze, I work him slowly...

Stop. Stop! You don't know who or what he is...

I laugh, spitting contempt at the frightened little girl inside, marvelling at how much a slave she still is, how much she'll always be, until the blue fire finds her, burns her to ash, allowing me to exorcise her in little more than a belch or breath.

Never known, not here, not in waking: a transgression I can no longer deny us. Urging me always to wander deeper, to trespass further. The ways he has shown me; places I might never have walked, that the little girl of yesterday would have fled from, making a coward of me...

Shuddering, moving against me, his moans distress the breeze.

The creatures of the surrounding desolation respond, their cries and laments broken, their eyes turning on us, our pleasure in this expanse of suffering perhaps reminding them of states they once knew, of dreams once enjoyed, before they allowed themselves to be claimed by desolation, forgetting the possibility of anything beyond.

Their attentions like spider scurrying over and beneath our skins, seeking out likely hollows in which to weave their parasite nurseries. Hunger, desperation... some eager to share in what we've found, others to smother it, smash it into the same blood and dust they writhe in, agonised to the point of denial by its potential.

His hands rake my back, nails biting. One of my persistent fantasies: to be scratched and bitten, to walk away from lover's beds bruised, bleeding.

Something he'll know in time, when we meet at last.

The winds stir at our sighs, whipping up the surrounding ash and filth, the things dragging themselves from below, from the surrounding ruins, alight, old stars in their skulls, their breasts, others tearing themselves free from the masses as they kindle, no longer content to rot and wither as one with the rest, clawing themselves to tatters in their eagerness to be apart again. Others rise from beneath the red waters; bulbous, swollen things, filleted and squirming and naked, some vaguely human, albeit hybridised with things decidedly not: octopoid, slug-like, traces of the most hideous, deep-sea life in their contorted anatomies. Others stumbling barely formed from the storm, from rents and ruptures in the stream's banks, from wounds in the flanks of the valley: things formed from ash and blood and refuse; slopping, seeping entities of shit and stone, of coagulated blood, spectral, fluttering, formed from the remains of ineffably ancient cataclysms, the dust of dead things and their murderers.

All call to us, demanding just an instant's relief, a breath of Heaven.

Wretched, contemptuous. Beyond pity. Like us; dreamed to this state, wandered blissfully through the ways only to mire themselves in shame and disgrace, to allow for disease and despair to overtake them.

Their *weakness* disgusts me beyond any deformity, any condition they wear. Choirs sing hymns of self-loathing, pleading with us, with one another, to help them, to show them a way to *be other.*

All they dreamed for themselves, a truth they cannot wear or express in waking: my Mother and Father, my brother, my little sisters… all the same, beneath their smiling masks, their proscribed, plastic desires: denying fundamental despair, drawing a tissue-thin veil over the abyss inside, in hope that it will somehow conceal it, prevent them from tumbling into it or keep the things that fester and breed in the depths from spilling out.

His are the same; some of the first stories we told one another, when we met amongst the ways. Stories we'll forget, when there's no distinction; when waking becomes a nonsense and we can wander forever, without promise or threat of home.

Not yet, not yet: a distant dream, but growing closer with every kiss and caress.

I urge him on, my fingers in his hair, his lips at my shoulder. A galaxy of red and silver stars blazes behind my eyes, his teeth sinking deep, deeper than most lovers would desire or withstand.

Lost in those woods, the milk-white innocent, scarlet trailing about her nakedness, whispering in the wind, as the wolves come, as they batten on her, bearing her to the ground amidst playful cries, contrived screams, the game becoming grave as they bite, as blood flows...

His bite lycanthropic, venom pulsing through my veins, searing in its urgency, as welcome as a hit of Heroin, far more narcotic, not intended to sear my nerves or stop my heart (though it does), but spreading a message of transformation:

Convulsions wrack us as we burst, *blossom* together, breathless gasps, tears stinging my eyes, new matter elaborating from my back; fluid, whipping tendrils that harden, becoming nascent limbs, the sensation as new nerves fire at once agonising and ecstatic, so far beyond the fluid, cartoon transformations I imagined as a child: flapping, though barely formed, his and mine, blood pulsing between my fingers as I grip him close, as he tears free, shuddering, weeping, a lavish grin, the expression breaking the bounds of his face, painting itself on the air.

Black feathers shimmer with nacreous colour, others white and pearlescent, scattering red beads with every motion. Carrying us up, up, away from the tainted ground, away from the ones that crawl and cry and demand our aid, though we never promised them a damn thing, never knew them.

He holds me close, as though afraid I might fall without his aid, that he might plummet without mine. A hand trailing over my belly, tentative, as though expecting to be slapped away, denied. An old anxiety, born of his first fumblings: a flash of them behind my eyes, in stomach churning, sweat-stinking anxiety and darkness.

No such refusal, here, no such uncertainty: gripping him tighter, working him more fervently, his fingers far more expert than the boy he affects to be.

"I have to meet you. I have to see."

The prospect makes my insides boil and writhe. What if we can't be what we are to one another here? What if we're too much apart?

"Yes. *Yes.*"

Anything, in that moment, swept about by the singing, howling storm, the hymns of those below rising, attempting to latch onto us or claw us back to earth, where their singers can fall on us, tear us wingless, flay us, set us to bleed and fester like the rest.

Twining up the tower, lost in one another, in promises of tomorrow, we laugh at the prayers and rages from below, tumbling and darting as the winds change, phantasmal limbs tearing at us in vain attempt to rip us apart.

We rise towards its pinnacle, the great molten-wax chamber, the blue fire at its heart. More intact than most surrounding it, the fallen or partially shattered spires, the minarets abandoned half erected, whatever apocalypse reduced them to ruin having spared it.

Or maybe originated from it.

He prises himself from my flesh, the smile he wears ruddy; a child rising from a meal of strawberries.

"Closer to the truth. Not its entirety, but closer."

No more confusions, no more concern of who and what our waking selves might be or if they'll ever find one another. This, *this* is all that matters: what we are amongst the ways and the forbidden places they lead to. This smile, this flesh, these shudders and sighs... these wings that beat against me, as though to batter me from my violations. That realisation makes me more intent to see him in extremis, to know him in that moment of obscene and utter honesty.

His own toyings match mine; the work of no virgin or adolescent, seeking out every spot certain to elicit sighs and shudders, making me a thing of water, of burning milk, flowing and breaking against him.

"Here."

Guiding his face down, away from my neck, leaving a trail of bite marks in his enthusiasm, to where he can make a Mother of me, where no babe will ever batten.

Still rising, still rising, describing increasingly lunatic circuits around the tower, part of me wanting to never stop, to never ascend and see what revelations he has in store: to linger here, in the dust and storm, the songs of despair rising from below, the blue fire spilling from above…

He takes my hand, drawing it from himself, at the point of his climax.

"Not yet… not yet; you have to *see,* first."

Reluctantly complying, though he continues his own play, my own climax building to catastrophe.

Prying himself from me before we alight, not quite allowing me to blaze and become a new star in desolation's heaven, he sets me down with all the courtesy of a lover leading his dance-mate from the ballroom floor.

The fire's source burns here, at the heart of the semi-molten chamber; a blue and green star, spitted by shards of silver that protrude from the inner wall, its fires channelled away by systems and circuits carved into the tower, many of them ruptured or partially melted, allowing the fire to spill freely, to flow in fluid or burning streams across the floor, to spill or billow over the sides, pouring down or painting the air with its lustre.

He grasps me by the shoulders, his touch causing me to shudder, arresting a suicidal stumble towards the fire. All too happy to be immolated, if it means drawing closer to the forms and figures seething at its heart: things writhing in lust and love, quivering in the throes of murder (victims indistinguishable from their despatchers, the two so intimately entangled), those whose intimacies transcend either: mouths swelling with each kiss and bite, happy to be devoured, engulfed as though by great snakes, their flickering anatomies crushed, consumed, the cannibals responsible quivering in throes of orgasmic digestion, taking on a semblance of their former lovers, the two (or three or more) made one in ways that no sex or surgery can equal.

So many states, so many *dreams,* more than any mind can contain or endure.

Staring at me, fidgeting uncomfortably, he's reduced to a child again, demanding that I be its maternal judge.

"Do you like it?"

"What *is* it?"

Laughing softly in answer, he urges me forward, the matter beneath my feet and decorating the ruptured, curving inner wall of the molten chamber intricately inlaid with minute scripture: testimonies, fragments of verse or poetry in some alien language, that makes my eyes and temples ache, writhing and rearranging beneath my efforts to interpret.

Fiery contrails illuminate the chamber; arcs of blue and green that burst from the star's surface only to curve back on themselves, returning to their parent conflagration. Enraptured, mesmerised by their births and suicides, I stumble forward, abrupt vertigo almost taking my feet from under me, making me more fuel for the inferno. He arrests me before I murder myself, before I pollute whatever art or experiment he has set in motion here.

My sight flies from its sockets as though in defiance of him, carried like embers on the breeze, towards the unfathomable engine, the alien process that fuels it: through layer on layer of mystery; infinite depths, numberless states of being, flaring and flickering out in less than heartbeats, the space of thoughts.

With me, his fugitive sight and mine intertwined, the bodies we leave behind so distant, his breath at my neck, his hands on my shoulders, just another dream, another *lie*.

Waking will take us soon, I feel it; a hideous sense of certainty, threatening to burst me like a soap-bubble, to end me here so that I can begin again there. Another unwanted day.

A distant bell, ringing out over every mechanical, bestial roar, every apocalyptic choir, every voice raised in want or despair, every sigh of lust or resignation: echoing in the darkness between stars and worlds, the empty or seething abysses between states of being.

Calling me back, to the bed where I lie, to the sweating, fevered, ill-fitting skin I wear.

Not yet. Not yet!

There, at the fire's heart, my fugitive eye swirling around them, attempting to fix on them, to impose definition they exist in denial of:

Conditions of living night and sunshine, clashing, grappling with and raking at one another, their relationship exhibiting all the intensity of infatuation, of violent hate. They come apart in their extremity, bleeding and flowing together, becoming a condition beyond a mere comingling of previous incarnations, for which neither I nor Crowther have any analogue.

Tearing apart again, the singular condition (or state, or entity) gives birth to its parents once more, but in wildly different permutations: contradictions of engine and anatomy, attempting to integrate, though they thrash and deny the communion, though they're pained by it.

Resisting their common urge to distinction long enough to allow assimilation, the two become one once more; a comingling of the machine and the biological, the male and female, the night and day, so perfect I wrench my eyes away, afraid that they might burst or combust at the sight of it, risking a glance back to witness perfection tainted, tearing itself apart out of fear of its own awful purity.

Principles that shift and transform too quickly to grasp: a flock of beautiful children painted in sunlight, a living engine the scale of a world's core, a thing of luminous eyes and gaping, perpetually bleeding cunts, a globulous mass of sentient excreta, shat from the sewers of Hell itself.

"What are they?"

Other questions echoing those that this one masks, that it suggests: *Who are you? What are you? Will we ever meet and know?*

His answer coming not in words, but a brilliant burst of impressions, hissing through my thoughts like lightning, making me writhe like a worm on a hook.

Others, like us, once upon a time: wanderers of the ways. . .

"Oh, God.*"*

Seeing, now; the humanity at the heart of the flux, the core of constancy from which it originates: foetal forms, sanguine as twins in the womb, all frustration, all want and desire, bled from them, siphoned to feed the fire and the realities it ignites.

"Don't pity them; they were born for this. They don't suffer, not in any real sense. When they wake, all of this will be nothing but a bad dream."

"You've done this before?"

I'm reminded of where we stand, what we are: his body moves against mine, his hard-on between my buttocks, working itself to frenzy.

"Oh, yes! Many times. Many times.*"*

The weary familiarity of an ancient in his barely-man's voice.

"Why? I don't…"

*"*To open the ways, of course."

Of course. The most anarchist soul I've ever met. What else could he possibly want other than to bring the bounds of our skulls and souls crashing down, to make us all trespassers in one another's most sacred and forbidden imaginings?

"Nothing else will work. We can't save ourselves in waking; too separate, too much apart. Humanity will murder itself, long before it realises what it can be. But here..."

Yes, my own convictions, spoken in his voice, with his words. Shuddered by them, fearing their implication, unable to deny them.

His love of this engine almost as bright, as burning as the fires that comprise it, of the twinned souls at its heart, sustained here by their mutual rapture, their fascination with their own being.

Myriad histories, coiling and twining amongst the flames; contradictory creation myths, dreams not only of what they might enjoy when they wake, but of how they came to be: seeing them, flickering like mirages, ephemeral projections around their heads, in the most intense flames: stories that they dream, that they tell one another, simultaneously truth and fiction, *neither*; absurd and banal and miraculous and impossible:

The perfect paradox, an engine of insanity.

"How? How have you made this? Who are you?" A question I've asked him and myself many times, which he hears, even as it forms and resonates in my mind. Nothing secret, nothing unknown, here, save that: the story he'll never tell, that he consciously keeps, that I ache to unravel more than any.

"Soon, I swear."

Murmured against my shoulder, his breath hitched, his urgency plain.

Watching, as the things that might have never been born or conceived outside of this, which might have existed since before the dream of even the waking world, quiver and cling to one another, seep and sing their confessions and contrivances through the flames.

Kisses, gentle bites against my shoulder, my neck, his hands trailing over the undersides of my arms, raising them in sacrificial pose. Barely feeling him, barely hearing; enraptured by the unborn lovers, the dreaming siblings, the stories in the flames:

Teased from myself, as before, sight flying along the unseen thread of its own fascination, plunging into the fires, the tempests of emotion and inspiration that fuel them.

Not merely seeing, now, but scattered amongst multiple states: simultaneously there, atop the tower, as he presses to me, as he embraces me from behind, within the fires, a mote of consciousness, a speck of sentient ash: so, so far, back through the caverns and labyrinths, the chambers and catacombs, in my bed, my skull.

I feel its gravity, even now; the summons of unwanted dawn, that will pluck me from this place, from his arms, that will make me singular and separate, yearning with every heartbeat for what morning can never give, what day will always deny.

There, with them in their contradiction, experiencing their myths and histories as though they're my own:

Unwanted, the semi-divine Mother in which they swell regarding them as cancers, diseased reminders of the rape that created them. Doing all in her power to abort them, to drive them to abort themselves... singing them lullabies of every horror she has witnessed, every insanity she has partaken in; nursings that only make them more eager to be born, to see the worlds she has walked and murdered in all their atrocity...

Contradictions from the first, conceived and coalescing here, not from any brute biology, but from the stray stories, the random inspirations lacing the air: consciousnesses born from consciousness, with no state or equivalent in waking. That dream themselves and one another over and over, aching to be born, reluctant to; held in place by the arts he has woven around them, that he has bound and sedated them with...

The orphans of a mad and murdered Mother, one so broken, she somehow came to wander here in the flesh, breaching the waking world with her desperation, her suffering. Not even knowing that life swelled inside of her, after the abuses she has suffered, not even knowing who or what might be the Father. Swelling here, amidst the monsters, the lost, the self-aborted; feeding on them and whatever filth she might scavenge, until the babes come, until the predators she has kept at bay find her, in her agonies, her labours…

Laughing, through his kisses, his hands interlacing over my lower belly, as though to soothe or stir the babes that might some day coalesce there…

Smiling, as I see: not just one potential, but myriad: those Mothers, those Goddesses, those whores and lunatics and disgraces… different names, different faces, but all fundamentally *me,* in one state or possibility. Not understanding how I know, how it becomes apparent; a spark of dreaming revelation, knowledge sifted from the fire's purple smoke, from rumour in the air.

These children *mine.*

"Ours. Always ours."

The dream of them made real, as myriad as the origins they conjure; permutations of the same entities, scattered throughout potential and possibility… drawn here, gathered by him, to form the core of his paradoxical engine.

Breathless, tears coming, as I attempt to tear myself from the flames, as I try to close my eyes, to be blind to them and my many selves.

"How many?"

Nuzzling my neck, turning my lips to his kisses.

"More than you could ever imagine. More than I could ever count…"

Raped and brutalised, abused and murdered, driven mad, to

depths of disgrace no sanity can endure. Those lost and lunatic women, those broken Goddesses... every single one ensuring that their madness and despairs saturated the children they cultivated in their bellies and brains.

"Is that why you came to me?"

He pauses, pulling away, though I meet his kisses, blinking at me through the blood and tears that stain his face.

"No. Never. You were the first; I didn't seek you out. You came to me. You showed me more than I could have ever found, alone."

Down there, amongst the ways. Remembering the dreams we've shared there, the wanderings... adventures that last for days or months, experienced in a single night, an idle afternoon's nap. And not just ours, the pair of us becoming invaders and parasites in other's night-time realms, often barely seen or perceived; merely part of the absurdity. Watching as the dreaming states of others unfolded and unravelled around us, as they unwittingly shared stories with us they would never confess to their most beloved, not even to their waking selves.

Understanding, in that recollection, why he has done this, why the atrocity is *essential,* however much it pains or appals.

"One more horror, before we wake. One more, before we never have to wake again."

Understanding, in that instant: why he brought me here, what part I have to play.

A moment of hesitation, in which the waking world attempts to claw me back, insisting on itself. Dawn so close, eager to steal this last chance. I'll wake, forget; disregard what little I do recall as nothing more than surreal fantasy, inspired by wine or cheese before bed, by some fault in the circuitry of my subconscious.

What that grey, syphillitic world wants, what it's always wanted: to parasitically sustain, to coil through and squat within us: a worm, a toad, a cancer. No promises it can provide, no potentials it might parade the equal of what we might make in defiance of it, here and in whatever conditions come after, when the ways collapse.

"You see why it has to be you? Why it has to be us?"

"Yes."

Still afraid, not knowing what our children will make of us, what the fires might do. The world I'm happy to abandon no longer content with passive summons, reverting to all it has ever known or been: violence, coercion, attempting to *drag* me back, rake me from the only place I've ever wanted to be.

I feel the first grey flickers of dawn on my face, hear it at the window: rain like ghostly fingers, entreating, engines firing, men barking and cursing. A world that spits on itself and calls it mana from Heaven.

His fingers dig into me, his arms enfold me.

"Don't. Don't let it, lover."

"I won't. I swear I won't."

No more time: what little we have left here measured in heartbeats.

I carry him forwards, though the fires blaze, though the storms howl, threatening to immolate us, to cast us back off the edge of the tower.

We reach for them, as the flames wreathe us, as we burn like them; not merely their creators, their tormentors, any longer, but their echoes, reflections of what they might become or once were.

Even that distinction dissolving as they face us, their flame-flickering eyes open for the first time to anything but one another.

The waking world sighs in our minds, not capable of screaming, of any expression save the weariest. Tired even of itself, at this point—as eager to come apart as it is to sustain in its cancerous condition.

Crowther and I unravel, but do not dissolve to ash or dust in the flames. A moment of obscene panic, the part of me that's still in love with my individuality, being enclosed in the asylum cell of my own skull, shrieking like a bird born to captivity whose cage is melting around it, an autistic child's distress at its daily routines being disrupted. Denying its hold over me so easy, now that it comes to it; to become smoke that passes through the child's fingers, for the bird to fly free, surrendering to instinct as it takes to the air.

He and I... idiot distinctions, dissolving as I part and flow, accepting him, marrying nerve-to-nerve, thought to thought.

A slow genesis, new stars bursting into being inside my mind, the notions of stars and being and all things new to me, perceived from a different suite of senses, through a filter of alien experience.

What madness must feel like; being alien to oneself, to be simultaneously a stranger yet so intimately familiar… but if so, a glorious state, the loss of sanity synonymous with the loss of shackles and constraint, with a transcendence that the prophet-following and messiah-worshiping can't conceive.

Seeing him, knowing him, as intimately as myself; the child he was, pale and sickly and isolated, friendless in his disinterest of others, his contempt for the stinking, yowling creatures he was expected to keep company with. Cruel, sometimes, casually so; enjoying their fear, when he told them stories no child his age should know, when he watched their faces crumple and eyes swell, the worms writhing in their depths parasites that would hatch into such hideous glory later in their cycles, after gestating in the haunted dark of bedrooms, the shivering terror of sleepless nights.

With him, in his self-imposed loneliness, his blissful isolation; the distant, delirious moments in which he learned how to slip through, to wear waking thin and find himself elsewhere, amongst the ways that lead to other's states of dreaming, that simultaneously bind us all, yet keep us separate; corralled from one another in our private Heavens and Hells.

A surprise to him, to learn that others don't walk there, at least consciously; that they don't recall doing so or refuse to acknowledge it on waking.

And how he tried! Just as I did, in those first, fleeting years, to explain to those who couldn't understand, even if we had the means to express: who refused to, who were so afraid...

His Mother. Hatred that seethes; a cauldron of cannibalistic snakes behind his eyes, her neglect, her betrayals... not even scarred by them; wounds that still bleed, that will never heal.

How she looked at him, when he tried to tell her, when he wrote stories in English class or painted pictures of what he saw and discovered in sleep! As though he were alien, some parasite-thing seeded in her womb by an extra-dimensional cuckoo, her true child, that he knew she dreamed of, ludicrous in its perfection, a saintly or messianic rendition of childhood, that would never be strange or sullen, that could never be unwanted in its disappointments.

That memory, the most sacred, most ardently sealed, that he shudders inside of me at the thought of my knowing:

*

Long since lost, having drawn deep tonight, not caring if he never finds his way back, if he never wakes.

Memory echoing, of what drove him to these depths: the idiot frustrations of home, the cruel blindness of those who pretend to love him.

His thirteenth birthday, not much concerned by it; his Mother harassing him for a week over what he'd like to do, what reluctant gifts to shell out for. A party, perhaps? His Grandparents and Aunts and Uncles could come... what about the cousins he's hardly seen since they were six years old?

Answering honestly, as he's been taught, though he knows she'll use it as an excuse for conflict:

"It's okay; I don't want to do anything special."

Happiest in his own company, always; the thought of the stinking, barking things from school invading what sanctuary he has here hideous.

As for family...

Those rolling eyes, that familiar sigh. Her most consistent expressions, where he's concerned.

"You never do, Liam. You never do."

Why ask? It's what *she* wants... not for him, not for anyone but herself; a chance to pretend normalcy, that her life with him is anything other than a haunted abyss.

Not answering, not knowing what she wants him to say.

"Why don't you just go to your room, if that's what you want? Go and stay there for the rest of your life."

The woman seating herself at the kitchen table, angrily fumbling cigarettes from her handbag as she stares out of the window.

One of his most enduring images of her; the portrait that he conjures when he thinks of her at all.

Light music, as the rain comes: Vivaldi, so low he can barely hear it, his body, that has become a source of such irritation of late, melting from him: the storms of Winter shredding his stinking school uniform away, tearing the skin and flesh beneath to tatters, leaving him gleaming bone, washed clean by Noahic fury.

Then nothing, for a time, until he wakes in familiar strangeness, in the alien absurdity more comfortable and welcome to him than the flat where he has grown to the outer-reaches of boyhood, where he has learned to lament and mistrust humanity.

A time when he would have been cautious, wary. Not tonight. Tonight, should he suffer an aneurysm or a stroke in his sleep, should his heart stop or his brain still, then so be it.

Strange ways... even stranger than usual; the darkened corridors flickering with nacreous luminescence, the corrugated walls resembling fossilized foetuses, surgically plucked from their Mother's wombs and cemented before the first stirrings of birth. Some staring into the corridor itself with dark, hollow eyes, their sockets made nests for life whose webs decorate their faces, whose coiled and huddled forms are barely visible within the darkness. Most turned away, their eyes scarred shut, never opened.

Matter flows and froths around his feet; dark, warm and viscous, the stink of it ripe, sharp, though not in the slightest nauseating.

A song in the darkness, drawing him deeper: through twisting, twining tunnels and corridors, through chambers where others dream, barely registering his trespass. A wordless lullaby, drifting and tuneless, Mother's voice: slurred, weariness-maddened, echoing through the labyrinth.

Not wanting to follow; a sincere part of him aching to surrender to curiosity as he has many times before, to take one of the silent ways or those that echo with different hymns, promising escape in the fantasies of others, the obscenities they unconsciously conjure.

There was a time he wouldn't have been able to resist, would have seen no reason to, allowing himself to dissolve into them, become part of them: lingering in the vast chambers where strange skies flicker orange and purple, filled with the fluttering, weightless forms of ragged and shapeless creatures, where the dreamer wanders through fields of swaying flowers, their whining song unsettling teeth and sanity, where nests of immense worms boil and writhe, ribbed and black-bodied, those caught amongst their knots not calling for aid, not screaming as they're enveloped, but laughing like children, sighing like lovers, calling others to join their play. The chambers of dark and boiling seas with circuits of mercurial rivers, with nothing but sky, that the boy who already calls himself Crowther (in defiance of the name imposed on him, that sounds like the whine of some animal thing to his ears) recalls skipping through, laughing as ripples expand across the clouded blue with every step.

Ignoring them, the displays of new miracles, new wonders he might partake of, in pursuit of that song, as it leads him deeper and further than he's ever strayed, through nightmares that he wouldn't have dared approach barely a year ago, for fear that they claim or consume him, that they might somehow infect him, taking root in his sleeping mind.

The corridors of stone gradually give way to those of warped and rotted wood, foetal forms still visible through rents and ruptures in their walls. Something scrabbles through the beams above, an attic or upstairs-dwelling beast, spawn of childhood fears, the terror of ascending to bed alone, of the darkness on landings or in the corners of nighttime bedrooms. Another partially swathed in the darkness ahead, a flitting, uncertain form, always just beyond sight...

Doorways lining the walls open onto surreal nonsense: a tunnel that blossoms into a flock of crows and swarming insects, the forms crawling and tumbling throughout infested, perpetually pecked and plucked at, whimpering in their desperation to wake. A state where bloated, mutilated engineers herd naked human beings into the wheels of a titanic machine, their pitiless grunts those of swine hunting truffles, screams rising with the red mist from the engine's vents and valves.

Not his nightmares, a ghost in those places, unless he wishes it otherwise: passing through with no more consequence than a rumour, not caring that the further he strays from his point of origin, the more likely he will never wake.

He slows as he drawers close, the lullaby echoing loudest in tunnels formed from contradictions of foetal stone and scraps of domestic familiarity: mismatched and broken patches of kitchen tile, peeling wallpaper still bearing shades of the anthropomorphised animals it once depicted about their play. The same that decorated his bedroom walls in his earliest years, that his Mother screamed curses at him for embellishing with crayons and coloured pencils. Jutting edges of oven and cupboard, alcoves open in the walls, containing old, lost toys: the two-headed rubber dragon he adored since his fifth birthday, that his cousin, Alfred, gnawed shapeless in his teething agonies, tooth marks still visible on its heads, necks and back, the motorized skeleton action figure whose eye-sockets glow with sinister purple light when a switch on its back is activated, accidentally trodden to plastic splinters by one of his Mom's boyfriends, who slapped him and told him to stop being such a girl when he wept.

All here, reminders of lost days, the earliest abuses. Signifiers that burst in his brain and threaten to wrench him from this place to other, older dreams, where he'll foment, stew and forget himself in familiar misery.

A defence, designed to keep him from penetrating deeper, from finding the singer.

The wraiths and miseries the items conjure grow momentarily florid, almost intense enough to take shape, dispersed before they can with little more than a thought.

The tunnel expands into a measureless chamber, its tiled floor broken and irregular, great rents gaping into which streams of milk and blood pour, feeding the children that snarl and wail in the depths. Fragments of familiar rooms protrude like bizarre fungi from the walls: portions of long-abandoned sofas and old beds, ancient ovens and chairs and vacuum cleaners. Amongst them, more of the fossilised foetuses, though here the process that transfigured them to stone occurs in reverse, wet matter trickling from their bodies as they twitch, slowly stirring to states of flesh again.

At the heart of the chamber, raised on a great mound of ephemera—more of the lost and the stolen, the broken and the abandoned keepsakes of childhood—is a creature he simultaneously recognises but has never seen in this condition:

An immense figure, splay-legged, streams of blood pulsing from the cavity between, multiple rows of breasts decorating its chest, swollen and seeping, the matter they lactate trailing down its pregnancy-bloated belly, mingling with its menses or spooling through the air in defiance of gravity. A pelt of fine, white wolf fur covers its body, three muzzles protruding from beneath the hood it wears, one singing the lullaby that led him here as the others growl, snap and froth, simultaneously coaxing children from the depths below and warning them of what their Mother might do if they should obey.

They come, regardless of the threat, clambering and slithering up through the streams that birthed them, squealing in delight as they batten onto her legs and thighs, as those that aren't swept or clawed away by her overlong, spidery limbs enter her by the same means they were shat out.

The creature cries with each inverse birth, its belly roiling and rippling as the forms it has already absorbed rearrange themselves to make space for newly abortive siblings, calming them with caresses and hideous lullabies.

A luminous thing sits cradled in one arm, a living renaissance painting of a messianic babe, its perfection somehow ludicrous, hideous in its inhuman lack of flaw: blonde curls of spun sunshine; skin purer than the milk its Mother lactates, a dusty halo of light shining from within, eyes of pristine blue radiating wisdom and innocence without contradiction.

Pawing at its Mother's breast, it turns away from its repast, fixing Crowther with a disarming smile, gurgling a welcome sweeter than any song.

Crowther shudders with nausea, almost doubling over, losing his feet, an antipathy more profound than anything he's experienced wandering the ways inspiring transformation, making him shift on the bone. For now, he resists the urge to let bile and bitterness rewrite him, make him the beast she and the world she brought him into have always insisted.

The creature raises her head, lullabies stuttering to silence. Amber eyes flash beneath her hood, lips peeling back from jagged teeth.

"So, you decided to join us after all?"

A voice leaden with weariness, as though it can't bear the fact of him, his trespasses and transgressions, his constant *disappointments* having reduced her to the point of abjection. Its other maws growl, drooling saliva, one of them barking the most elaborate curses in a tongue he can't understand, but whose venom blisters the air black.

The babe laughs as it reaches for him, Crowther recoiling at a hideous urge to accept its hand, to allow its light to soothe and placate him.

The streams of milk and blood shift as he steps closer, rewriting their courses to flow around him, as though to contain him, preventing him from fleeing or drawing too near. The children below flow with them, though many shrivel and die, deprived of the darkness they crawl from, the sustenance of her touch.

"I followed your song."

Laughter erupts, all three maws expressing the same sarcasm, the babe chuckling with infantile delight.

"Did you? I'm surprised. Since when have you been concerned about us?"

The children echo her sentiments as best they're able, each and every one a deformed, moron thing, slurring or squealing its Mother's words or producing shapeless noise where they cannot.

Crowther resists the urge to kick out at the closest, to send it tumbling back into the abyss.

"I don't know you."

The creature throws back its head, howling, blood tears streaming down its face. In its arms, perfection flickers, its light momentarily dimming.

"No, you don't. You never have."

The creature shifts on its altar of nostalgia, items popping loose, tumbling away into the abyss. Memories echoing after: old arguments, old abuses.

Opening its arms to him, it proffers a place beside his perfect sibling at her breast.

"But you can, here. I know I've never been the perfect Mother, but we're not lost yet, are we? We can be new to one another again."

Crowther closes his eyes, every cell, every instinct, screaming for him to accept: a mouthful of her milk, a night in her arms; of her lullabies, and all will be different: he'll wake as the son she's always desired, a blessed prince, her only love in the world.

Not just a dream, but something they can make true, both here and there, in the waking world.

He hates himself for wanting it, for almost surrendering.

The children part as he stumbles towards her, as realisation pricks his soul with bitter splinters.

What he's resisted thus far, the urge to be more than a projection of his waking self, exploding: his flesh becoming molten on the bone, bone itself restructuring: an agonising rebirth through which his blood and matter mingles with his Mother's, that the abortive siblings she endlessly shats and denies scramble to bathe in and devour.

His perfect sibling flickers, its light fading along with its smile. A moment in which the painted sham betrays itself, revealing the truth beneath: a thing drowned at sea, blue-skinned, worm-infested, bloated with rot, its flickering eye-sockets and blackened mouth seething with parasites, worms of a far greater size protruding from its swollen belly, piercing it through wounds in its back and flanks.

The thing snarls at him, its mask of innocence momentarily failing, as it realises its nakedness.

Flickering again, its perfection returns, but even more absurd, making him laugh through the pain as he swells and distorts to the same scale as the Mother-thing, similarly lupine, but black against her sullied white, blue fire blazing in his eyes and throat, the same flickering through his fur, burning on every breath.

The bastards flee, realising the threat he poses, but many not quick enough, squealing as he crushes them to a pulp beneath his talons.

With every death, an echo of bitterness, a wish on her part for her child to be other: more handsome and outgoing and athletic, more sociable and scholastic and sweet.

All frustrated, failed desires, ways he can never be. Their impossibility realised here, in these deformed and witless things, bastard creations with no purpose or business in being, other than to parade their pointless grotesquery before the Mother who will never be satisfied with them.

The same Mother that howls at his defiance, now, raking at the mound on which she perches with talons that beckoned him only moments ago.

The lie in her arms sings to her, pleading with her:

"Don't let it, Mother! Don't let it hurt me!"

Its voice so serene in his thoughts, so guileless: that of a child destined to be a prophet or prince, whom men will follow and women weep for.

A smile that can inspire genocides.

What will walk from here, if he lets it; what might wake behind his eyes: the child she has always wanted, but can never have: a sadist and serial killer behind a mask of sainthood, a monster that revels in its duplicity, the idiot perfection that others make from it in their weakness, their need to be sheep.

No. His denial one of violence, not even finished shedding himself as he lashes out, claws ripping through her fur and flesh, snapping her head aside.

The Mother bleeds, reaching up to her rent open face with trembling claws, one mouth sobbing whilst the others snarl, gnashing their teeth.

"How could you? How?"

"Ungrateful shite! How dare you touch me!"

The babe in her arms wails, the Mother distracted by its hideous din, taking a moment to coo and placate it.

Crowther wretches as sewage rises inside; every inch of bitterness and bile she has cultivated over the last thirteen years of his life, every rejection and neglect stirring, a vomit of living scorpions.

Agonising, so vile it blisters and tears his distended mouth: a stream of black blood, filled with the clawed and venomous children she seeded inside his mind. Every one telling the story that conceived it as they leave his mouth: the little cruelties, profound neglects, each and every one significant, setting his feet on deeper steps into this abyss.

The vomit explodes against her, rocking her on her perch, the parasites clawing and stinging, seeking out her eyes, her mouths, her wounds, carving ingresses where there are none to be had. Some trail down to the babe in her arms, raking and plucking at its cartoon perfection, tearing it to tatters.

Their mutual Mother screams, her abandoned, partially aborted babes rising from the sewers to aid her, clawing and biting at his ankles, attempting to drag him from his feet down into their filth.

He stamps and rakes at them, the fragile bags of distorted flesh and bone bursting at his touch, still vomiting gouts of infested bile that sear on contact with the source of his nausea.

In its arms, the babe that could never be, plucking and peeling at itself, shedding its luminous exterior to dislodge the parasites attempting to burrow beneath, revealing the truth of itself, their Mother weeping, hugging it close to her breast.

Crowther, unable to bear it, leaps across the abyss, rocking the mound of memory, the Mother-thing reeling back, scrabbling to keep a hold of the living lie it nurses.

A thrill of the most savage cruelty, boiling from him in spurts of blue fire, his black pelt blistering open with it as he grasps the squealing babe, tearing it from its Mother's grasp. Her shriek rattling his bones as she rakes at him, slurring threats and promises, whore's seductions and saint's salvation, if he'll only return the child to her.

Her pleas more traumatic than the violence she inflicts on him, making him bleed more profoundly than any gash or wound. Raising the squirming, struggling babe up, as though to comply, the urge to do so instinctual, so strong he can barely deny it.

Of course, Mother. Anything, anything to make you smile.

Shuddering, a self-loathing snarl, he stops himself, his talons closing around the bitch-thing's throat, choking off its cries, its hollow promises.

Ensuring that it sees, as he raises the sibling that never was or will be to his lips.

Foulness. The most delectable poison, the babe's filth flooding his mouth, its rotten meat sliding down his gullet. Worms and hissing matter fall from his jaws, his eyes never leaving those of the Mother-thing as they flicker and fade, as all volition drains from them.

It crumbles in his grip, the creature sloughing to filth, tatters falling away as its abortions weep and whine, as they dissolve to pools of noisome mess and drain into the abyss they crawled from.

Beneath the mock-divinity, a naked and shivering woman, a bruised, bitten and bleeding thing, abused by all who've ever loved her, by herself more than any.

"I'll be kind to you, Mother. Kinder than you've ever been to me."

The woman not even looking up at him, not capable, her frame rag-doll as he lets it go, watching as it tumbles away, not even screaming in farewell.

*

He wakes without regret for the first time in memory, happy to feel consciousness seeping through its familiar channels, the sensation one that usually disgusts him to the point of tears.

Lying in the dark for a time, he still sees her in his mind's eye: a white and red worm, writhing in the depths, still tasting the foul dream of Motherhood on his tongue.

Closer, not quite so lost, the lie that would have consumed him, had he let it, that would have *become* him, if she had her way. The neverborn babe, the cannbalised sibling. Feeling it squirm in his mind, chewed up and ragged, rotting and foetid, unable to conceal it, unable to pretend otherwise. Calling to him in its disgrace, no longer attempting to pretend perfection, promising so much, if he'll only vomit it up, permit it some small trespass in his mind.

Closing his eyes, he wallows in its impotence, its unspoken fury that it will never be what its Mother-thing promised, the princedom it would have ascended to burned to cinders, collapsed into the void.

Promises, seductions becoming threats and curses as he leaves it to its tantrums, delighted in the certainty that it will consume itself with them, that it isn't long for sanity.

The flat so still, so quiet, save for the rain against the windows, the faint gurgle and hum of the central heating system. His breath and thoughts.

He smiles, brighter than the moonlight or synthetic glow of streetlamps invading through the curtains. Happiness that verges on delirium, knowing what he'll find when he rises, when he goes to her.

He sustains the moment, allowing possibilities to bubble and seethe in his skull: what he can do, what he can make...

Revolutions and renaissances unlike any in human history, which will break the very notion, undoing and re-weaving the species in its most fundamental self. All of them... the weak and worthless, lost and pathetic... those like himself, unwanted and disregarded, he can find them, now, bring them together amongst the ways, wage war on the tainted soul of his species...

Breathing hard, an asthmatic rasp, he calms himself before he has to reach for his inhaler.

Rising from the bed, a sensation of floating, quilts and coverlets peeling from his sweat-slicked body, every inch of him twitches and trembles, as though in the aftermath of lovemaking, a nightmare that shudders his heart in its cavity.

He hears her, gurgling, slurring in the darkness next door, surprised she's even still capable, after what he's done, where he's cast her.

The landing is dark, cold. Moonlight streams silver through the curtainless window. Outside, dark windows, sleeping homes. All his... every dreaming mind a playground, where he can make games without fear of censure.

Opening her bedroom door, a thrill of taboo runs up his spine, the darkness within musty and dust-scented, lingering traces of old perfumes and skin-creams. The shape on the bed is twisted and trembling, caught in a mummifying knot of its own quilts and sheets, the face peering from beneath twisted, lopsided: a rubber mask partially melted away.

An eye appears, black and beady as a rodent's, reflecting the moonlight. Reaching for him, her arm spasms, fingers curling into a spider-leg knot. She slurs nonsense, spittle streaming down one side of her mouth, a frustrated grimace, reducing her to a child, unable to express its irritation.

He doesn't speak, though a million fantasised celebrations rise in his throat, stinging his mouth raw. He's imagined this moment so many times... for her to know even an inch of the disgrace he's felt beneath her eyes, at the point of her tongue.

Shuddering, exhaling that bitterness, he imagines he can almost see it; a billow of flyblown black in the dark.

Unable to keep himself from crying out, yelping laughter, as she slips from the bed, collapsing in a gasping, moaning heap to the carpet, trailing umbilical cords of bedding.

Every curse and accusation, the litanies he has prepared... impotent, in the face of this. She knows, he feels it; her despair and contempt, her fear of him, now.

No more boyfriends to help her, no cold-eyed, hard-handed men to call him pussy or queer, little bastard or worthless shite. None for so long, now. None ever again.

Lingering a moment longer, he watches her writhe, hears her in his thoughts, screaming up from the abyss where she still wanders, blind, forgotten to herself.

Where she'll wander forever or until he forgets her too, letting her fade to phantasmal nothing.

Tears prick his eyes as he steps out of the room, closing the door, the night blossoming around him with possibilities he can't discern or define, ways opening in his mind and waking life.

A long time before anyone will think of calling; her friends, what little family she still entertains, keeping her at arm's length in recent months.

Maybe, in a few days or so, someone *might* come calling, but even then, he doubts they'll break down the door out of concern for her.

Time. In which to pack a travel bag, his backpack. Time in which to shower and brush his teeth and dress.

All new, every process, experience and sensation, never laughing so much at warm water on his skin, never crying out with such intensity as he orgasms again and again.

He doesn't linger on the front doorstep, the night new but soon growing old. He needs to be away, to forget all he's been here; the only way he'll ever be free and whole enough to kindle the revolution he has in mind, that he's cultivated since he was a child, unable to articulate the dissatisfaction that inspires it.

Locking the front door behind, he walks down the broken concrete path, ecstatic at the certainty that he'll never see its familiar weeds and ruptured paving slabs again.

Laughing, as the moon grins down at him, returning its Bitch-Goddess flirtation, knowing that he'll be smiling long after it has gone to toothless senility.

*

I tremble, tearful at his honesty, at what he and I now share. Strange even to think of it in those terms: *my* memory, now; *my* Mother lying stinking and abandoned in her filth, choking to death on the sheets knotted about her neck.

My joy, as the night caresses me with its frost-bitten fingers, as its denizens catch my eye, watching me pass with predatory assessment, uncertain as to whether I'm a rival or potential prey.

As open, as honest with him: nothing I can conceal, now; nothing I can feel shame in: every idiot betrayal, every childhood cruelty, every moment of unthinking, adolescent hideousness... his to experience, to obsess over, as I have, in the sleepless, undreaming hours before dawn, when all my life is nothing but sewage and waste. Every decision undone or turned on itself, every attempt to stray beyond my bounds met with defeat and disappointment, every love affair turned to filth...

I let him see, let him wander there. No choice in the matter; no discerning now where he or she ends and I begin, this new and nameless thing, this strange and sexless parent.

Oh god... all of them, all of them new: every defeat, every

calamity and collapse… here, with me in the flames, remembered and relived, as though for the first time.

The children stirring, smiling, enamoured of our miseries, attracted by the momentary ecstasies they far outnumber:

With me… in the sweating, self-loathing aftermath of love, my first since the original, idiot fumblings of late high school, which I swore I'd never repeat:

This man… this impossible man, with his laser-beam intelligence, that pierces through shit and obfuscation like a lance through a boil. This twitchy, energetic, perpetually dancing beauty, this thing of anxious appetites, always hungry, always thirsty, wine and coffee and cake never far away in his company.

Never knowing this… not realising how self-deprived the previous twenty years of my life had been.

Until he showed me how to burn. Until he gave me a better reason for being. Until…

Closing my eyes, trying to sustain the sensation of being molten inside, of boiling like a kiln of mercury. The breathlessness, the abandon. His eyes on me, drinking me as he does wine, with the same relish, the same need. My strange and hungry beast, my indefatigable boy. James Medrith, Jim or Jimmy to his friends, though he's been christened with a different nickname by every acquaintance, from the casual to the intimate.

Burning…what it felt like to be with him: like burning inside, every moment one of new stars, whose fires needed to be fed, with food, with drink, with sex...with raw experience. The fuel by which he blazed, but also what the fires gave birth to: a process of perpetual motion, infinitely renewable, but which none could emulate.

So strange... that it fractured and faded so quickly. Months, only—the longest relationship I've had; so few comparing to it; the raw intensity, the breathlessness, the walks and climbs and spontaneous holidays, the beaches and strange cities; the towers and markets and deserts. Stopping into cafes and restaurants just so that he could enjoy the local cakes and pastries, what passed for coffee, into whatever seclusion we could find to satisfy other appetites.

My beautiful, wild creature, my insatiable fool. Remembering...the rain in which we ran, on hillsides fast turning to sludge and slurry, where he laughed rather than cursing the weather. The days he made himself sick with wine and cakes and confections, never once bemoaning the appetites that drove him to it (often indulging them once again the very next day, the instant his system was purged). The long, langurous days we spent together in hotel rooms and on beaches, in woodland and lost places. Never knowing it before; such appetite for my company, my conversation, my body. A trembling addiction, a narcotic need. Days when he would call in states of utter distress, begging for me to attend him, to abandon my work, my studies, my lectures and lessons: to come to him, soothe him with my presence, if not my kisses.

To be balm to another soul, to know that I could make him whole with little more than the fact of myself...a state I'd never known before, a role I never knew I could play, until he taught me otherwise.

A mentor, in many respects: teaching me my own wants and loves, that I'd never been allowed to explore, that I'd denied myself, out of some idiot, puritanical fear, some sense of unworthiness. Regarding such as the remit of others, until him: so apart from the waking world, so out of love with it, I had no right to make demands of it, especially concerning my own indulgence.

His loss is still a wound, never healed, bleeding since the moment of its infliction. His intensity… too much to sustain, to endure. A point at which it began to drain me, to leave me sagging, nearly empty.

He didn't understand; I see that. Boundless, some strange fission in his soul, a star that would never collapse on itself, probably even after his death, becoming as frustrated with my lassitude as I was with his energy.

My choice, a coward's way: not knowing how to end it, having never made these decisions before. Choosing poorly: a casual affair, allowing him to realise it, by and by. Wanting him to; somehow so much easier than ripping out his heart with words. The hysterics that resulted as much a pantomime as I realised the rest to be, nothing but part of a life-long play-act: his apparent loves, his desperate energy, his appetite for any and all, diversions from fundamental despair, an abyss of uncertainty that welled through, boiled out, at the point of betrayal's discovery.

The truth that he kept hidden from me, the secret face that his handsome mask concealed, as much as mine did the secrets I could never share with him, the insanity he'd never comprehend.

Threatening so much; to slit his wrists, to throw himself from the cliffs where we loved to walk, to consign himself to the ocean, let the fish and tides take him.

Realising, then, why I could never be what he desired, why he could never be what I need. Too wounded in himself, just like all of us.

I let him go, refusing his texts and telephone calls, blocking his number and e-mail addresses. Hoping against hope that he'd never turn up on my doorstep, that I'd not see his face at work or university.

Hating him, for a time, not allowing myself to realise what I truly despised: my own cowardice, my casual cruelty to him, my sickening weakness...

Crowther is with me, in those moments; knowing me at my most vile, my most insular and depressive. The near-suicides, the temptations of cliff-edges and sleeping pills and railway bridges. The self-deceptions, when jobs and relationships fail—as they always, always do.

Weeping and sick and self-excoriating, recalling, reliving my consistent hideousness, over and over, as he does, as we do.

The children rising, swelling as the flames lick them and illuminate their interiors: children no longer, but young adults, the fires flickering in their hearts and eyes, between their legs, their forms and sexes inconsistent, one seeming male an instant before he buds with pubescent breasts and child-bearing hips, the other female before she wavers, shrinking on herself, curves becoming angles, her features craggier and more severe.

Most abidingly, neither one nor the other, androgynous as we are, *as I am,* in this new condition, where no such accident of biology defines or divides, where such restrictions are the concerns of children, the fears of infants.

Laughing, their humour ripples out, beyond the tower's pinnacle, blistering the sky, blue flame catching in its dusk, spreading, eating away the ugly, ominous cloud as though scouring a wound of infected tissue. Trailing from them, now, flowing out from every pore and orifice, down the sides of the tower, ceaseless in its voracity, carving luminous streams through the desolate filth, the dust and ashes, the unliving rock, down through the ruins, the remaining shrines and temples, to the scarlet stream curdling in the valley below.

Red filth kindles like gasoline, scarlet swiftly becoming azure as the fires spread, those at play or lamenting below burning with it, tearing themselves from the moaning, tortured masses they've become, stumbling, but standing free for the first time in what may be seconds or centuries.

The children regard us, seeing us as clearly as we know and see one another, now. Shame, yes, guilt, yes; so, so much, but already fading, dissolving as we... *I* swell into this new state, as the fires we have kindled, that they have fanned and cultivated, fill us, as I am scoured clean of memory, of trauma; of reluctant Mothers and absent Fathers, of treacherous, unsatisfying loves and ephemeral friendships.

I blink at the newly burning sky, at the star-flecked delirium, the kaleidoscope of colour and light and matter, the raw potential...

The children are laughing, so close, now, their fire envelops us, igniting my breath and skin. As I laugh with them, they embrace me, the fire invading, devouring, melting new formed flesh from bone, reducing bone to embers.

I come apart in an incestuous embrace, all that remains of me—the intention that has burned between my constituent parts for so long— racing through the streams and circuits, touching everything they emblazon and ignite.

The children turn their eyes heavenwards as wings burst from their backs in wet, flailing ribbons, luminous structures as much of light as flesh, and they soar, the tower collapsing beneath them, the engine that sustained them flying apart, its genesis finally complete.

*

Limitless. Directionless. Lightning consciousness, divorced of parameter. A thinking fire, spreading, spreading: no dream or thought free of me, no way I don't illuminate, whose walls I cannot melt or erode or blast apart.

Spires and temples crumble, melting to lambent filth at our passage, self-tormented forms and flesh remade, minds that have been reduced to insanity not restored but suffused with fresh purpose, new coherence, the filth that reduced them to disgrace scoured by my passage.

Screaming joy, singing hymns of ecstasy, the ways crumbling around us, leaving the states and places they cordon to burst their banks, to bleed into one another. Fantasy pollutes fantasy, nightmares and dreams, metaphysical flights and erotic longings become one. All of humanity stirs in its bed, its barely woken condition. Some deny us, some defend their fortresses and temples until they are all that stand in the ocean that follows fire.

Let them; let them fester and devour themselves in their isolation, let them become lords of rats and cockroaches as the rest of us ascend to stars, as we become God above and the Devil below.

They will always be, even in the new condition we make; those who choose to remain untouched, sealed and scarred in their own corpses.

We will forget them, when it is time for new dreams, when realities bloom around us like weeds, when we are reforged in the hearts of storms and drowned stars.

When the ways between this and waking finally burst open and the fire spreads through concrete and plastic and flesh as well as minds, when all distinctions die and we celebrate our communal unravelling…

We will forget.

*

Wake with me.

An echo, an old, old imperative. So strange, now, knowing what I know, seeing as I see. Always waking together, though seas and cities might separate us, though we might not be part of the same whole, as we are there, in the unseen ocean, the spiritual storms we've inspired.

I feel him so keenly, so tangibly; a presence in my head, in my body and blood. Just as I feel myself within him, stirring likewise, on the other side of the world.

Parasite infatuation.

Tears. A sensation of vertigo, of tumbling. Not just him, but a million others waking with us, stirring inside of us, as we stir within them.

A human revolution that will drive some mad, that already does; feeling them slip away, as they allow the miracle they have made and become part of to destroy them. A time, perhaps, when they might claw themselves back together or when others will gather their scattered sanity, when they might be restored, thread by thread, shard by shard.

But not today. Today, some wake to delirium, frothing, gibbering, weeping in lament for the era they know has passed, the isolation they can no longer enjoy, what suspended their shape, what held them in place, gone, leaving them to flow without proscribed purpose or direction. Some so unwilling to accept the death of tradition, they die with it; hearts rupturing, brains boiling themselves to oblivion, those whose bodies refuse the call to suicide taking more active hand: slitting their own throats with shards of broken mirror, stabbing their own hearts, hurling themselves from the tops of parking lots and tower blocks. Some so repulsed by what they've woken to, they lose whatever delusions of sanity they maintained, murdering their husbands, wives and children, setting fire to themselves and their homes, engaging in acts that shame the atrocities of the world they endlessly lament but refuse to let go.

Feeling it all, in the space of those waking hours: every pain, every confusion and derangement, distantly, for the most part, but sincerely enough to know that more will follow, before the last of humanity withers, before the last wall of the ways collapses.

Fleeing, I take what little I need to sustain myself, as we all do: survivors of the first stages of the revolution—leaving our homes, our jobs… everything that binds us to who and what we were, the ghosts of those who died in the night.

Some try to sustain, somehow hoping that the ways will accrue again, that they'll become isolated and alone in their skulls once more. Others become traitors to tomorrow, wanting to reverse the most fundamental revelation our species has ever known, allying themselves with the lonely few in love with what was, who too often hold positions of old power (money, politics, religion), who pursue us, condemn us as terrorists and anarchists and monsters to those still uncertain, who require time to realise themselves.

We fly to meet one another, in the midst of chaos, under conditions neither he nor I dreamed. Learning, by and by, how to move lightly, how to go unseen, thanks to others who have always lived shadow-lives, whose experience we share as though our own, now.

There are times when we're almost caught, when the furore they've raised against us results in lynchings, mass murder, the confused and meandering turning on one another, on their kin and neighbours, as they always have: the morality of cannibals still holding some sway.

But they are few, so few, and we are many: we learn that, as we travel; we meet them, they shelter us, in their attics and cellars, in their garden sheds and bunkers, from those so in love with their slavery that they hate us for breaking it, who would kill us for the crime of their liberation.

What structure remains disintegrates, slowly, day by day; there isn't enough will to sustain it, the last of the reluctant, the wilful lonely, either surrendering to the new status quo or following those who can't abide it into oblivion.

Crowther and I don't seek one another out when we sleep, now; we always wake to that new condition, in which there is no he or I, gestating in the depths where tunnels and chambers once stretched forever: those labyrinths gone, now, eroded, melted, blasted to ruin, allowing the rains our children precipitate to cleanse them, to flood and submerge them, creating secret depths where stars fall and drown, but do not flicker out: where they burn perpetually, becoming the furnaces in which we are remade, where dreaming souls descend to dissolve all they know of memory, becoming something new in their plasma-hearts, rising from the ocean as wonders, even to themselves.

We watch as they do, as others flock or plummet from the skies, enjoying a different gestation or metamorphosis, their wombs of storms and lightning, of rain and sunlight: other species born and reborn there, our children the first, soaring and fluttering through the Edenic orchards, tending to and guiding those that come after, teaching them the means of dreaming themselves anew.

Others join them, in the days and nights after; dreamers

seeking to emulate them, to be like them; conspiring children of their own.

We watch, as we swell to our state of completion, as they sing to us, becoming strange midwives to their own creators, cajoling us to emerge and join them in their play.

Soon, we promise them, *soon.*

*

Here, in one of the few places we've been safe and still since that first and last waking, one of the few places we've had the luxury. So far from the world, in its lunacy, the last thrashings of the old and cancerous, that wishes to be old and cancerous forever.

We still feel them, even this distantly; their rage and frustration at being denied, at the orders that sustained their power and comfort rotting at the roots.

So little is left, now, their gambits so desperate: contrived acts of terrorism, atrocities that make 9/11 look like a dumpster fire, the old games of scapegoating no longer holding great sway, those the lonely and teeteringly powerful seek to coerce no longer blind to the manipulation, knowing it for what it is: experiencing the horror and agony of those who burn, who are bombed and shelled and ravaged by chemical agents as though such is their pain, atrocities inflicted upon them.

The powers that were -the churches and nations, priesthoods

and governments- unable to sustain, no longer able to make threats or promises that people believe, the dreaming minds of humanity opened in ways they've never been, what they desire swelling to fresh abstraction with every passing day.

Time, yet, before the atrocities cease entirely, time before the castles collapse. Still enough of humanity that was, of *tradition,* to poison us.

But not for long.

Wood crackles as it's fed into the burner, Lemuel sitting cross-legged on the carpet, the rings and jewellery threaded through almost every part of his anatomy glittering in the firelight, the stories he sings accompanied by the sighs and echoes of those who not only listen but *live* them, sharing his dreams while partially awake.

That sense of gravity so strange, yet so familiar, now; of being *drawn* from inside my own head, streams of consciousness waiting to break their banks, to flow unfettered into his tales, to be cast as part of them, woven into myths and fables as though they're the instances of my own life, which have become increasingly diffuse, since the children took flight from the tower.

Lemuel...a storyteller born, a performance artist, poet, playwrite, before his awakening, scavenging a meagre living from his unique brand of street-side theatre, what roles he could find amongst Derry's independent theatre scene (hardly enough to pay for the tobacco in his pipe or the rum in his flask, to hear him tell it, both more essential to his continued survival than bread or shelter).

I found him almost dead on the streets of that city, thrashing and convulsing with snares of silver around his throat, his wrists, his would-be kidnappers keeping their distance, repulsed by the stories that streamed from him, that he screamed into the freezing night in defiance of their silence, their imposed peace.

Knowing him already, more intimately than through any face to face meeting: having found him, like the rest, amongst the wreckage of the ways, not lost or lunatic, but riding those swells, celebrating in the dissolution, enraptured at knowing the stories of others so immediately, weeping in delight at the renaissance he has ached for unbeknownst to himself since his first conscious fantasy.

One of my closest encounters with them; the vile, wounded things that the dreamless send against us, that others, far longer in this fight than Crowther or I, call variously *The Severed, Hollows, Isaac's Bastards,* amongst other epithets.

So afraid, so repulsed by them, reduced to a shivering, abandoned child in their presence. The condition that they would have us all occupy: one of perpetual dread, of abuse-fostered obedience, until our times to be finally fed, flesh and soul, to the engines of history.

Engines that Crowther and I fundamentally vandalised, in our passions: the renaissance we inspired far beyond even what he imagined, in his dark and trembling cot on the other side of the world.

Remembering how afraid I was, not knowing what to do, having always fled before, using whatever means I could to obfuscate or throw off their pursuit.

Acting on instinct, on fury and disgust, more than conscious thought: screaming at them as I emerged, the pair too focused on Lemuel to respond.

The stories I vomited at them...not mine, but ones borrowed or gifted, drawn from the seething depths of the ocean where the ways once stood. Stories of old things, of sorcerers and the creatures they conjured, of fey things in ancient woods, glowing hunts and bachanals, where the naked and tattooed flickered brighter than the moon, dancing around fires in which horned gods blazed, their hymns of abandon echoing throughout the night.

The first wounded, bursting and bleeding beneath the assault, stumbling before righting itself. The other struggling to hold onto Lemuel as he took advantage of its distraction, flickering from one point to the next as my stories seethed and coiled around it, seeking anchorage in its mutilated mind.

The wounded one rising to face me, the lashes with which it held Lemuel torn free, whipping from its fingers in hair-fine tendrils, its bland features melting, eclipsed by its eyes and mouth, that swelled to become black holes, vaster than the face that framed them...

Lemuel shrieking, a war cry that would have ruptured his throat barely days before, hurling himself at the one that still held him, bearing it to the ground, his scrawny, pierced frame flickering with azure and orange fire as he wrestled with it, slamming his fists into its unbearably bland face over and over, until it was nothing but a bleeding mass of ink and bone splinters.

Even then, the thing still thrashed, emitting its hideous, mechanical whine. Lemuel combusted, the fires he wept and drooled erupting from every pore, every wound, the creature he straddled not blazing to ashes, but becoming a vessel for them, the fires seeking out the void at its core, illuminating its emptiness.

How it screamed, then, the Severed no longer sounding mechanical and monotone, but spluttering and shrieking like a wounded animal, its purity tainted, the other turning to regard its ally, its attention no longer mine...

Barely even thinking: the killing art rising in my throat, lacing my spit as it flew, making it a hail of silver needles that caught the Severed in the side of its grotesquely pulsing face, carrying it off balance, screaming, clutching at itself.

No need to summon Lemuel from his violence, the man exhausted by it, on the verge of collapse, his fury expended.

Helping him away, a limping, circuitous route through Derry's narrow back alleys and abandoned districts; places the Severed would find disorienting by dint of their natures, resonant with echoes I couldn't perceive before Crowther's gambit, but which were fast becoming part and parcel of my new reality.

Lemuel weak, disoriented after his recent expressions, skin and hair still flickering with embers of orange and azure, lambent tattoos pulsing beneath his pale skin.

But silently celebrating at being found at last.

Amongst the eldest of those I met in the early days of my transience, when I was still learning this new status quo, my shifting place within it. Closer to my own age than most; in his late thirties, not exactly handsome, but compelling by dint of his strangeness; a face that draws the eye, with its piercings and tattoos, scrawny to the point of starvation, yet with an appetite for confection that would shame the sweetest-toothed child.

An anchor in the storm, some solidity in the escalating flux. Essential, given my confusion, my uncertainty: still not sure of my part in it all, at that point, what the rest would demand of me. One who sooths as much as Crowther arouses, who calms my nerves and smothers anxieties with his tales, his music, his poetry. The part he's come to play in the tribes we've drafted and accrued, those that follow us like the children of Hamlin charmed by the Piper's music, almost paternal, adoring each and every one of them in ways that his former, dreaming and divorced self would never have credited.

As for the rest..?

Young, for the most part; younger than either of us, closer to
Crowther in that regard. Raldin and Domino pottering around the
kitchen, their natural domain, preparing food, baking bread; the
arts with which they made their living, once upon a time. In the
freezing cellars below, Romo and Lucia, Elias and Laura, play
their games, tell their stories, make love in the darkness. Strange
creatures, all; runaways and exiles, prodigals and isolationists, out
of love with their humanity, as Crowther and I were. Wanderers
of the ways, before they came crashing down. Not drowned or
swept away in the resultant floods, at least not unhappily so:
adapting to them, celebrating the new condition, as Lemuel did;
an inversion of evolution, men and women becoming fish again.
As enraptured by their newly awakened states as they were
despairing of the previous, strange to themselves, as I am, still not
knowing what capacities they might demonstrate in their awoken
conditions, but learning with every passing day.

With them in the dark, as Romo conjures a display of burning
lions, their manes of green flame, their eyes shimmering like
stars, as Lucia swathes the shadows around her, weaving them as
a spider might its silk, forming a coccoon of pulsating darkness at
which the lions claw and rake, until it erupts around her, swarms
of black butterflies smothering their flame. With Elias, as he
watches these displays, sprawled out on a ragged, barely-held-

together sofa, Laura perched cross-legged on the carpet before him, staring as though hypnotised into the shifting mass above his head, a phenomena like smears of thick and muddled acrylic paint that squirm and interbleed, vague forms sometimes visible in the flux, dissolving or subsumed by others before any sense might be made of them.

More than allies, more than friends; beyond any notion of family, accrued over the days and nights of my flight, most having saved my life more than once, as I have theirs.

More than that, far more. Not merely *saving* one another's lives, but making them worth living; showing one another in ways we never could before what we know, what we dream, desire and dread. Minds as open books, as theatres, as cinema...beyond those and all mediums humanity has contrived: a means of meeting fantasy to fantasy, paranoia to paranoia, regret to regret.

That intimacy redefining us all, undoing any notion of species we once clung to, any separation of sex or race, religion or nationality.

Their thoughts singing to me even now, as I wait, as I silently call him home through the snow.

He's so alone, now. Shivering, breathless and terrified, making his way up the mountain by ways he knows only because his lost companion did. Taken, before he even realised they were hunted; a bullet through her brain, the vicarious pain almost enough to make him faint, holding onto consciousness only for fear that he'd be next.

With him, an adoring ghost, sharing the biting cold in his bones, the hideous, buzzing numbness that has claimed his hands and feet, weariness that recalls the excesses of the cot, when all he or any of us did was gurgle and shat and sleep, sleep, sleep.

The snow calls to him, singing lullabies: *lie down, lie down and sleep. Lie down and let us sing you quiet dreams.*

Calling him through, drowning out the sirens in white: *Don't listen to them! Come to me, Crowther. We're so close, now.*

So close. Though I still don't dare open the door, for fear that I see nothing but the white that sings so sweetly, whose seduction will soon override any I can contrive.

Luana approaches, handing me a steaming mug, the chocolate it contains several shades lighter than her skin. No words, none necessary; the woman takes me in her arms, hugging me close and kissing my head. A comfort to us all, her maternity compensation for the son she drove to suicide.

Staring into the steaming chocolate, silently calling, not to Crowther, knowing he can't hear me any longer, but deeper and further than that: into nameless state where the ways once stood, where the ocean churns, where new shores form and accrue with every heartbeat.

Into the storm that rages there, amongst the ones that swell and dream of other conditions, so far flung as to be beyond alien, to the children that soar and sing to them, in their apotheosis, that rouse those that have slept overlong.

Afraid. So terribly, terribly afraid: of them, of how far beyond us they've grown. As our parents were of us, I've come to realise: the fuel for their every cruelty, their consistent neglect.

Calling to them regardless, singing lullabies that they remember from our time atop the tower: the memories and experiences they sapped from us to fuel their gestation, their cataclysmic birth. Knowing the milk they love: the more intense and extreme, the better. Trauma: those nights when I raked my own wrists and throat until red welled, when I stared up at the clouded night sky from the filth and petrol-stinking street, ignoring the barks and bilious cries of drunks, the wails of police sirens, begging the moon to shine through and take me, for other-things from the stars or other dimensions to sweep down and pluck me up, even if their only intention was to devour my flesh and mind, leaving gibbering abomination in their stead.

Those miseries a black, pulsing summons, the children's song faltering as they turn from their charges, flocking to me. So different from what I recall: transformed by their transgressions, the others that they've touched and inspired to states of abstraction:

Flickering, luminous forms of blue and amber light, their bodies one moment fluid, shot through with sunlight circuitry, the next fractal shards sprouting, grinding against one another with every motion, swathing them in rainbow robes.

Wings are their only constant features, every state they occupy boasting at least one set, some formed of the same light that flows in their veins, others of smoke or mist, of flesh and feathers.

Coming to me, they dance around my projected state in an elaborate performance, singing to me of all they've done in my absence.

I'm barely able to meet the eyes that blister the air around them, their wings and bodies, our children having grown too absurdly beautiful, beyond any dream he or I ever had for them.

Mother. You are afraid.

No question; the children seeing me, knowing as I know.

Yes. I'm afraid for him.

They pause in their dance to regard one another, communicating obliquely.

What do you want of us?

An impotent question; part of some ceremony or ritual. They already know—their eyes penetrating inside, reading me as they might casually flick through a book or comic.

Help him, please.

The pair flutter, flickering, as though uncertain, afraid.

We cannot touch him, there. He is beyond us.

A serrated knife twists in my entrails.

No, not after everything. It can't end like this…

Sorrow billows from me, painting the surrounding storm infested, pulsing black. The children recoil, fearful of being tainted by it.

Mastering themselves, they move in balletic concert, dispersing the filth with a scented breath, a beat of their wings. Comfort and sunshine wash my insides, calming my thoughts. Despair becomes cigarette smoke, nothing more than a lingering acridity.

They approach, embracing me, enveloping me in their wings, their touch suffuses me, ecstatic, agonising light invading my every recess.

We cannot reach him, but you can. Bring him home; let him sing to us again.

Their essence… comingling with mine, flowing on their spit as they kiss me, on their sweat as they rake me open, caressing my wounds.

Altered by this incest so fundamentally, I already feel a transformative urgency in my waking mind and body: a sensation of blossoming, as I experienced when Crowther embraced me atop the tower, when I woke from the inferno we sparked, so many contradictions whispering in my thoughts: fungal, parasite memories blooming…

A similar transgression that I will carry to him, when I wake, through the ice and snow.

Unable to sustain it any longer, they bring me to the point that I almost burst, becoming like them, the gestating demi-gods they tend.

Letting me go, letting me fall, singing to me as I plummet towards the black and boiling ocean, the pregnant stars that flicker in its depths…

*

The cold bitter enough to murder me after a few steps. The others don't protest, seeing the change in me, sharing my desperation to finally meet him in the flesh.

None except Lemuel, who can no more hide his horror at what I intend than he can the silver glittering throughout his face.

He follows me to the door, whilst the others hold back, knowing full well that I'll brook no intereference.

"This is insane. Even if you find him…"

"I will. And I'll bring him back. Believe me, Lem. Please."

A plea he can't fulfill, even if he has a mind to; hearing every unspoken urge, every desperate dread, feeling them as though they're my own.

His hand on my shoulder, gripping, burning even through the layers I'm swaddled in. A promise of fire, a seduction of warmth and affection it hurts to deny.

So many words, none either of us can speak. I leave him in the doorway as I step silently out into the cold.

Even with my children's gift, the cruelty of these mountains is more than enough to sap the life from me, to freeze the blood in my veins should I lose myself, should I wander overlong.

Their sunlight flickers inside, lacing my blood, beading on my brow and fingertips like sweat. Enough to keep me from total exposure, to hold frostbite at bay, for a time.

His song is so faint... flickering, on the verge of snuffing out. Focusing on it, scenting him like a wolf following a blood trail, away from the house, with its light and warmth, with its songs and stories.

They beg me, in my thoughts: *Let us come, let us help you...*

The young ones in particular, who still have little notion of their mortality, even after everything they've experienced.

I deny them, demanding that they wait for me. None resist, seeing that I won't be responsible for them out here should they fall, should they break their ankles or backs. Should the cold take them. Not if it means leaving him to the snow.

A dense woodland of immense, black pines decorates this flank of the mountain, falling snow almost luminous against the dark, trees and rocks cracking, whispering, the eyes of wild things alight in the shadows.

None approach, none dare. Even those that linger, faintly rabid from hunger, considering their chances only for a moment before slinking sadly away to gnaw old bones, to lay down and die in the cold.

Their hunger tangible, jagged teeth rasping my mind, gnawing my entrails: lone wolves, expelled or separated from their packs, left to die for some infirmity or disease, starving or losing their animal minds. Great bears, black and slow and perpetually hungering, seeking anything to swell them with fat before they slumber.

More distant, but more acute: the world we fled, devouring itself, so close to collapse, now: most cities become hives of anarchy, those like us taking to the streets en masse, not in violence, but in song, *invitation*, while the lords in their castles hunker, herding the dreamless and broken against them: the soldiers and the killers, those whose only dreams are to exercise power and obey.

Where the violence begins.

Feeling the bullets as they blaze through me, as they rip and whir and puncture, the explosives as they hurl me into the air, tear the limbs from my body, open me, spilling me out, the tanks grinding me to pulp beneath their treads.

Still not enough to disperse them, not enough to even slow their advance, stunt their celebrations. There are too many, too many who ache and suffer and dream of more, though they hadn't the means to articulate it to themselves, until now.

The fear of those behind the walls is delicious, in its own cruel way. So, so afraid, at last; after so long insulated from fear, all want or loss. Trembling at the songs outside, pissing themselves, turning on one another in their desperation.

Not long, now. Not long before the walls are torn down, before the rats are dragged from within, exposed to searing sun and merciless moonlight.

A smile spreads beneath the scarves and layers of fabric swathing me as I slip and skitter down the slope, testing every step for fear that the snow might give way beneath me, plunging me into some chasm or off the edge of a ravine.

The cold steals my breath, familiar numbness already seeping through my limbs, warring with the children's sunlight. Crowther's candle-flame gutters, his thoughts misty and incoherent. No longer climbing, no longer driving forward, the snow's seduction too much, in his weariness…

Don't. Don't you dare sleep, sweetheart.

Singing to him between the trees, promising him what awaits, if he'll only drive a little further, if he'll only force his heart to beat a little longer.

Something else pulses at the edge of perception, following him, scenting a similar trail. Unlike anything I've ever felt.

More monsters than any would know; creatures the lonely ones in their castles have kept and cultivated for such an occasion, made from broken men and women, from lost and abused children.

Severed. Sentient holes in the world, sucking wounds in our thoughts. Dreamless creatures, deprived of inspiration, ritually, surgically stripped clean of all self, save what their masters proscribe.

Mercifully rare encounters, the sight of them, the *fact* of them, more debilitating than any bullet or beating, more terrifying than threats at the point of blades or guns.

Those that almost stole Lemuel away...the closest I've ever come to them, the most intimate confrontation.

The closest I ever will, I pray.

This one... strange in its isolation, the bastards tending to move in pairs at the least, difficult to get a bead on, its *emptiness,* its ragged, mutilated condition repulsive, arousing antipathy akin to phobia.

But close, so close, now.

Losing my footing, the snow shifting beneath me. The forest blurs, dissolves as I tumble, precipitating a small avalanche. Protruding rocks and branches bruise and tear me open, red stars of pain bursting inside with each impact. Familiar sensation; having experienced it vicariously a million times, from car crashes never lived, from trips and sprains never suffered, breaks and fractures and dislocations, whiplashes and internal bleeding.

This barely a stumble by comparison, a spar of stone thrusting from the snow bringing me to a halt with a sickening crack. Black momentarily blooms behind my eyes, threatening to drag me down, swallow me away from the endless white.

The children's gift flares inside, riding my blood as it seeps from me, *igniting* it, urging my flesh to knit, my bones to repair. What injuries I sustain already scar, scabbing over as I claw my way to my feet, shrugging off the snow that threatens to bury me.

Still wincing, regardless of the exaggerated healing, barely able to stand without the stone's support.

Dripping barely melted snow, I blink, my vision clearing. Through the distant trees, I glimpse a figure on the slopes below, similarly swathed, every inch insulated against the lethal chill.

Stumbling as he climbs, he reaches for trees and branches, any handhold that he can haul himself up by.

Knowing him without seeing his face.

Ignoring the grating, splintered sensation in my chest, I weave around the rock, tripping and stumbling down to meet him.

Not crying out, though I ache to, a million unspoken welcomes and confessions swarming against my lips, sealed in silence for fear of drawing what hunts him. Hunts *us*. Not needing to, his masked and swaddled face turning up to me as I descend, his hands reaching out. I hurtle forward, catching him as he falls, holding him upright, though the agony of it sears me like lightning.

I've got you, I've got you, sweetheart.

No spoken words, none necessary. Raw thought and impression lacing the air between us, glittering like spider silk.

Cold... I can't...

The candle flame fades to little more than a blue ember, his body growing slack in my arms.

No, don't. Please, don't.

After everything, all we've done, the dream that has undone the world… it can't. It can't be like this.

Laying him in the snow, I fumble the gloves and layers of wrapping from my hands, the cold biting my fingers violently enough to make me cry out.

I tear away the fabric swathing him, the visor around his eyes, seeing his waking face for the first time.

The most beautiful death mask, the corpse of a fairytale prince that no kiss might wake.

Pale, so pale, skin almost blue; a face surprisingly redolent of what he wore when we met amongst the ways: an attenuated, effeminate youth, features drawn and tapering, lips sallow. A sickly, scholarly boy, almost a decade my junior.

Tears freeze on my face, burning my cheeks. I plant a maternal kiss on his forehead, exhaling, attempting to fan the ember within to a semblance of its previous fire.

Barely a flicker, my kiss rousing the merest moment of blue.

Crying out with what breath I have left, I no longer care if the Severed hears, if it emerges at my back, plunges one of its hideous blades between my shoulders. Anything, even that emptiness, welcome compared to this.

Kissing him again, prying his cold, unmoving lips apart, I breathe into him, a process almost violent in its intensity.

Happy to surrender what little warmth I have left, if it only means we freeze together here on the mountainside.

Wings flutter in the boughs overhead, spectral children laughing in the woods.

More than mere breath and spittle pass between us: the children's gift rises, washing my entrails, searing in its concentration:

His body convulses in my arms as it pulses down his throat, threads of luminous fluid seeping from our interlocked lips, streaming down his face. A sensation akin to orgasm, to bleeding out, to giving birth.

The ember blazes blue, swelling to its former candle-flame condition then beyond; a kindling in my thoughts, his own dimly punctuating them, as blood and thought thaw, beginning to flow again.

Reaching up, a freezing hand strokes my face, his eyes flickering open, a dusting of ice crystals falling from overlong lashes.

He gives me a tooth-chattering smile, his breath billowing silver in the frigid air.

Not... how I wanted it...

Laughing, though not with my mouth.

What ever is? Can you walk?

He strains to rise, using me as leverage, surprisingly light, despite the layers upon layers swathing him, leaving me to wonder if his bones are hollow—a bird's bones.

You... went to them? You saw them?

His legs tremble like those of a newborn foal, his first steps uncertain, the snow shifting beneath.

Don't think about that, now.

Needing every ounce of his energies for the journey ahead, neither of us daring to entertain the delusion we can possibly make it.

His weariness is infectious, a disease that threads through me like tendrils of grey mist. Hearing that same siren song, now; the snow a sweet bed, calling us to lie down and make love until we freeze in it, as one.

Forcing ourselves on, Crowther gritting his teeth, snarling at the imaginary creatures as they sift and dance around us, as they partially form from billows of snow and deepening shadow.

Part of the world we've made that has yet to fully realise itself: an erosion of the waking and dreaming, the actual and abstract. We glimpse them as they dance naked between the trees, beckoning and gesturing for us to join them, their blazing, beautiful eyes full of the most obscene promise.

How long before they don't have to merely beckon, before they come to us in flesh coalesced from our own frostbitten delirium?

I force myself to look away, though they're so beautiful; youths with skin as black as shadow, as white as the snow, eyes that blaze blue and amber, that promise the most sublime peace, if we'll only accept their embraces…

We share a spurt of defiance, the blue blazing, fed by our children's fire. He is no longer reliant on me, dragging me along behind him, though it's clearly an agony to him, the figures dancing between the trees demanding my eyes...

As one, our dreaming state no longer divorced from itself, closer to realisation than ever before...

My cold -numbed fingers slipping from his, I fall face first in the snow. Turning, he takes hold of me before I slip back down the slope, his eyes narrowing as they fix on something behind us.

Don't.

An impotent warning, seeing it well enough through his eyes. Scrabbling to my feet, following as he resumes his climb, I move as fast as the snow and our frozen muscles allow.

A hideous void aches at our backs, a sense as of inverted gravity, causing us to fall forward, clutching at the ground as though it's a sheer cliff face, trying to keep ourselves from tumbling back into the abyss.

The thing is so hideously *silent,* not a whisper of thought or inspiration from it, not even a suggestion of what it might dream.

A hollow thing, filled with other's echoing imperatives, its own long abandoned and forgotten, its outer appearance that of a man, the clothes it wears nondescript: grey on grey, little to swathe it against the cold, nothing the mountain can throw at it that matches the void inside. Pale-skinned, milk white, its features bland as unbaked dough, a face so instantly forgettable, it's difficult to keep in mind.

Seeing us, its dark eyes unblinking, the serenity in its expression more terrible than any wolf's snarl, any assassin's threat. Worse for being wanted; a promise that it perpetually pulses, that echoes from the absence at its heart:

Let us bring you peace, let us soothe the chaos in your souls...

Spitting in the snow, snarling through clenched teeth, we redouble our efforts as though a fire blazes at our backs, a tsunami of diseased filth and toxic waste rising to drown the world.

The Severed draws closer with every heartbeat, its hideous *serenity* dulling the woods, muting the sounds of creaking boughs, of padding paws, of animal growls. *Infecting* us, the desire to simply stop, to lie down and sleep, so strong... a surrender that will sweep us away, reduce every struggle, every concern and desire to blissful silence.

An old and familiar temptation, that we have fought our entire lives, simultaneously disgusted by the unthinking, bovine passivity of our species and yearning to share it, to lie down with the other cattle and no longer think of life beyond the pen.

The Severed is an avatar of that principle, just as the children we have made are the opposite: a creature that might still the ocean, smother the stars in its depths, quiet the storm and make what gestates within stillborn.

A hideous realisation striking us like bolts of black lightning, shuddering us to a halt: *We can't lead it back to them.*

Crowther almost weeps, bathing in the remembered warmth that is so recent for me, a forgotten dream to him.

But he stops, nonetheless, turning with me to face what follows.

What little breath remains to us snares in our lungs, the Severed almost floating up the mountainside, weightless, making no impression in the snow.

We cling together as it pauses, the smile it affects as hollow and insincere as the promises it exudes.

"My name is Dumolo. I'm sorry it has to be like this, sorry for everything you've suffered."

A soft voice, paternally soothing, so sure, so serene.

"Please, don't be afraid of me. Look, I'm unarmed."

Spreading his arms, allowing us to see that he wears nothing around his waist, nothing concealed beneath his grey clothing.

Meaningless, already having seen what harm they're capable of without blades or firearms.

"Leave us alone, please."

Dumolo closes his dark eyes, sighing. "I can't do that. Not with things as they are. Besides, if I leave you here, you're apt to freeze to death. That can't possibly be what you want?"

Everything he says is effortlessly reasonable, a parent coaxing addled and idiot children from a cliff edge. Almost enough to make me question myself, question Crowther. What if all we've done since the breaking of the ways is nothing but the idiot vandalism of disaffected youth? What if we've achieved nothing with our little displays and defiances other than to arouse those in authority to our presence, to bring their stern eyes to bear?

That sense of being a child again, errant and wilful and foolish beyond belief, so strong; enough to make both of us quiver in one another's arms, to almost weep in apology for ourselves.

"Come, please. Come down from the cold. Even if we can't be companions, we can at least discuss things by the fire."

Its play of being cold pantomimic, exaggerated in the manner of a child treading its first boards. Its words so reasonable, with a Father's edge of kind command.

I hold Crowther back, in his extremis, his mind billowing with warm temptation, honeyed surrender. Unspoken promises of open fires and warm brandy, of sighs and forgiveness at the misunderstandings we've had of one another. Of a new way going forward, in which we do not need to be in perpetual conflict, in which we can work together towards a more...amicable solution.

The sense of that...so clear as to be overwhelming, as to make every urge and inspiration that has brought us thus far seem nothing but the tantrums of entitled children.

No.

The Severed physically staggering beneath my denial, Crowther almost tearing away from me, going to it, as though afraid it might flicker away, taking every offer of reconciliation with it.

I hold him fast, consciously stoking the blue fire inside, reminding him of the promises he made amongst the ways, the stories he told me atop the tower, that live now, in the forms of the children that the *thing* below would happily murder.

Smiling, though his lips crack with frost, weeping, though the tears freeze on his cheeks. As much at his own desire for the lies as the lies themselves.

Not so very different from the rest, in the end, are we?

No, not so very different.

So many things learned during our flights from them; tricks and feints, arts the like of which my former self could scarcely imagine.

So weak, aware that it's nigh suicidal, but drawing upon them now, willing the wounds I've suffered to cease scabbing, to bleed afresh.

Crowther senses it, though he doesn't urge me to stop. A wave of pure adoration unsettles the air between us, making the snow at our feet swirl and steam.

The Severed senses it, too, its face melting, becoming blank as a store-front mannequin's as it steps back, wary of imminent assault.

I almost falter, allowing what tingles at my fingertips, what burns and buzzes in my throat, to dissipate harmlessly at the sight of its transformation: its mouth and eyes swelling, becoming perfectly round hollows in its face, all other features melting and swirling towards them, reduced to liquid effluent, draining into the most dismal of sewers.

Crowther gestures wildly in the air, deflecting the silvery lashes that spit from those holes, that seek to bind and restrict us.

That same sense of gravity inverting, the holes swelling beyond the bounds of its face until they become one: a great, pulsating abyss, into which the snow pours, into which the wind diverts, towards which we stumble, unable to maintain our footing…

A vomit of blue-burning butterflies erupts from my throat, filling the air between us, the Severed lashing at them, sweeping hundreds from their flight. No fury or disgust inspires its violence, no genuine aggression, the creature incapable even of that. Only a mechanical imperative, a robot's need to fulfil its prime directive: to pacify us, sedate and drag us back to whatever Limbo birthed it. To make us *like* it; others amongst the dreamless, without a thought or inspiration the lords in their castles don't proscribe.

Crowther takes advantage of the momentary distraction, though he's on the verge of collapse, his legs threatening to crumble, the candle flame already fading once more:

Throwing back his head, he emits a cry that staggers the Severed, the creature clutching at its pulsating head, a spider's egg sack on the verge of hatching.

A song that shudders me, that momentarily ripples the woods as though they're little more than a reflection in water. As they still, the cry dying, Crowther slumps to one knee, the shadows between the trees stirring, distressed by the sound, made more substantial, as though the mere absence of light congeals, becoming fluid, sculpting itself into suggestions of flesh.

The Severed rights itself, whatever mask of humanity it affected ruptured, peeling, an inky black filth pouring from its wounds. Beneath, its egg-sack head pulses more furiously, whatever gestates within desperate to be born, though it never will, the abysses that constitute its only feature swelling again, the butterflies I vomited swallowed, dispersing as they swirl into the void.

I feel each and every one flicker out, their deaths shuddering me, what little strength I have left draining away into the snow.

The Severed slumps towards us, no longer so elegant, its clothing hanging from its featureless, sexless frame, revealing little more than a distorted mockery of humanity, as a child might make out of salt-dough or white clay: nothing to distinguish or define, nothing between the legs. The sheer blandness of it a horror beyond anything we've encountered in nightmares, amongst the broken and polluted ways.

Still bleeding, it ascends the slope, staining the snow blue-black as it turns its abyssal eyes on us.

Clutching at Crowther, I attempt to drag him back. Nothing

left, now, nothing either of us can do…

Why? Why do you deny peace? We can show you such sweet surrender…

No anger or frustration, not even honest disgust: just the same monotone imperatives, the same wash of parasitic comfort, easing us down, making a welcome bed of the snow.

Drawing close enough to reach for us, its fingers too many, overlong, its hands immense…

A chorus from the woods distresses it, eliciting hisses as it turns from us. Our gazes drawn past it, to the unsettled shadows, the *beings* that emerge from them, sloughing off the murk like lingerie, the remnants of some chrysalis or placental sack.

I know them, saw and defied them during my descent: the siren-things my cold-addled mind projected between the trees, summoned into states of shadowy flesh by his cry, by my simultaneous fear and fascination of them.

Eyes blaze, those of cats and wolves in the dark, the forms that emerge so beautiful, they steal what little breath I have.

Look. Look, sweetheart!

He does, though it pains him to raise his head. Seeing with him, through him, as he sees through me: dancing couples and troupes, their performances making no impression on the snow. Slinking, sultry individuals, smiling as they emerge, baring themselves to the snow and moonlight. Each and every motion calculated to arouse, seduce, to draw the onlooker deeper, deeper into the woods, into what dreams it promises. Lycanthropic smiles, silvery teeth flashing, serpent's tongues flickering.

The Severed hisses, casting its gaze from one to the other, then back to us, realising its jeopardy.

End this. End this and you'll never know pain again.

A promise of Heaven to many, no doubt. To us, a threat of Hell.

The creature reaches for us once more, its proximity enough to make Crowther convulse as though in the grip of a *petite mal.*

I cling to him, spitting curses at the thing, what murderous art they inspire slathering unrealised down my chin: "Don't you *dare!* Don't fucking touch us!"

Such pain, such distress… you have no idea what it is to be free of them.

But it does, doesn't it? It gave them up to become *this.* Dreams and ambitions, whatever affections it once expressed… gone, leaving it without bliss or agony, without shape or distinction.

Hideous. What they would see all of humanity reduced to: dreamless cattle in the grey garden they call Eden.

Almost feeling the scrape of its talons, the porcelain perfection of its skin, before it recoils, staggering back, clutching at its pulsating head. Gently, I shake Crowther, attempting to whisper him from his fit as the thing bursts and bleeds, inky filth pulsing between its fingers, portions of its awful perfection peeling away, steaming and squirming on the snow.

The sirens laugh, dancing around it, assaulting it not with teeth or talons, but *song,* a hymn of seduction that should, by rights, have no purchase on it. But *does,* arousing anatomy it no longer possesses but remembers, deep, deep in its mutilated soul, that it howls and claws at itself rather than acknowledging, tearing what little clothing it still boasts away, ripping at the nondescript flesh beneath.

Flashes behind our eyes, Crowther gasping in response to them, vicarious sparks and embers of sublimated desire, of fantasy so ingrained, even its mutilation isn't enough to excise them: an infant's gurgle in the dark, a gently opened door. Lingering, breathing the same air as the sleeping one, basking in the ludicrousness of his own parenthood...

Music. Dust-tasting wind whipping by, drawing his lips back from his teeth, sweeping sweat from his brow. Americana blasting from the radio, the MDMA in his system painting the air with faint ribbons of coiling colour.

Shudders in a darkened cinema, fighting back tears, the images on screen so perfectly realised, he can hardly bear it. A hand gripping his in understanding, her face already shimmering.

White and red, splinters in his mind, pain so momentarily intense, it flays the world from his eyes, allowing him to see a veiled truth: a scarlet, pulsing intensity that fades from view and memory as he masters himself, grips his rent open and shattered arm.

Impressions. Experiences. Sensations. What the sirens remind him of, what they rouse in the shell that's left.

Anger, lashing out at them blindly, sweeping up the snow with his silvery lashes, spitting his filth at them.

The sirens laugh, dancing from his assaults, taunting him, teasing him, drawing in close to caress, to brush their bodies against his.

The Severed screams, a keening, hollow note that ruptures what remains of its egg-sack head, leaving it to stagger, to spill out as the sirens descend, their touch causing it to blister as they drag it away, still laughing, still smiling, into darkness.

*

A drowned, dreaming moment, the sea warm, effervescent, currents and minor maelstroms fed by our gestation, the dreams we experience there, swathed in starlight.

Roused from slumber, from those other places, by a familiar lullaby. The children...*our* children, dance and dart around us, reconfigured here to swim the ocean depths, leaving trails of light and colour in their shimmering wake. Smiles blister the waters, tinting them pale blue and warm amber, their delight requiring no words, their affection likewise.

They beg us to share our dreams, to know of the states they might one day fly or walk or swim.

We oblige, unable to resist, even if we were of a mind: stories of states that have yet to be, that might never. Of peoples and places so far removed... where others suffer and make their own playgrounds. Where the revolution we have ushered in is nothing but a distant dream, an impossible fantasy, where children still weep in their beds and call out to us, begging to be free.

Can we do that? Can we show them the way?

I smile, though we lack all anatomy with which to do so. Our pleasure, our *anticipation,* seeps into the waters, swathing them, lending them a measure of the same.

Of course. Of course we will, in time.

In time.

Their impatience is tangible, the children aching to transcend even this near-limitless condition, to walk forgotten, in ignorance of themselves, on alien shores, in unknown streets, in skins they do not know.

They don't require our permission or blessing—so far beyond that, born to be better. But they want us to join them, to be essential parts of those new stories, to know us in ways and frames no parent has ever been known, to be strange to us in their turns.

Go. Go, and let us follow, when we're born whole again.

The children laugh, their dance becoming more agitated and erratic in their delirium, lingering a moment longer to silently embrace us, to coil about us in the burning heart of our womb, to kiss the unknown stories from our lips and minds.

Tearing from us, trailing seepages of amputated myth, they take flight, into conditions where they'll forget and be born again, where we will follow and find them, in time, eager to see what atrocities they've sewn.

*

Waking, an empty bed, voices from outside, above, below. I shiver beneath woollen covers, snow still falling beyond the window.

How long..?

Panic at his absence, a sense as of being wounded, wrenched in half, some fundamental part of my anatomy ripped away in the night by celestial surgeons.

Flinging back the covers, I swing my legs over the side of the bed, momentarily struck breathless by the ugly bruise-blotches covering them from the ankles down. No pain, only a familiar numbness, the same not true of my hands and fingers, whose frostbite has already receded.

Attempting to stand, supporting myself against the bedside cabinet, I tumble, squawking as I go to my knees against the wood-panelled floor.

Hurried footsteps from the hallway. The bedroom door bursts open, a wash of vicarious concern, Lemuel sucking air through his teeth as he bends to help me up.

Foolish, my love. Very foolish indeed.

Others cluster at the door, Lemuel gently urging them back as he supports me to limp towards it.

You're lucky not to have lost toes or fingers. Like I said, very foolish.

The man smells of sweet smoke and spices, sweating vanilla and cardamom. The others draw back, smiling greetings as I emerge out into the corridor, the barrage of welcomes and relief overwhelming.

I accept their hugs and kisses, such casual affections become second nature to us in the aftermath of collapse.

There's no concealing it from them, though I try. I love them all, but ache to see only one face, to feel only one pair of lips.

Lemuel leads me through to the living space where the majority gather, lounging on chairs or sofas, stood at the windows, watching the snowfall.

A figure sits hunched and cross-legged on the carpet before the fire, clutching a mug of steaming coffee.

The strangest sensation, like meeting my doppelgänger, a long lost twin, some simulacrum stepped from a mirror dimension, though he doesn't resemble me at all.

He turns, hair hanging lank over his face. In a flash of scintillating, sea-storm grey, his pupils hone to pin-pricks.

Catching my breath in the same instant as he does, our hearts beating in synchronicity.

Strange. So strange, moreso than anything either of us has experienced or encountered since we brought down the ways, since the apocalypse engine he spent several sleeping lifetimes cultivating fulfilled its purpose.

A smile, struggling to stand, several of the others approaching to support him as he trembles, staggering towards me. He's taller than I imagined, than he ever appeared amongst the ways. Taller and far older looking than his twenty-three years: eyes deep and sunken, features faintly drawn, as though with some sickness or withering despair.

Smiling, laughing nervously, we pull away from those that hold us, fall together, into the first touch not made in desperation, not insulated by fabric or numbed by cold.

No lightning flickers between us, no starburst from colliding atoms, the reunion far quieter than either of us anticipated, but also far stranger: feeling his hands on me, my skin beneath them, simultaneously and vice versa. This state of separation, of being divided between two brains and bodies… the more absurd condition, now. An ache, a fever that transcends any sexual urge, any cannibal appetite: to be *one,* as we are in soul, in that state that is more real to us now, where we aspire to be, when this idiot, self-fancied *waking* has realised its paradox.

My fingers at his cheek, in his hair, his at my neck, my shoulder. A kiss that carries seawater and sunlight, that momentarily casts us there, into that state of *I* waiting to wake, to be.

Smiling with new-formed lips, we turn our mutual eyes up, seeing through the teeming fathoms, the boiling depths, to the storm overhead, the path our children carved through them.

Resisting an almost undeniable urge to force our birth, to burst from starlight prematurely and rise ragged, wounded, to feel red rain on raw nerves and barely formed skin, to come apart, even as we ascend, a bleeding angel, following in its children's wake.

A sensation of physically ripping apart, as though our flesh has melted and fused during our embrace, making us one. We laugh through the pain, embracing even more fervently, the kiss that follows far more traumatic, accompanied by a familiar imperative that resonates through us all: *Wake with me.*

Understanding what that means, at last.

Printed in Great Britain
by Amazon